The Last Gift

The Last Gift

A Novel

Abdulrazak Gurnah

BLOOMSBURY

NEW YORK · LONDON · NEW DELHI · SYDNEY

Published by Bloomsbury USA, New York

All papers used by Bloomsbury USA are natural, recyclable products made from wood
grown in well-managed forests. The manufacturing processes conform to the environmen-
tal regulations of the country of origin.

LIBRARY OF CONGRESS CATALOGING-IN-PUBLICATION DATA HAS BEEN APPLIED FOR.

ISBN: 978-1-62040-328-0

First published in Great Britain 2011
First U.S. Edition 2014

1 3 5 7 9 10 8 6 4 2

Typeset by Hewer Text UK Ltd, Edinburgh
Printed and bound in the U.S.A. by Thomson-Shore Inc., Dexter, Michigan

One Day

I

ONE DAY, LONG BEFORE the troubles, he slipped away without saying a word to anyone and never went back. And then another day, forty-three years later, he collapsed just inside the front door of his house in a small English town. It was late in the day when it happened, returning home after work, but it was also late in the day altogether. He had left things for too long and there was no one to blame but himself.

He felt it coming, the collapse. Not with the dread of ruin that had idled by him for as long as he could remember, but with a feeling that something deliberate and muscular was steadily bearing down on him. It was not a strike out of nowhere, more like the beast had slowly turned its head towards him, recognised him and then reached out to smother him. His thoughts were clear as the weakness drained his body, and in that clarity he thought, absurdly, that this must be what it felt like to starve or freeze to death or to have a stone crush the breath out of your body. The comparison made him wince despite his anxiety: see what melodrama tiredness can induce?

He was weary when he left work, with that kind of weariness that sometimes descended on him inexplicably at the end of the day, more so in recent years than before, and which made him wish he could sit down and do nothing until the exhaustion had passed away, or until strong arms came to pick him up and take him home. He was old now, getting old, to say the least. The wish was like a memory, as if he remembered someone doing just that a long time ago – picking him up and taking him home. But he did not think it was a memory. The older he became, the more childlike his wishes at times. The longer he lived, the nearer his childhood drew to him, and it seemed less and less like a distant fantasy of someone else's life.

On the bus, he tried to work out the cause of his fatigue. He still did that after all these years, tried to make sense of things, looked for explanations that would diminish the fear of what life allowed to happen. At the end of each day he retraced his steps until he found the right combination of mishaps that had left him so feeble at the close of it, as if such knowing (if it was knowing) really alleviated his distress. Ageing, that was what it could be for a start, wear and tear, irreplaceable worn-out parts. Or hurrying to work in the morning when no one cared or was troubled if he was a few minutes late, and when sometimes the effort and the anxiety left him breathless and aching with heartburn for the rest of the day. Or a bad cup of tea he had made himself in the staff kitchen that had made his gut bubble with incipient diarrhoea. They left the milk out in a jug all day, uncovered, gathering dust and breathing in the corruption they brought to it in their comings and goings. He should know better than to touch that milk but he cannot resist the lure of a sip of tea. Or simply he had expended too much inexpert exertion, lifting and shoving things he should have left well alone. Or it could be heartache. He could never tell when that would come, or where from or for how long.

But as he sat on the bus, he knew that something unusual was happening to him, a gathering helplessness that made him whimper involuntarily, the flesh on his body heating and shrinking and an unfamiliar emptiness taking its place. It happened unhurriedly: his breathing changed, he trembled, sweated, and saw himself curled up into that familiar slump of human abandonment, the body expecting pain, dissolving. He watched himself beside himself, a little panicked by the sly, irresistible dissolution of his rib cage and his hip joints and his spine, as if body and mind were separating themselves from each other. He felt a sharp stab in his bladder and became aware that his breathing was rapid, panicky. *What are you doing? Having a seizure? Enough hysterics, breathe deeply, breathe deeply*, he told himself.

He stepped off the bus into the February air, a day of sudden cold, shivering and weak, breathing deeply as he had instructed himself. He was not dressed for it. Other people around him were wearing heavy woollen coats and gloves and scarves, as if they knew from practice and familiarity how cold it really was, which he, despite many years of living here, did not. Or maybe, unlike him, they listened to weather reports on the TV and radio, and then were only too happy to fetch the heavy garments they kept in their wardrobes for just such purposes. He was wearing the coat he wore for most months of the year, enough to keep off the rain and the chill, but not too warm when the weather was mild. He had never been able to make himself pile up clothes and shoes in a cupboard for different occasions and seasons. It was a habit of frugality he no longer needed to practise but had never been able to break. He liked wearing out the clothes he was comfortable in, and liked to think that if he saw himself approaching he would recognise himself from the clothes he wore. On that cold February evening he was paying for his abstemiousness, or tight-fistedness, or asceticism, whichever it was. It was his restlessness perhaps, the habit of mind of a stranger unreconciled to his surroundings, dressing light so he could throw the coat off quickly when the time came to move on. That was what he thought it was, the cold. He was improperly dressed, for his own stupid reasons, and the cold was making him tremble out of control, with an inner trembling that made him feel that the timbers of his body were about to give way. Standing at the bus stop, at a loss about what to do, he heard himself groan, and understood that he was beginning to lose track of events, as if he had dozed for a moment and woken up again. When he forced himself to move, his arms and legs were boneless, and he breathed in short, heavy sighs. His feet were leaden and numb, opening up into stinging cracks of frozen flesh. Perhaps he should sit down and wait for the spasm to pass. But no, he would have to sit on the pavement and would be taken for a derelict, and he may never be able to get up again. He forced himself to move on, taking one laborious step after another. It was now important to get home before he ran out of strength, before he fell down in this wilderness where his body would be torn to pieces and scattered. The walk from the bus stop to his home usually took him seven minutes, five hundred steps or thereabouts. He counted sometimes, to drown out the racket in his head. But on that evening it must have taken longer. It felt as if it was taking longer. He was not even sure if his strength would last. He thought he passed people, and at times he staggered and had to lean against a wall for a few minutes or seconds. It was no longer possible to tell. His teeth were chattering and he was sweating heavily by the time he reached the door and, after opening it, he sat down in the hallway, allowing the heat and the nausea to overwhelm him. He could not remember anything for a while.

His name was Abbas and, although he was not aware of it, his entrance had been noisy. His wife Maryam heard him fumbling with the keys and then heard him bang the door shut, when usually he slipped in quietly. Sometimes Maryam was not even aware that he was home until he stood before her, smiling because he had caught her out again. It was one of his jokes, making her jump, as she always did, because she had not heard him come in. That evening, Maryam started from the noise of the keys in the door and felt a moment of quite ordinary pleasure at his arrival, and then the door banged and she heard him groan. When she went out to the hallway, she saw him sitting on the floor just inside the door, his legs open in front of him. His face was wet with sweat, he was panting for breath and his eyes were opening and shutting in confusion.

Maryam knelt beside him, saying his name, 'Oh no, Abbas, Abbas, what is it? Oh no.' She took his hot wet hand in hers. His eyes closed as soon as she touched him. His mouth was open as he struggled for breath, and she saw that the insides of his trousers legs were wet. 'I'll call an ambulance,' she said. She felt his hand tighten slightly on hers, and then after a moment he said, groaning, *No.* Then in a whisper he said, *Let me rest.* She sat back on her heels and waited beside him, alarmed by his helplessness and unsure what to do. His body heaved in a spasm of pain or nausea, and she said his name again, tightening her hold on his hand. Then after a short while she began to feel his agitation subsiding. 'What have you done?' she asked softly, murmuring to herself, murmuring to him. 'What have you done to yourself?'

When she sensed that he was trying to rise to his feet, she

put his arm over her shoulder and helped him struggle up the stairs. Before they reached the bedroom he was trembling again, and Maryam took his weight and forced him over the remaining few steps to the bed. She undressed him hurriedly, wiped him where he had soiled himself, and covered him. She did not think why it was necessary to undress him and clean him first before covering him. Perhaps it was just an instinct about the dignity of the body, a superfluous courtesy she had not reflected upon. Then she lay beside him on top of the covers while he shook and groaned, sobbing loudly and saying, *No, No* over and over again. When the trembling stopped, and Abbas was no longer sobbing, and even seemed to be falling asleep, Maryam went back downstairs and called the surgery's emergency number. The doctor appeared within minutes of her call, which she did not expect at all. The doctor was a young woman Maryam had not seen at the surgery before. She hurried in, smiling and friendly, as if nothing exceptionally frightening was happening. She followed Maryam upstairs, glanced towards Abbas and then looked around for a place to put down her bag. Her every movement was considered and seemed to be telling Maryam not to panic, and she did feel herself growing calmer now that the doctor was here. The doctor examined Abbas, took his pulse, listened to his breathing with her stethoscope, checked his blood pressure, shone a light in his eyes, took a urine sample and put a litmus paper in it. Then she asked him questions about what had happened, repeating her questions several times until he gave satisfactory replies. Her voice and manner were courteous and solicitous rather than concerned, and she even found time to share a smile with Maryam as they discussed what needed to be done next, her teeth dazzling white and her dark-blonde hair glowing in the bedroom light. How do they teach them to do that? Maryam wondered. How do they teach them to handle wounded bodies with such calm assurance? As if she was dealing with a broken radio.

The doctor called an ambulance, and at the hospital they told Maryam that Abbas had suffered a diabetic crisis, short of a coma but serious enough. They told him it was late-onset diabetes, which happens to people as they grow older. Normally it was treatable, but because he did not know he had it and had not received any treatment, he had developed a crisis. It was too early yet to tell in full what damage that might have caused. Was there diabetes in his family? His parents, his uncles or aunts? Abbas said he did not know. When the specialist physician examined him the next day, he said that the diabetes was not life-threatening but that, judging from his motor responses, he had probably suffered some brain damage. There was no need for alarm. He might regain some of the lost functions or he might not. Time would tell. He had also suffered a mild stroke. Regular checks would clarify his condition and treatment, but in the meantime he would remain under observation in hospital for another day and if there were no further events, he could go home. He was issued a long list of prohibitions, was put on medication and instructed to take sick leave from work. He was then sixty-three years old, although that was not all there was to it.

Maryam rang their children Hanna and Jamal. She told them about what had happened, going round and round with her reassurances to keep them from hurrying home. If there are no further events he will be home tomorrow, she told them. 'What do you mean *events*?' Hanna asked. 'That's what the doctor said, if there are no further events,' Maryam replied. She was taking her cue from the hospital

7

staff, who seemed to want to keep everything calm, so perhaps that was best for Abbas, and having Hanna and Jamal rushing home would only excite him unnecessarily. She worked in a hospital herself, and knew that people sometimes made too much fuss about their sick relatives. 'They are treating him now. They say he is stable. No, there's no need to rush down. He's not going anywhere. Of course you can come and see him any time, but there's no need to rush. Come when you want. He's all right now. They're treating him. No, he will not need to inject every day, Jamal. He does so at the moment, but not for much longer. He will take medicine and follow a diet and there will be various things I have to check regularly. Like what? Oh, cuts and grazes on his feet, blood sugar, and other things. They'll teach me all about it. He'll be all right. It'll take him a little while to be strong again. Don't worry, he'll be all right. Yes yes, come and see him soon.'

The illness left Abbas exhausted. Even small efforts made him shake and sweat, and made him whimper with frustration. He could not even sit up without help. He was always hungry but food made him queasy. His saliva tasted poisonous and his mouth smelled like a drain. When he forced himself to swallow food, he gagged and retched. A nurse from the hospital diabetes team came to visit and explained to him (and to Maryam) how he needed to look after himself. She laid down the law and gave them pamphlets and advice, before grumbling her way out again. He was even more exhausted after she left. After several days he still could not walk the few steps to the bathroom without help, and when she left the house, Maryam had to bring him a plastic bucket and put it beside the bed in case of an emergency. He had to use it once, and he sat on that bucket like a baby, groaning and moaning as his body spluttered and squirted, shaming him after a lifetime of waste and lies. Then when he was finished, he could not clean himself properly, could not wash himself as he usually did. He had never got used to cleaning himself with paper, still felt soiled afterwards, and now he had to get back into bed feeling as if his bum was scaled with dried waste. Sometimes he drifted away, into sleep or away from his moorings, into those deep silent places that he could not help returning to, that he hated returning to. Even in his daze he knew that he had left things for too long, as he had known for so many years. There was so much he should have said, but he had allowed the silence to set until it became immovable. There were times when he thought he was already gone, that he was out of reach, hanging on to a thin rope that was unwinding from a spool while he slowly dissolved. But he was not gone and he came awake again, and he remembered that dream he had had at times when he worked at sea, of hanging on to a piece of rope as his body dissolved in a rush of water.

When he started to get better, he became easily irritable, especially with his own feebleness, but it came out in the ill-tempered words he spoke to Maryam. The words hurt her but he could not help himself. Sometimes he could not bear it when she came into the room, chattering to him, fussing around in the wardrobe or in her bedside table, looking for what, putting her palm on his forehead, lifting him up to swap his pillows, bringing him the radio from the kitchen. Leave me alone. Stop fussing. Sometimes he could not bear for her not to be there, for her to be somewhere else while tears of self-pity and self-loathing slid down his face. I cannot bear this. I cannot bear this any more. He was the sinful traveller fallen ill in a strange land, after a life as useless as a life could be. Talking hurt him, it gave him a pain in the chest, and he was too weary to explain. His words did not make sense, he could see that in the incomprehension in her face. He could not make himself say the words so that they would make sense. He wanted to be left alone, but when he tried to tell Maryam that, he only uttered spluttering abuse and could not stop himself from weeping.

But he was getting stronger. He could go downstairs on his own, and return upstairs when he needed to, although that took him longer. He was able to keep the food down and was getting used to the new diet, which he did not find that arduous, except for the loss of salt and sugar. He would be able to look after himself, he told her. It was time for her to go back to work. He was not an invalid, just a little weak. So long as he took his time, he would be fine. It was a relief when she returned to work after three weeks, even though it left him the long silent day to himself. He tried to read but his concentration was poor, and the effort of holding up a book was tiring. He was getting stronger, and when he was well enough, he would speak to Maryam about all the things he had kept from her.

Maryam did work in a hospital but not doing anything glorious or life-saving. She worked in the staff and visitors' canteen, and she knew that if she stayed away any longer she would lose her job. The canteen manager had told her so on the phone, kindly, when she rang to ask for another two weeks off work. Oh come on, she was not expecting to be paid, just two more weeks to be sure that Abbas could really look after himself, but the manager said no, sorry but they were short-staffed. Maryam had been working there for a long time, as had the canteen manager, but times were hard and jobs were not plentiful. Neither the canteen manager nor she were going anywhere. It was not as if Maryam was qualified to do anything else. She had been working in the hospital for twenty years: first as a cleaner until the children came, when they decided she should stay at home to look after them, then when they were old enough, she found a job in the hospital canteen. She often thought that she should do something else, something more challenging that would make her feel better about herself and very likely pay her better, but she never even got round to looking. When she mentioned the thought to Abbas, he nodded or made agreeing noises but he did not encourage her. She had no idea what that other challenging work might be, and perhaps neither had he. This was the kind of work she had always done, and she knew many people at the hospital. People came and went, but a small group of them had been there for a long time. She did not want to lose her job, not at this time with Abbas as he was. It was not as if she could say to the canteen manager, stuff your miserable job, I hate it anyway, I'll go find myself another one in a bank. There was nothing else she could do. And also she had become used to the way the job filled her life. That was how she was all her life, always settling for less, always doing what was best, and it was too late now to start being awkward and taking risks. She never had that kind of strength.

In those first few days after she returned to work, she felt again the shock of what had happened to Abbas, he who hardly ever fell ill and now was so weak and confused, so angry, so quickly reduced to tears and sobbing for no reason. It was more shocking to think of him like that when she was away from him. Somehow when he was there in front of her, she could lose herself in the details of what needed to be done, even if it was an ordeal at times to go close to him. But at a distance he came to her in pieces, in shocking episodes that she could not get out of her mind. Her friends at work asked after him, and she told them briefly, making the best of her bulletins from sick bay. The bulletins helped her to reduce her shock into something more ordinary, to fit what had happened into familiar dramas. Who did not know a father or a sister or a husband or a neighbour who was struggling with a lingering illness or waiting for a major operation? After her bulletins, she listened to those of her friends and between them they made tragedies tolerable, blaming doctors, fate or even the unfortunates themselves for the miseries they described. It was better that way. They were not the kind of friends she could open her heart to. She did not have that kind of friend except for Abbas. She was afraid that if she spoke openly she would release a torrent of empty sympathy, which she guessed would be the best her friends at work would be able to offer. Which was probably also the best she could offer if one of them were to open their heart to her too. It was enough to feel the human gestures without probing too much, it was enough.

If anything, she did not want to think about how he was now. She wanted not to think about that for just a few hours in a day, but she could not manage it. It was not right to leave him on his own all day, but the doctor said he was getting better and it was worth a try. The medication is doing its work and he will be fine. Don't fuss over him all the time, she said, let him look after himself a little, let him learn. Stop fussing, that was what he said too. She knew he wanted her out of the house so he could be alone with his silences. But it was not right when he could not manage, when he spilt things and soiled himself and sat weeping all day in his loneliness. It hurt her that he spoke roughly to her, which was not his way, but she had to get used to it. He was not well, and anyway, she would fuss if she wanted, what else was she supposed to do.

It was their regular doctor, Dr Mendez, who said don't fuss over him all the time, let him look after himself, as if she was not a champion fusspot herself. She was very firm with Maryam, as she had always been from when Maryam first took the children to her all those years ago. Her instructions were to be obeyed in full, and her diagnosis often had a hint of blame, as if Maryam were at fault. Dr Mendez was a Spanish lady doctor, and a very stubborn one, in Maryam's view. She was about Maryam's age and had been their doctor for years, growing more and more like a rugged lady wrestler as she grew older and filled out. Perhaps it was Maryam's own fault, that she had not found a way of preventing the doctor from bullying her, but she spoke to Maryam as if she was not very good at looking after herself. After the diabetes diagnosis, she lectured Abbas about his negligence too. Older men are too vain to go to the doctor until something terrible happens to them and then they are a nuisance to everyone, she said. He should have had regular blood tests as a matter of course, a man of his age, and then they would have diagnosed the diabetes years ago and would have had his heart problem under control too. Now the children must have blood tests at least once a year. These conditions are passed on in families, she said. It was as well that Abbas was so weak; doctor or no doctor, he would not have taken that tone of voice from her when he was well. As the stubborn Spanish lady doctor lectured him, Maryam thought she saw Abbas briefly smile, and she preferred to think that it was his mischief smile, saving up some mockery that he would deliver to her later, when he had the strength.

She thought of him then as he used to be, as he was when she met him all those years ago in Exeter. She often thought of him like that since his illness, the man she met when she was seventeen, not to compare or grieve that he was no longer like that, but as a pleasure, as a memory that came to her on its own and which made her smile. Perhaps it was also to mourn that ease that was now so completely past.

She saw him for the first time in Boots in Exeter, such a long time ago, in an almost imaginary life. They were both standing in a queue and he smiled. People did not always smile when they caught her eye that way, or she did not think they did anyway. More often than not she looked away before she could read what was in their eyes, so perhaps they did smile after she had broken eye contact, but in those days she was afraid of their despising, sneering looks and their angry faces, and preferred not to know. He was a slim, strong dark man, wearing a light-brown, polo-neck sweater and a denim jacket. He was ahead of her in the queue, and she had time to have a good look at him as he looked this way and that way while he was waiting his turn. Then he looked back and saw her, and looked again and smiled. It made her feel good, that smile, as if she was someone he had recognised, as if they were part of an understanding, of something the two of them knew that no one else there did. She was not surprised when she found out later that he worked as a sailor. It was the way he looked, like someone who had been places and had done things, someone who had known freedom. She was born in Exeter and had never been anywhere else or done anything. She was living with Ferooz and Vijay then, and that life was becoming difficult. The thought of Ferooz and Vijay made her wince, as it always did even after all these years, and she stretched her shoulders and neck, and then gently eased that memory away.

She knew, just by looking at Abbas then, without knowing anything about him, that he had done things. He had a certain look in his eyes, a mean look, a look that said I am not taking it quietly, whatever you have in mind. She had to say it was a mean look. When she knew him better she saw that it was not in his eyes all the time, only in passing when he did not like what he heard or saw, or when he suspected he was being treated with disrespect. He could not bear disrespect, all his life, even to the point of silliness. Sometimes that look was like something burning, his eyes glowing, and his face would be angry and determined, as if his mind had taken him somewhere else. When he was not about to burst like that, his eyes were calm and big, like someone who liked to see, and when she first met him she thought he was someone who liked to please.

Yes, that was how she would always remember him, while memory lasted, that slim restless man she met in the first summer after her last year at school. She had a job in a café at the time . . . and here she was still doing the same sort of thing a whole lifetime later. She thought then that if she could earn enough she would move out of Ferooz and Vijay's flat and into lodgings with one of her friends from work. But the money was no good and the work was a drudge, although she liked her mates. It made a difference then, when everything was so hard, to work with people you got on with, people who laughed at everything as if all their lives were a stupid joke. Later she got a better-paid job in a factory, which was where she was working when she saw Abbas again. She still went to the café sometimes to have a cup of tea and meet with the people she used to work with, and always got a cream cake on the house. That was where she saw him the second time. He glanced at her and recognised her. He hesitated for a moment and when she smiled at him, he came over. He hovered for a moment with his tray and then sat down.

'Boots,' he said, smiling.

'It's a pleasure to meet you, Mr Boots,' she said, and they both laughed.

They chatted for a while and then he said goodbye, see you again some time. He told her his name and said that he worked on ships. She told him her name too and said that she worked in a factory. Even that exchange seemed somehow amusing. She knew, without knowing how, that she would meet him again. She could not remember much of what he said or what she said in return, only the feeling of it remained and she was not sure if she could name it: excitement, anticipation. She remembered the way he looked at her and the pleasure she saw in his eyes and the way that made her feel.

And the third time she met him, the blessed third time as he said later, because blessing always comes the third time round, was in the factory. It was such a surprise to see him there and she could see from his sly, pleased smile that it was no coincidence. He had taken a job there because he wanted a rest from the sea, he said. He was in Exeter to stay a few days with a friend and was having such a good time that he thought he would stay on for a while. In the meantime he took a job in the factory because a person had to work or become a burden on someone else. He spent so much time hanging around where Maryam was working in the line that the supervisor told him off in the end, but he still came to talk to her. The supervisor was a thin weasly man who strode about querulously, looking for provocation and bickering with everyone. Abbas was an immediate provocation to him, and it took a day or two before Abbas learned to evade his attentions. His work was supplying several of the lines with what they needed, so he could roam about whenever he was not in demand, charming the women and keeping out of the way of the supervisor. Afterwards he walked her home, still talking, making her laugh, flattering her outrageously. She knew she was being courted and she lay awake in the dark afterwards, thrilled by what it meant. All that week they went around like that, talking all the time, holding hands by the third day, a good-bye kiss on the fourth evening, and they made love for the first time that weekend. It was the first time for her altogether. She told him before, in case something happened. She was not sure what could happen but from what she had heard something was going to be broken and there was going to be blood, so she wanted him to know. He asked if she was sure, and she said she was. He was so handsome.

Maryam would have preferred to stop her memories there for a while, to linger over the image of the Abbas she had just met, but she could not supress the presence of Ferooz in the vicinity. She was still living with Ferooz and Vijay at the time, and they did not like what was going on with Abbas. At first they did not like the idea of a boyfriend. Then they did not like his age, old enough to be her father. He is twenty-eight, she told them, which is what he had told her. Then they did not like that he was a sailor. They are wild, irresponsible people, Vijay said. Drunkards. He's just using you. There's only one thing men like him think about.

It was a terrible evening. She was supposed to meet him at the cinema but they would not let her go out, talking at her with such alarm that she dared not move. The next morning, before anyone was up, she collected a few clothes in a carrier bag and went to him, to Abbas, to where he was staying with his friend. He must have guessed that she would come, that she had not been allowed to come the previous evening. He was standing at the window, so early in the morning, looking out for her, and as soon as he saw her, he ran downstairs to let her into the flat.

'What happened to you?' he asked, pulling her into the house and shutting the door gently so as not to wake up his friend. 'I thought . . . I thought you no longer wanted to see me.'

'They wouldn't let me come,' she said, thrilled, despite the tension of the moment, to see him so agitated.

She told him about the arguments and the abuse, and he said let's get out of this place, and she thought fine. She was happy to go far away from the mess, get away, leave it behind. She did not know if she had any rights, or if Ferooz and Vijay could have her brought back. So when Abbas said, *Yallah, let's get out of here*, she said count me in, I'm coming. It felt glorious, not to stop and think, not to go back to the belittling life she was used to.

She had thought of dying when she saw his collapsed body by the door, his dying, her own dying. Later, his collapse made her think of him gone, and then of her own life, of its beginnings and its endless furtive turnings. It was Ferooz who had told her the story of her arrival in the world, the story of her beginnings. She was found outside the casualty doors at Exeter Hospital, an abandoned baby. A night-duty porter, whose name nobody bothered to remember, stepped outside to see the dawn and to smoke a cigarette, and saw a bundle at his feet. It was wrapped in a cream-coloured crocheted shawl and had a brown envelope pinned to it like a delivery address or a label. When he saw that the bundle was a baby, the night-duty porter may have smiled or he may have been uncertain whether he should pick it up and take it inside in the warmth, or whether to call someone who would know exactly what to do. The nurses sometimes became annoyed when the porter tried to help, as if he might break something, or hurt the patient, or just generally be uncouth. He put his cigarette away without lighting it and went in to tell the other porter on duty. They called the duty Staff Nurse, who swept up the bundle and hurried inside with it, and Maryam expected that the nurse gave the porters a rebuking glance and that they exchanged a look at the fuss she was making.

She was tiny when she made this dramatic arrival, weighing just over four pounds and was no more than two or three days old. The doctor who examined her said that she had been well looked after. Her mother was possibly a teenager, the doctor said, to judge from the size of the baby, but that was only a guess. Maryam wondered what faces the doctor and the Staff Nurse would have made at each other as they shared this information. What word would have described a girl like her mother at that time: scrubber, slag, slut? She was not told that kind of detail, and she had no choice but to add in some extra strokes of her own to fill in the picture. She was not sure about the cream-coloured crocheted shawl, for example, whether that was there in the story she was told or whether she added it because that was what she imagined an abandoned baby would be bundled up in. She had a cream-coloured crocheted shawl for her own babies, and sometimes thought *my mother* as she handled it, and felt tender towards the absent one.

In the meantime, while the doctor continued his examination of the baby, the Staff Nurse called the police in case the mother was still nearby. Also, she did not think anyone should touch the envelope in case there was some evidence that would be useful to the police. One could not be sure what horror lay behind such cases. It was most likely that the mother had relinquished her baby out of the shame of being unwed, or out of desperation at the thought of a despised and lonely motherhood, but it was just possible that the baby had not been left by the mother but by a relative, or by someone who had harmed the mother. In any case, whoever had done it, it was a crime. Offences Against the Person Act 1861, Ferooz told her. She had looked it up.

The police came immediately but could not trace the mother or whoever had left the baby outside the hospital. The envelope was unaddressed and contained a sheet of lined paper, a page torn out of a school exercise book. It said, *Her name is Maryam they won't let me keep her.* Judging from the name and from the baby's complexion, the police thought the mother must have been a foreign woman, or rather, they said, in the elegant phrasing of the time, that she was probably a darkie of some kind. As the police knew, some of the foreigners had worse prejudices than Christians in matters such as unwed mothers, and sometimes hurt their own daughters out of shame. So the first job for the police was to locate foreign families in the town and begin their enquiries there. This was easier to do then because there were so few of them, before the floodgates opened. However, they also found copious evidence of blonde hair in the shawl, and the baby's little tuft of hair was fair, although this was not unusual for babies who grew dark hair in adulthood. So it was possible that it was the father who was foreign, and he had abandoned the teenaged girl he had made into a mother, who in turn was forced by her relatives to abandon the baby.

The police made their enquiries, had their suspicions but could not announce a definite identification of the mother.

If there had been another crime associated with the incident, they would probably have tried harder, but this looked like another case of a girl who had been foolish and had paid the price, and what information they had, which was nothing more than rumour, suggested that the strongest possible suspect was no longer in Exeter. Maryam was put out for long-term fostering with a family in Exeter. Her date of birth was estimated as 3 October 1956.

The family she was put out to foster with were Mr and Mrs Riggs, an elderly couple who were already fostering two other little girls. Maryam would think of them always as her mum and dad, even though she was only with them for the first few years of her life. For practical purposes, their name filled the empty space in her own name, and she became Maryam Riggs. Her own earliest memories were of the time she lived with them and shared a room with two little girls.

Their mother was a large, tall slow-moving woman with a mole on her cheek. It was a large mole, and sometimes their mother worried it until the skin around it became red and angry. She talked to them in a kindly grumbling monotone, talking all the time, and she even carried on talking when she was on her own. When she was angry, her voice was sharp and painful to listen to, as if she was hurting. When she started talking like that, it took her a long time to stop, and the shortest word or the lightest sigh set her off again. She cooked them vegetable stews and watered down the milk to save money, and she filled them up with sweet suet puddings and scones that were hard as rock. They were to call her Mum.

It was a cold house. They all wore several layers of clothing and Mum's dresses reached all the way down to her ankles. The dresses made her look as if she was someone from another time, and Dad sometimes called her Queen Victoria. She kept their hair cut short to avoid nits, as she called them, and gave them a shallow bath, once a week, all of them in the same water. They were bathed in the kitchen, in a tin bath which Mum filled with water heated in saucepans. Mum had big hands, and scrubbed the children hard with a thick grey flannel, kneeling on the stone floor beside the tub, sometimes with a cigarette in her mouth. The only room with a fire was the living room. The kitchen kept its warmth from cooking and from heating the saucepans, but the water quickly lost its heat and their baths were hurried and brief. Their dad got into the bath after them, and they had to get out while the water was still warm enough for him to use. Afterwards, the children ran upstairs to get under the covers as quickly as they could. Maryam smiled when she described this bathing routine to her own children, and she made them see that some of it was fun.

Their dad worked in a carpet store not too far away, and he was often around the house. He had been a van driver for the carpet store, but he was disabled in the war, wounded in an air raid, and he was not allowed to drive because his eyesight was bad. A thick scar ran like an underground tunnel just below his right eye. The store kept him on for odd jobs, sweeping, small repairs and generally helping out when he was required. When he went to work, he wore a suit and tie, an old herringbone suit that was the only one he possessed. Maryam did not know at the time that Dad's job was probably a kindness by the store and that he probably received poor wages. That was something she worked out for herself when she thought about him later.

At home, Dad was always fixing something, pottering he called it, and he smoked a pipe. They called her Mary and it was only much later that she learned that her name was

Maryam. The eldest of Mum and Dad's three girls was Maggie. Maggie's name was always on Mum's lips: fetch this, stop that, you'll come to no good, that's for sure. The other girl was Gill and she was not well. The children were allowed to sit in the living room while their parents listened to the radio after tea. Dad liked to have one or other of the girls sitting on his lap, and he stroked them and kissed them on the cheek and called them you little nig nog. At seven in the evening they were all sent to bed, even if the sun was shining. She did not remember being hit or being shouted at, although Maggie was, for answering back and for being nosy. She used to peep through keyholes and rummage in forbidden drawers. Mum said there was nothing worse than someone who was nosy. Nosy people caused all the trouble in the world.

There was an outside flushing toilet just beside the back door. The toilet door did not fit the frame. There was a large gap at the top and bottom, and Maryam remembered times when there was a skin of ice in the toilet bowl first thing in the morning. The toilet had an animal smell, as if something else lived in there, and she was terrified of using it after dark. By the time she was five, the other children had been sent away. Mum explained that they had been adopted and now had families of their own. They belonged to someone. She asked five-year-old Maryam if she would like to stay with them for good. Maryam said she would. She did not really know what she was being asked. It had not occurred to her to wonder if there was anything differ-ent about the way she lived with Mum and Dad compared to the way anyone else lived. It had not occurred to her that she could be sent away from them.

But when her mum and dad asked to keep her for good, they were not allowed to because they were too old. Her mum grumbled about that for days, describing to Maryam the stupidity of saying they were too old to adopt one child, a child they loved like their own, when they weren't too old to bring up three as their fostered children. Dad said he was flabbergasted. He always said that when he thought something silly had happened. They even considered appealing, but when this idea came up, Maryam was taken away from them, because the social workers said the whole episode was upsetting the child. That was how she lost Mum and Dad. A man and a woman came for her in a car and took her away, and she had no idea because Mum was talking to her in her usual way as if nothing strange was happening.

Maryam was fostered with another family. She did not remember very much about that family. She thought something bad happened there to the other child they were looking after, a boy older than her who looked hot and often trembled. Their house was cold too but it also smelled. The windows were never opened and the beds smelled bad. Her new father was a big man and when she got in his way he pushed her away hard. Once he threw his beer at her because she was crying. Her mother was thin and had long hair, and was always hurrying them and tugging them, and telling them they were the bane of her life. When she thought back over her childhood, it seemed as if she was there for a very short time, but when she counted carefully in later years she knew she must have been there for a good while because she started school when she was with them. Maybe she just did not want to remember.

Her memory was very confused about this time. She stayed with other families but her recollections were vague. Sometimes she was hit, she remembered that, and once she was locked in a room on her own all night while the family went out. Maybe it was not all night and she just fell asleep on the floor in the end. When she woke up in the morning the door was unlocked. She cried all the time and kept asking for Mum and Dad, but she never found them again. She was sent to live with another family that had two proper children about the same age as her. The mother was dark and had asked for a dark child to foster, so they had given her Maryam, because by then her complexion was darkening more than ever. But Maryam would not stop crying for long – you are not a baby any more, her dark mother said – and she did not want to play with the proper children. She was in big school by this time and was being bullied constantly. One day she hit a girl who was tormenting her. The teacher had put a vase with flowers in water on their table for them to draw but the girl kept moving it and scribbling on Maryam's paper and calling her smelly. Then the girl spat in her face, and Maryam snatched the vase and flowers and water from the girl's hands and hurled it at her. It hit her in the face. The headmistress sent her to sit on her own in the school hall until her mother came to collect her. Her dark mother said she did not want her any more and she was fostered to another family that was going to put her right.

Maryam could not please them. They had a daughter of their own who was a year older than Maryam. Her name was Vivien, and she kept an eye on Maryam and reported on her if she broke any of her parents' many rules. The father was a teacher, and he gave Maryam reading tests and intelligence tests, and told her that she was backward for her age. He organised routines to improve her ability to learn and gave her practice tasks to do as homework. The daughter reported any infringements of this regime, after giving Maryam her own scolding first, pinching and slapping her for her stupidity. The mother taught her table manners and where to put her hands when she went to bed and how to wipe herself throughly so she did not leave soil marks in her knickers. In the end, the family could not really come to like her, even though she stayed with them for more than a year. They tried but could not put her right, so they sent her back.

By this time Maryam was nine years old and had a good idea of her worthlessness. So when they found another family to take her, and her new mother called her Maryam and stroked her hair and said what a lovely little girl, she knew that she would have to do everything she could to be lovely, so that she would never stop liking her. She was given a small room of her own, and her new mother decorated it with pictures of animals and a crimson and gold butterfly mobile, which hung over her bed. She was a thin smiling woman with a laugh that seemed to bubble out of her. It made Maryam laugh just to hear her laugh. She was a nurse, and her new father was an electrician in the same hospital. It is a psychiatric hospital, do you know what that means? That was how she talked to her from the beginning. Nobody had talked to Maryam like that before, not that she remembered, expecting her to ask questions, to want to know about things. At least that was how Maryam wanted to remember her, as someone who spoke to her differently from the way anyone had spoken to her before, someone who expected her to be curious. Her name was Ferooz, she told Maryam, and she was from Mauritius. Her husband's name was Vijay and he was from India. Ferooz got the atlas out and showed her where Mauritius was, and told her how it got its name and how no one used to live there, and who lived there now and what they did. She also showed her where India was, and pointed to the city where Vijay came from, or rather to the city nearest the village he came from.

In any case, she showed her a map, and told her about places she had never heard of and gave her a glimpse of the world.

She also told her many things about their lives. Vijay limped badly because his body had not healed properly after he was knocked over by a car when he was a child. Their families thoroughly disapproved of their marriage, because of religion. Her family were pious Muslims with a position to uphold in Mauritius, and forbade her to marry a Hindu. Vijay's family were ignorant villagers and could not bear to have anything to do with Muslims. Perhaps it would have helped if they had children, but they could not. Perhaps they had offended their families too much, and without their blessing could not deserve the gift of a child of their own. But now they had a lovely little girl and did not care about those horrible families. They would be a family themselves.

That was Ferooz, and that was the story Maryam told her own children. She did not tell them everything, not about the things that went wrong and how later she lost Ferooz and Vijay so completely. There were some things she did not know how to talk about, not to her children, not yet. She ended that part of the story by telling them about their father. He was a sailor then, visiting Exeter to see a friend. After he met Maryam he got a job so he could be near her, but Ferooz and Vijay did not like him, so they ran away together. *Yallah, let's get out of here*, that's what he said. That was the story of their love. That was what she told them. They met and ran away together and he never went back to sea. They loved what he said: *Yallah, let's get out of here*, and when they were children they sometimes said that to each other as a joke.

Maryam tried to get in touch with Ferooz after Hanna

came but she could not find her again. Her letters went unanswered, and once, when she found the courage to ring her number, she discovered that it was dead. She wished that she had not waited so long.

They were beginning to get into a new little convalescing routine. Of course, they already had a routine, one that grew and changed over the years as their lives changed. That was the thing about growing old together, you shuffled and made space and learned to be comfortable with each other, if you were lucky. Maybe she did not really mean growing old together. She did not feel old, and did not think of Abbas as old, even though there were so many unmistakable ways in which he showed his age even before this illness. It was not their ages that made them comfortable with each other. It was more like being so used to living with someone that you did not need to speak about some things, and other things you never mentioned, out of kindness, out of what they provoked. She saw people coming to the hospital, couples who looked battered and worn out, so that it was impossible to tell which was the one who was ailing. Yet first this one hovers over the other, steadying her as she stumbles slightly over a bubbled-up floor tile, and then she waits patiently while he hesitates whether to go left or to go straight ahead, or whether to ask someone for assistance. Then she steps up, links arms with him, and somehow something is agreed and they set off again.

She got up first in the morning as she had always done, went downstairs and made them tea. They drank their tea in bed, hardly exchanging a word, dozing for a few seconds now and then. She loved the ease of it, the unhurriedness now that it was just the two of them, and sometimes he promised that he would get up earlier and make tea for them the following week. Yes, she said, when you are feeling better. Then she got up, washed and hurried downstairs to make herself breakfast and get ready for work. That was how it always was with her, a moment's ease followed by bustle and tumult, the story of her life, she just could not get the tempo to steady. She laid the table for him to have his breakfast later. Even when he was well, he only had a cup of tea before leaving for work, picking up an apple or a pear on his way out, the frugal habits of a lifetime. She knew that when he came down, he would put the breakfast things away and make himself a cup of tea. By the time she was ready to leave, he was out of bed, washed and dressed, and sitting in the living room with one of his books. In those days, after he began to get better, it was *The Odyssey* again, and that was how she left him, thinking that soon he would have to go back to work and that would be the end of his enforced holiday. Some mornings he went to the newsagent to get a paper, but he could not bear reading about what was happening in Iraq, so some mornings he did not and went for a short walk instead.

Then late one Saturday morning, when she was in the kitchen unpacking the groceries she had just brought home from the supermarket, she heard a small noise in the living room, and had time to think to herself that he had dropped his book, before she heard him say in a muted voice, *Oh yallah.* She hurried to the living room, and found him sprawled in the chair panting for breath. His face was twisted in agony, and his whole body was leaning to one side and shaking uncontrollably. She did as she was instructed, wedged his teeth open with a spoon to check that he had not swallowed his tongue. Then she called the emergency number, laid him out on the floor so he could breathe properly, and was ready to give him mouth-to-mouth if he faltered. By the time the ambulance arrived he was unconscious but still breathing on his own. In the ambulance, Maryam was shaken by a panic whose name she knew well. He is going to die.

Hanna and Jamal both came down the same day, and they all learned from the doctors that Abbas had suffered a stroke and that it would take a few days to assess the damage. In the meantime he was sedated to allow his body to recover some equilibrium, although he was probably out of immediate danger. They went in to see him together, and saw him lying shrunken in his bed, a thin brown man with tubes coming out of his nostrils and his arm, but breathing on his own. *He is not going to die*, Maryam thought firmly, *He is not going to die*. She wanted to say this to her children, but perhaps it had not occurred to them how close he had come. The doctor had been very reassuring in his report. Perhaps to the children Abbas looked even stranger than he did to her, because they had not seen him since he fell ill, and had seen neither him nor her for weeks and must have imagined them well and at ease in their absence. But perhaps she was being sentimental, assuming her children were more innocent than they were. They were probably not at all surprised to be standing around their father's hospital bed despite her reassurances that he was getting better after his collapse. They knew quite well enough how old he was, and maybe had been secretly dreading that something terrible was yet to happen.

The shock of their Ba's illness made them solemn when they got home, but drew them closer together in a kind of mourning. They followed her to the kitchen while she prepared supper, talking about their Ba and remembering his antics. After a while, Jamal went into the living room to watch their *ancient TV*, as he called it.

'Have you got a drink in the house?' Hanna asked, looking into various kitchen cupboards. Maryam nodded towards the right cupboard and watched her daughter turn towards it with a resolute look. She really wanted that drink. Hanna was then twenty-eight years old, had been teaching for five years, and was about to give up her job to follow her boyfriend Nick to Brighton where he had just got his first job as a university teacher. Each time Maryam saw her, she seemed more assured: in her voice and in the movement of her eyes, in the way she dressed, as if complicated choices were involved in the way she looked as she did. Well, yes of course complicated choices were involved, but it was as if she was deliberately remaking herself from someone she did not like. Maryam thought her speech was also changing, leaving one voice behind and taking up another one, still warm (most of the time), but with an undertone of challenge and worldliness that had not been there before. It was the voice of a young Englishwoman making her way in the world. Is this what parents do, she wondered, study their children as they turn into men and women they learn to grow cautious of? And what do they think as they look at us? Do they think how difficult, how tedious, how she's failed me? She had never had parents or family, not really, not so she could compare what she knew now with what she thought she knew before. And Abbas never mentioned (or almost never mentioned) his parents, so it was all guesswork for her, making things up on the hoof.

'He'll have to retire now, won't he?' Hanna said, and then took a sip of wine. 'Will you be able to get all his paperwork in order or do you want help with that?'

'Yes, yes, he'll have to retire now,' Maryam replied. If he lives. The questions were meant kindly, but Hanna had taken to speaking to her in this insisting way, as if she was likely to be forgetful. 'We'll have to wait for the doctor, but I should think they'll say he must retire,' Maryam said.

'All right, tell me if you need help,' Hanna said. She stepped forward and gave her mother a quick embrace. 'Nick sends his love. He's sorry he couldn't come. He's commuting to Brighton and it's wearing him down, but we're moving in a fortnight. He's found a place to rent and I've got some supply teaching all set up. It's going to be hectic for a while, but I can come if you need me.'

'Yes, I will, but now I just want him to get better,' Maryam said, and could not prevent her voice from quavering.

The next day they went to see Abbas before Hanna returned to London, and afterwards Jamal stayed behind at the hospital while Maryam went to drop Hanna off at the station. He sat beside his father's bed, looking at his face, tranquil and composed despite the tubes, and he smiled. He didn't think he was going to die yet. He was breathing regularly, his eyes closed, silent and unreachable, as if he was in one of his distant places. But the ashy skin on his face, the wrinkled hands, the shallow rising and falling of his flaccid neck told him that he had been through pain, was going through pain. His father was often silent, and preferred solitude, so perhaps he was not in agony where he was. It was just a fancy, a bit of wishful thinking on his son's part. Ma often said how alike they were in their love of silence, Jamal and Abbas, and perhaps they were, but Ba's silences were sometimes dark and his solitariness had a feeling of menace, as if he had gone somewhere where it would not be pleasant to meet him. At those times, his face turned sour, turned down, frowning, his eyes glowing with a kind of ache or shame. When he spoke in that state, even when he spoke to Ma, his voice was harsh and his words were cruel. Jamal hated that, but most of all he hated that he spoke to Ma like that. It made him shudder with anxiety for what that voice would lead to, for the unhappiness he knew it must cause Ma. He sat beside his father's bed, looking at his lean face, serene after suffering, and thought that he did not want to think about those dark silences and those growling words. He wanted to think about his other Ba, so that if he could feel his thoughts as he sat beside him, it would give him strength to fight off the assailant one more time.

When they were children, and Ba was in the mood and they were not being too boisterous, he loved to tell them stories. (He would think about that Ba, the laughing story-teller who lost himself in his tales.) He just started and they immediately fell in. He sometimes even shouted *fallen* to hurry them to their places. *Fallen* was what children said when they played soldiers, he explained. Fall in. What children? Where? But those were questions he did not bother to answer. He just hushed them and motioned for them to come closer. They sat as close to him as they could and stared with wide-open eyes while he revealed his little wonders. He told them the most absurd incredible stories, and they swallowed them whole, Hanna and he. He knew how to draw them in, and they could *see* in his face that the stories were true. They were not, but he told them like that and they believed him, and perhaps he believed them himself as he told them. There was one story in which he was chased for hours by a troop of laughing elephants. He described them to his children, the great beasts thundering behind him, lumbering leather-cheeked pachyderms laughing their trunks off, their double chins and their huge bellies swinging as they trotted after him, cackling and snorting.

Do you know why they are called pachyderm? Because they have such thick skins. He outwitted them in the end by lying flat on the ground. They stood around him not laughing any more, but puzzled and sad, and then wandered away. You have to understand, their Ba told them, that it offends elephant sense of fair play to stamp on something lying flat and still on the ground. Only you have to lie *completely* still otherwise it's curtains, the end, squelch.

Another time their Ba was forced to play hide and seek with a hungry shark in a coral reef in Sulawesi. The sharks in Sulawesi are famous, he told them. They are big bullying brutes with a huge appetite. They just love their work, swaggering in the ocean and barging into whatever gets in their way. If you watch them carefully, keeping your distance, of course, you'll see them smile as they open their huge jaws to chomp a little friendly parrot fish that's swimming by. But they are not very clever, they can't resist knocking into things, so as long as you don't let those huge teeth get too near, you have a chance. In the end, after being chased by the Sulawesi shark for ages, their Ba tricked him by swimming through a narrow coral alley, and the shark barged in and wedged himself in there while Ba escaped.

There was another time when he spent a week in a tree while a pack of barking hyenas patrolled beneath him, raising their bums and firing streams of their poisonous shit towards him. Did you know that hyena shit scalds? It's one of their deadliest weapons. Hyenas fire shit into the eyes of their prey and then pounce. Their Ba had no choice but to climb as high as he could on that tree and hope that the hyenas would empty their bellies and run out of ammunition. He did not even dare doze in case he slipped off the tree, because then those powerful hyena jaws would crack his bones with one snap.

Their favourite was the one about a talking camel. Their Ba was a sailor before he met their Ma, and he went everywhere, and in India he met a talking camel. Everything fabulous is to be found in India: unexpected and magical creatures, ladhoo and halwa badam, precious stones that hatch out of birds' eggs, marble palaces and rivers of ice. The talking camel told their Ba stories, and they became such good friends that Ba invited him to come and visit. So maybe one day they might meet him, although India was a long way and it might take the talking camel a long time to walk all the way to England. In the meantime, Ba told the children some of the stories the camel had told him. They were endless, because the camel's supply was infinite. There were no hyenas or sharks in the camel's stories, but baby camels and monkeys and swans and other small friendly creatures.

Sometimes he told them proper stories, ones that he knew from childhood. He only told them on special occasions, when they were younger, on their birthdays or at Christmas. Birthdays were a problem at first, because Ba said celebrating birthdays was conceited, something foreigners did to spoil their children. What was so important about them that their birthdays should be celebrated? He did not celebrate his birthday. Their Ma did not celebrate her birthday. He did not know anyone apart from these European foreigners who celebrated birthdays. Were they more important than their Ma and Ba and everyone else in the world who was not a European? No birthdays. But he had to give in in the end, because their Ma made them a cake every birthday and put candles on it, and cooked them special meals, and one year he came home from work to find the kitchen decorated with balloons and a little party in full swing. So he had no choice but to grin in defeat and watch the solemn happiness of his children. *Yallah, we have become civilised*, he said. Christmas was just as troublesome at first, a wasteful festival of pagan drunkenness, he called it, but one year he secretly bought a small silver tree and some lights, and he laughed with them when they leaped around him with surprised delight. Then after the frenzy, they sat on the floor in a circle, their Ma, Hanna and Jamal, and he began. Hapo zamani za kale. In the old days of antiquity. He had different voices for all the characters. When the cruel man laughed, Ba was raucous and ugly, twirling his pretend moustache and swaggering his skinny shoulders like a brawler. When the beautiful young mother begged for help, he was piteous, wringing his hands and fluttering his eyelids. When the good man put the world to rights, he was commanding, his chin held up in determination and his eyes flashing. It was the crudest play-acting but they loved it, and when he finished he and Hanna applauded and showered him with kisses. He loved it too, their Ba, and smiled and chuckled and called to Ma to rescue him from the children.

Jamal smiled as he remembered the performance, and leaned forward to touch his father on the arm. What made these moments so funny was that their Ba was not a jolly or loud sort of person. He did not join in and laugh when they were playing their games as Ma did, and he did not like it when they were noisy. Perhaps that was because he was so much older than her. Ma did not mind playing the child, but it seemed a long way for Ba to come down to that. When it was time for TV, he left the room and went upstairs, although it has to be said that it was children's TV or old musicals on weekend afternoons that drove him away. He stayed for the news. Often he was tired from work, and he was not at home during the day, so perhaps he was not used to having them around so much, yelling and tugging and bickering in the *sweet* way of children. But he was quiet anyway, and perhaps became quieter as time passed. As he grew up, Jamal sometimes felt that his father's silences meant that he had disappointed him in a way he was not sure of. How tiresome offspring must be, so you can't even sit quietly without them thinking that you disapprove of them.

Anyway, Ba did not like to talk that much. He never answered the phone, or almost never. If he was alone in the house, the phone could ring and ring without interruption until the caller got the message. There's nobody here, my good sir. Their Ma devised a code to get him to answer when she needed him to. A couple of rings then hang up, another couple of rings and then hang up again, then the third time let the phone ring until he answered. He always answered that call. When they were all at home and having a bit of fun, he would sit there with them but did not usually join in. It was not that he grumbled or disliked it, or not much, he just sat there in his own place, sometimes smiling, maybe throwing in the odd remark, or occasionally grumbling. Unless he had one of his bees in his bonnet, and then you could not stop him until he had had his say. He just talked over any attempt to interrupt him or change the subject, the way you see politicians do when they are asked a question they do not want to answer. Otherwise he sat with his newspaper, or a crossword or a book, when it was quiet enough for him to read, not saying much. That was it, not saying much. He loved reading books about the sea, histories, novels, marine life, stories of wandering and travel and endurance. That was why they loved it when he threw himself into the stories and acted up. It was so funny when you knew what he was like at other times.

When they were little, up until about the time when Jamal was ten or eleven, they went on a lot of outings. Their Ba loved that. He found events in the local paper and said: Children, how about an outing to see whatever this Sunday? When Sunday morning came, they cleaned up and got dressed as if they were going somewhere far away, packing a spare blanket to sit on for their picnic, a towel to mop up any spills, and raincoats in case of rain. They never went far, but the previous evening Ba would have studied the road map as if they were headed for an expedition and he was the leader. They visited ornamental gardens, animal parks, old churches, market shows, even caravan exhibitions. Ma never contradicted his choice. Outings were his thing. She just packed some snacks, tomato sandwiches, which Ba loved but everyone else hated, cheese sandwiches and grilled meatballs and yoghurts and crisps and lemonade, and a thermos of milky sweet tea for Ba. They always had the same picnic, and Jamal knew that for the rest of his life he would always remember those outings whenever he ate a meatball. When all was ready, they got in the car and off they went. Sometimes they had to turn back after a few minutes because Ba asked one of his questions: Did you lock the back door? Is the heating switched off? Have you got my wallet? Once on their way, Ma always drove while Ba looked around him like a tourist, drawing the children's attention to the most ordinary sights: sheep in a field, a windmill, a line of pylons marching across the countryside. Even if his choices of outings were sometimes strange, Hanna and Jamal made faces at each other and had fun anyway. There were always treats during an outing, sooner or later. Ma sometimes led them in raucous songs and Ba did his best not to mind the noise.

Hanna used to say to Jamal that they were a strange

family, an odd family. Their mother was an abandoned baby who had no idea of her real parents, and their father never spoke about his. Jamal did not really think they were strange or odd, although he agreed with Hanna when she said that. She made them sound odd. He couldn't remember when he first heard his mother's story, and whether he heard it first from Ma or from Hanna. Hanna was always telling him things when they were small. He seemed to have known that story all his life though, and as time passed the meaning of it seemed to grow, as did the oddness of his father's silence. He didn't know if they were told not to speak about their mother's story to other people, but he didn't. He never told anyone about it. Over the years, their Ma spoke about it now and then, and sometimes he learned a new detail he had not known before. It was not told as one of those stories their parents returned to and recounted to each other as part of their shared history, laughing at memorable set pieces that may not have been accompanied by laughter when they happened, tales of their courtship and love, of fortitude and absurdities and near disasters. The stories of their Ma's childhood came out in bits and pieces, an episode recalled or a feeling recollected in the middle of telling another story or driving home a scolding, or an incident she drifted into as her mind wandered. And Jamal too had his own way of listening, not one he learned or practised, but one which came to him without thought. He listened in silence. He did not ask for any details and he did not interrupt. He wondered now if that is how children listen to stories, or if he was just a docile and solitary little boy, and what his Ma was telling him was curious enough and did not require further questions. His mother sketched a moment and he pictured it, and found a place for the image among the others he already possessed.

He was not sure if at first he thought the story of his mother's abandonment was real. Probably not. When he was a child everything felt so unlike the world he knew in some other place in his mind, that he did not know how to disbelieve anything. But at some point he must have realised that it was a real story and he clutched at any new detail that his mother released. By the time he was a teenager, and could be spoken to with greater openness, his mother had settled into her own style of disclosure. Jamal was nervous of disrupting the pattern, of making her wary of speaking about such things to him. Hanna was less obedient, more confident of getting what she wanted from her Ma. She asked for events to be made clear, for names to be repeated, and to be told what happened to people who figured in the stories. How far is Exeter from here? Where were your mum and dad living now? How did Mauritius get its name? Her questions forced their mother into asides and explanations and out of the confiding tone in which the most intimate details emerged. When Jamal was on his own with his mother, he let her speak uninterrupted, relishing the deliberate way she added depth to the picture, pausing to allow a forgotten detail to emerge, surprising herself with something she had forgotten to remember before. And Jamal did his best to make no challenge when he noticed any contradictions. He did not know then that stories do not stand still, that they change with new recollections and rearrange themselves subtly with every addition, and what seem like contradictions may be unavoidable revisions of what might have happened. He did not know this consciously, but he had an instinct for listening, which amounted to the same thing.

Once, while he was still living at home, Ma was talking about Exeter and a bad winter there when everything froze.

40

One thing led to another and she began to reminisce, and as she talked she grew sad: about how she never visited there since they left in 1974, about friends she had lost touch with, about Ferooz. Ba was also in the room and he looked up from his crossword as he sensed Maryam's mood and boomed out, *It's a pleasure to meet you, Mr Boots*, which was one of their jokes about when they first met.

Ma smiled. 'I do wish I could find Ferooz, though,' she said, looking at Ba.

Jamal knew that her mother had tried to get in touch with her adoptive parents but could not find them. They all knew that, she often talked about how after Hanna was born she had wished for a reconciliation more than anything, how she regretted losing touch with Ferooz. She did not talk in this way in front of Ba, at least Jamal had not heard her do so. Then when she did, he looked at her with a discouraging look.

'Why do you worry yourself about those people?' he said, snapping at her. He must have heard the snap, because when he spoke again he made his voice sound sane and persuasive. 'They did not treat you well. At least you tried to find them, which is a great deal more than they will have bothered to do for you, I can assure you of that. You tried to find them and you failed, so now there's nothing more you can do. Forget them.'

It was a tense moment, and Jamal saw that his mother held his Ba's look for a moment before he dropped his eyes to his crossword. He understood that the look she had given Ba was a kind of challenge: *I don't want to forget them. I don't want to be like you.* What could have happened that was so bad that it made her run away, yet was not bad enough to prevent her yearning for reunion? Maybe nothing in particular. Perhaps she had just been impetuous, a girl of seventeen making a romance of her life, and then she waited too long to admit her regrets. It was in such moments that they seemed a strange family, these moments they approached and then retreated from, these stories and events which made brief unexpected appearances and then disappeared amid long looks and drawn-out silences.

Why was Ba so silent about his time before? Jamal gently patted his father's thigh as he lay there on the hospital bed. 'What did you do? Can you hear me? You can't be that ill, or they'd have punched holes in you and filled you up with tubes and hitched you to a machine,' he said aloud.

Abbas opened his eyes suddenly, stared blankly for a moment and then shut them again. It shook Jamal, that sudden bloodshot stare, as if the dead had spoken, and then he felt unkind for the thought. You're not that ill, look at you, huffing away like some pasha in his hammock, he said softly. But then he noticed that his breathing had changed, had grown slightly agitated. Should he call someone? He could hear staff moving about the other side of the curtain that surrounded the bed. After a moment, Ba heaved a small sigh and his breathing gradually became regular again. It was strange to be sitting beside his sleeping father, who lay there defenceless as he had never known him to be before. Usually he was such a light sleeper that, should you by some unusual chance have caught him dozing, he stirred as soon as you approached. Maybe those taut nerves of his were still working, and Jamal's voice had penetrated through the drugs and made him open his eyes.

Jamal patted his father on the thigh once more. *Don't scare me like that again. Just rest now. Why do you never talk about your family?* Because he never had, at least never to do much more than draw a sketchy picture of a miserly father and a put-upon mother. Sometimes, often, he talked

42

about being a sailor and the countries he visited, or the various bad jobs he had had to do over the years before he settled into the one he did for the rest of his life, as an engineer in the electronics factory. But never about his family or even about where he came from. When they were younger Hanna or Jamal asked, in the uncomplicated way of children, about where their grandparents were or what they were like, or other questions of that kind, but most of the time their father brushed their questions aside, sometimes with a smile and sometimes without. You don't want to know about that, he would say. Now and then he would tell them things, precious little things as they seemed to Jamal, but nothing very precise, nothing very concrete. It was as if he spoke out of a reverie, unguarded for a few moments, holding up a fragment of a whimsy before letting it float away into the blinding light.

He remembered how one Christmas he told them about rosewater. This is how we greet each other in our celebrations. On the first day of Idd, people called on each other to offer greetings and share a cup of coffee and, if they were well off enough, a small bite of halwa. In some houses, the host sprinkled his guests with rosewater as they arrived, shaking it out of a silver fountain into their hands and sometimes lightly showering their hair with it. When Hanna asked for more, because she wanted to know about these people and which houses they visited – as did Jamal but he did not have her fearlessness about asking – he told them about how rosewater was distilled from rose petals and how it was used in various foods as well as in religious ceremonies in all parts of the world from China to Argentina. He told them about Idd and gave them a travelogue: how Idd was celebrated in that country as opposed to another one, in which month of the lunar year it occurred, what a lunar year is. When they asked him about his home country, he said he was a monkey from Africa.

It did not take very long for them to learn not to ask him certain kinds of questions. Jamal could not bear the look of irritation on his face when they persisted with their questions. It was Hanna mostly, because she felt the deprivation more than he did. She preferred to pin down details, and sometimes she found Ba's evasiveness so intensely frustrating that she had to leave the room.

'No, not evasiveness, evasions, Beautiful One,' she said later when they were old enough to talk about such things with bitterness, and when the undergraduate Hanna had acquired enough language to analyse what she called her dysfunctional family. Long ago he had asked his father what the name Jamal meant, and he told him it meant the Beautiful One, and so that became the name Hanna used as his ironic nick name. She herself preferred to be called Anna, and that was the name she used outside the house.

'They are lost,' she said. 'Ba deliberately lost himself a long time ago, and Ma found herself lost from the beginning, a foundling. What I want from them is a story that has a beginning that is tolerable and open, and not one that is tripped with hesitations and silences. Why is that so difficult? I want to be able to say this is what I am. Yes, I know, so has every human being who has ever given the matter any thought, but I don't want to crack the mystery of the soul or the nature of being. I just want some simple boring details. Instead we get snippets of secret stories we cannot ask about and cannot speak about. I hate it. Sometimes it makes me feel that I am living a life of hiding and shame. That we all are.'

Jamal recognised the feeling she described. It came to him at unexpected moments when he too felt he had to dissemble and fudge. That feeling – that there was something to be ashamed of – had been with him most of his life, even when he did not know of its presence and had only slowly begun to understand its several causes. It added to the sense of difference and oddness that he had grown up with, a sense of strangeness. He had learned to recognise that feeling in many ways, and not just in response to hostility and unkindness and the teasing at school. He saw it in the stilted and careful smiles he received from some of the mothers of other children he knew, in the way people tried hard to prevent him from noticing that they had seen something to notice, in the ingenuous and sometimes insistent and cruel questions the children asked about his country and its customs. It was years before he learned to say *this* is my country, and it was Hanna who taught him to say that.

Even when they tried to, they could not forget his difference and nor could he, even though he pretended to. How could it be otherwise? After two or three centuries of unrelenting narratives about how unalike one another they were, how could it be otherwise? Sooner or later, the meaning of their difference would be there in a look or a word or the sight of someone walking across the road. The teacher might be talking about poverty in the world and would not be able to resist a quick glance in his direction. Poverty is to be found in places where people like him lived, and we, who have redeemed ourselves from this condition, must learn not to despise those who have not yet found the means to save themselves. We must do what we can to help them. That is what he took the teacher's pained look to mean, Jamal (and Hanna and those others who look like them) is one of those poor wretches but we must not despise him or say cruel things to him.

Whenever someone old and dark-skinned came shuffling

along the pavement in the way of old people, hair dishev-
elled perhaps or a grubby coat buttoned up askew, they
chuckled, the children he grew up with, and glanced at him,
embarrassed for him. He pretended that he did not feel any
discomfort, pretended he was not any different from the
chucklers.

'There are times when I hate that they brought me here,'
Hanna said. 'That they did not find another place to have
me and to have you. Not because other places are free from
cruelties and lies, but just to be saved from so much demeaning pretence. Not to have the chore of pretending to be no
different from people who are full of shit about themselves.
But I suppose they did not have any choice in the matter,
really, only an appearance of choice. They could have
chosen not to have me, but after that the matter was out of
their hands.'

It was after they both left home that Hanna raged like
this, about the secrecy and their suppressed and dissem-
bling lives. For a while, the matter seemed to possess her,
then somehow she found some way of coping with it. It
was university that did that, and the new friends she met
there, and the love affairs, and academic success. As she
made her way in the big world, the frustrations of being
Hanna Abbas, growing up in a small modern house in
Norwich with parents who seemed to her to be out of their
depth, became less urgent. She was fully Anna now, and
hardly ever talked about her difference in the same way.
Instead it became an embellishment of her Britishness.
Once he teased her and said that perhaps he should change
his name to Jimmy, and maybe that would make him less
fretful. He saw that he had hurt her, that he had made her
seem treacherous to herself.

'I hate the name Hanna,' she said. 'I don't know where

they got it from. Anyway, you're the one who called me Anna.'

'I know, I know,' he said, placating her. 'When I was a baby and couldn't say the whole thing. Only teasing.'

Jamal had not got to where she was yet, but perhaps prudence led inevitably there. He could not quite make himself say *home*, when he meant England, or think of *foreigners* without fellow feeling.

He used to think that there were not many people who knew as little as he did about his parents. He used to imagine that other people knew who they were, and who their grandparents were, and where they lived and what they did. They would have uncles in Ireland and cousins in Australia and in-laws in Canada, and perhaps an awkward and disreputable relative who had cut himself off from everyone. They had obligations and get-togethers and tiresome relations. That was what normal family life was like, from what he could tell, whereas they were a vagabond family, wanderers without connection or duties. He had learned different since he started his doctoral research on migration movements to Europe, had learned something of how precarious, how mean, how resourceful the lives of these strangers were, how blood-soaked some of their stories were. He learned to be patient for the story that he knew his Ba would tell him one day. He looked at his father, breathing regularly in his drugged sleep, so recently close to departure, and thought perhaps the time for the telling was not too far off. If you stop struggling so hard against it, life can be quite tolerable, he whispered to his father, but he was not sure if he believed that himself. Why didn't his Ba do more with his life? Why didn't he want more? But was it so little what he did and what he wanted? It was not so little to spend so many years waiting in patient silence, knowing that one day he would be struck down just like this.

What did you do? Jamal whispered to his father. *Did you kill someone? Were you a torturer? Were you a crusher of souls?*

Maryam came back from dropping Hanna off at the station, and Jamal gave her the chair he had been sitting on. She touched Ba's hand and Jamal expected the eyes to fly open again, but nothing happened.

'He opened his eyes while you were were away,' he told her.

'What! Did he speak?' she asked.

'No, he just opened his eyes wide and then shut them again,' Jamal said. 'I don't think he woke up. I think it was like a twitch.'

Maryam went to tell the Sister who came to have a look and assured them that he was sleeping and was doing fine. Why didn't they go and have a rest themselves and come back tomorrow? The way he was going, the doctor may well let him wake up tomorrow. On the way home, Maryam asked Jamal how long he was staying for and he said for three or four days. He'd see how things went. He was moving to a studio flat in a few days. He said *studio flat* with a self-mocking inflection. It was just an upstairs bedroom with a partitioned shower and toilet, but it would be a change from living in a small room in a house with two other students he had come to know too well: less interruption, and more work and emotional space.

When they got back to the house Maryam went upstairs and brought down a photograph of Abbas in a frame. It was taken in Exeter by the friend that Abbas was staying with, and in it he was wearing a light-coloured, polo-neck sweater and short denim jacket. Maryam put it on the shelf above the gas fire and then turned to Jamal. 'So handsome. You look just like him,' she said. 'Except for that craggy beard.'

He thought she meant scraggy but he did not correct her. It was disconcerting, the way she mispronounced certain words, as if English was a language she had learned imperfectly when in fact she had lived in England all her life and only spoke English.

'Where was that taken?' he asked. He knew, but he sensed that Ma wanted to talk about the old days.

They went to Birmingham first. Abbas said they were more likely to find work there and she did not know any different. If he had said Newcastle she would have gone, and that was as far as she could think of then without crossing the sea. Somehow Scotland was not a place you went to but came from. That's what she thought in her ignorance. He was the one who had roamed the world and knew its ways and knew where was safe. Birmingham was as exciting to her as anywhere else because it was far from Exeter, and because she was with him for company. Sometimes she was fearful about what she had done, at other times she could not understand why she waited so long. But maybe she did understand; she would not have known how to run away on her own. She would have been too frightened of what life could do to her, without money, without charm or daring. Without. Abbas had a little bit of money, so they were not completely broke and were able to find a room and look for work. It wasn't too bad. Work wasn't easy to find in those days of inflation and strikes and trade-union wars. She found work as a cleaner in a hospital because it was the kind of work no one wanted, and he got work on building sites at first, and then found a factory job. It was confusing to live in a big city, and to do that kind of work, but it wasn't too bad, and it was too late to think about what she did not like about it.

Her life became completely different. She felt nervous at times because she was not sure how things were done and Abbas was not always there for her to ask him, but he was always there at the end of the day and she could not have imagined the pleasure of living with a loving companion. The company. He was full of talk and laughter . . . well, when they were on their own. He was more careful when they were with other people, but he wasn't shy, he wasn't afraid. At least that's what he said: I'm not afraid of anybody or anything. The first time she heard him say that, she did not believe him. She thought he was swaggering for her, trying out those words to see if she liked him more for it. She must have done because he kept saying them for several years. Honestly, though, he was such a battler in those days. No one was going to bully them or take advantage of them, he said. She thought he talked like that to give both of them courage and confidence, and it did, it did. When he was not doing his big talk, he was so gentle and perhaps a little bit anxious, although she did not know what of, or even if it was of anything in particular. She was young enough to take everything in her stride, and she did not worry too much about anything, not when she had Abbas telling her hilarious stories about his journeys and some sad ones too, and on weekends they could stay in bed until early afternoon. They went to the cinema when they felt like it, and had a roast meal at the café round the corner if they wanted. She thought he would miss the sea, but he said no, he'd had enough of that. They were so lucky, she thought, to have found each other like that, just imagine the chances.

Their lives were good in Birmingham. They both had work, even if it was poor work, and those first three years just flew. She thought of Ferooz and Vijay at times, and felt guilty and sick for running away without a word. When she said this to Abbas he said nothing. He did not sympathise or discourage, not in those days. He just looked down and waited silently until her hurt went away, as it always did after a while. There was so much pleasure in such ordinary things: buying pots and pans for the kitchen, decorating the bathroom of the flat they rented, learning to listen to music that she thought she despised. He loved reading, which was not something she could take to. It took too long when there were so many other things which did not. Sometimes he told her about the books he was reading, and that was enough for her. She loved to hear him talk about places he had known, about his experiences, which sometimes sounded impossible enough to find their way into books. She noticed that he always stopped short at some point, that he was holding part of the story back, and she soon worked out that he was not telling her about his childhood or about his home. When she asked him about that, he found a way of slipping away without explaining himself and she let him do so when perhaps she should not have done. After all these years, when so much of their lives had happened to them together, she did not know how to make him speak about what she had allowed him to keep silent about so long ago. It did not seem so important then, before the children came. That was what she wanted in those years in Birmingham. She really wanted her Hanna straight away but Abbas said she was too young and that they should wait for a few years. They argued about that. She knew that he was older than he had told her, that he was really thirty-four when they met in Exeter, and she thought that he did not want children any more, that he had become used to his roaming life, but he said no, it was because she was too young to burden herself with children yet.

After three years in Birmingham – it did not feel anything like three years, it went so fast – they moved to Norwich. Abbas applied for a job in a new electronics firm and he got it. He had to do training for it and then they sent him there. It was a much better job with good pay and a pension scheme, and by then they both decided they would prefer to live in a small town. Abbas liked the water being nearby too. At first they called him a fitter, and then as times changed he was called an engineer, and then as even more time passed he advanced to chief engineer. When she went for work at the Job Centre, the man asked her what work she did in Birmingham. She said she was a hospital cleaner and he smiled and said you are in luck, so she ended up as a hospital cleaner again. She told herself that being a cleaner had its own satisfactions, you cleaned things, and she took the job. When she was a child living with Ferooz and Vijay, she wanted to work in a hospital, to be a psychiatric nurse like Ferooz. Well, she ended up working in hospitals most of her grown-up life, even if not as a psychiatric nurse.

Maryam looked at the picture for a while and then she said: 'What do you think? He still looks quite good, doesn't he? He was almost never ill, you know. But it happens like that, you're fine all your life and then one day everything descends on you.'

He thought he would probably never get better. Years ago he had dreaded this coming, the coming of this dread, dying in a strange land that did not want him. That was years ago, and the country still felt strange. It still felt like somewhere he would one day leave. In some of the port cities he found himself in all that time ago, there were whole neighbourhoods of Somalis or Filipinos or Chinese, and it was possible to forget that he was in England for a short while. Despite their ragged appearance, these neighbourhoods were watchful and alert for strangers. They were people who were a long way from home, now huddled together for safety, and they had to keep a sharp lookout to protect their honour, which is to say their women and their property. But away from the big old ports, he sometimes passed dark-skinned old men on their own (old men more often than not, not usually old women) and he felt sorry for them. They looked so strange, those old men with their crinkly white hair and leathery dark skins walking English streets, like beasts out of their element, pachyderms on concrete pavements. I'll never let that happen to me, he said to himself then, I'll never let myself die in a strange land that does not want me, and here he was, more or less on the crematorium trolley.

The doctor, Mr Kenyon . . . He thought at first that he said his name was Mr Kenya, and thought how funny, they get everywhere this lot, and feel no shame about naming themselves after land grabs, but he had said Kenyon. Why do they call themselves Mr and not Dr as they get more senior? Mr Kenyon told him he would lose some function. Paralysed. But some of it might come back. Physiotherapy and a good attitude. Did he say a good attitude or a good diet? Hearing is not one of the lost functions, speech is. He can make sounds but not words. Makes you wonder at the cleverness of it, making words out of these gurgles and whistles, making sense. We'll get it back, Mr Kenyon said. Yes bwana, you and I.

He had never known such fatigue. He felt as if a vital

fluid in his body had been drained out, and when they first sent him home, he sat for hours without energy or volition, unable to lift his arm or rise to his feet or even close his mouth. He could not always keep his eyes open, and his mind wandered in and out of stupor. To his astonishment he found that hours had gone by in the blink of an eye. He could not bear voices or music on the radio, and so a silence enveloped him and oppressed the air around him.

He did almost nothing for himself. Maryam cleaned him and fed him and medicated him, and he paid no attention. She took him to the surgery once a week, dressing him and then taking him downstairs one step at a time, and then driving him there. He sat silently while she debated his symptoms and his treatment with the doctor. They had been adversaries for years, and Abbas smiled as he watched them battle over his sick body. He expected that it was an inward smile, which did not show on his face. The doctor wanted him to do exercises, take a walk every day.

'You like reading,' she said, speaking each word clearly as if he had trouble hearing her. Hearing function not impaired. 'Walk to the library and read there for a while. Exercise is very, very important for you. You must make more effort. You must tell yourself that you will get better. Attitude is very important in therapy.'

Mr Kenyon must have said attitude, then. 'I can't sleep,' he wanted to say to her, not properly, everything is uncomfortable, my head, my throat, my belly, but when he spoke only thick slurred noises came out of his mouth. He lay on the bed with eyes open, keeping as still as possible. Maryam slept on a camp bed, which she wedged between the wardrobe and the window, and left him the whole bed to himself. It was to give him room to sleep in comfort, she said, but perhaps it was also to get away from his smell and his decrepitude. Even then, he often could not sleep. The small-est sound woke her up so he had to lie rigid until he heard her breathing change. But sometimes he could not help himself, and the nausea and stomach pains overcame him and he heard his voice shrieking in the underground cham-bers of his mind, on and on like an animal dying. Then on other nights he lay still, unable to sleep, and in the corners of his mind he saw pulses of red and green light where the pain lurked, waiting for him to draw near.

There was a tangled path from the road, easy to miss when you did not know what you were looking for. He was on his way home from school. It was a long walk on the narrow country road, stepping into the verge now and then to allow a cart or a passenger lorry to drive past. The verge was dense with palms and trees, and gave him shelter in the early afternoon heat. It was an hour's walk from school to home. He was the only one in his family who was sent to school. What a battle that had been, going to school. His father saw him as he came out into the open. He was weav-ing a basket for the vegetables that would go to market the next day, and he paused in his work to shout at him. 'Get to work, you maluun. Do you think you have slaves here?'

That was his father. His name was Othman, a hard mean man who gloried in his toughness and who always spoke in a shout. Now, as Abbas lay there in the dark, broken by disease in a stranger's land, he saw his father standing in the yard in the afternoon sun, his saruni rolled around his thighs, a half-woven basket on a tree stump in front of him. The short hoe that he always took everywhere with him lay at his feet. His short, muscular body was as hard as a fist, and he stared at Abbas with careless ferocity. That was how he looked at everything, ready to scrap with everyone, animal or human, and his appearance of rage was not diminished by the large thick-rimmed spectacles he wore at all times except when he went to sleep. Whatever he did, his father managed to look dangerous and comic at the same time. Abbas had been looking forward to his lunch, but he knew that to say anything would be to provoke his father intolerably. Instead he asked if he could say his prayers first, thinking he would be able to sneak a few mouthfuls of whatever his mother had put aside for him. He saw his father grin at his wiliness, but he was a pious man, and could not refuse anyone his prayers. 'Hurry up,' he said. 'Don't keep God waiting, and don't keep me waiting either.'

His father had a smallholding, a couple of acres with some fruit and coconut trees, all growing anyhow, as if they found themselves there by chance rather than anyone having planted them that way. He also grew vegetables to sell in town, and no one in the family could be spared from the daily labours of this work. He never tired of telling his children that he had grown up poor and had worked hard all his life, and he did not want to be poor again. No one in his house was going to eat for free. Everyone had to work for the food he stuffed into them. His boy children were his labourers on the land and he made them work as hard as he did. His wife and his daughter were like servants, watumwa wa serikali, as his mother liked to say. They fetched water and firewood, cooked and cleaned, at everyone's bidding all day long, from sunrise to sunrise. God damn this life of a dog.

His father's one indulgence were the pigeons. There was nothing exceptional about these pigeons, no trailing tail feathers or cocky plumes. They were the ordinary dark-grey plebeians to be found all around them, in town and in the countryside, but he built houses for them, which he tied to the trees, and scattered handfuls of millet for them in the yard to see them descending to feed around him, and chased away crows and cats with passionate hatred. He protected them as he did not protect his children. He allowed none of his children to molest them, and so one of their rebellious pleasures was to catapult a pigeon to the ground and roast it over a fire, which they made far away from the house. But even the pigeons did not distract him for long from the unrelenting supervision of his labour camp.

They worked like that, all of them, the whole family, but they lived a hard and poor life without comfort or luxury. It was because their father was such a miser. He hated spending money. He had dug a hole in the ground under his bed where he kept a locked chest for hiding his money. Then he built a trapdoor over the hole, which he kept padlocked. It was like a vocation, or something he had sworn to, an oath taken as a penance to spend as little money as possible. They wore ragged clothes and slept on mats on the floor. They hardly ever ate meat, and even then it was only the knuckle bones of a goat boiled for soup. He was a mean man, all right, mean with money, and mean in the way he saw things. Allah karim, he said if any of their neighbours asked to borrow money for some emergency. God is generous. Ask him for a loan, not me. But still, they were better off than most of their country neighbours, because they lived in a stone house with a latrine at the back rather than a hut made of mud and sticks, and doing their business in a hole in the ground in the bush. The meanness and labour in their house made Abbas feel different from other children. Their lives were just as poor, but they seemed to have time to roam the country roads and raid fruit trees and play long games of mwizi na askari, when he was always hurrying home to sneak a couple of mouthfuls of cassava or bananas and work on the land. Parsimony – it was a word he learned later, but when he did, it truly described his childhood, and even its sound reminded him of the sinister and unnecessary poverty they lived in.

He was the youngest, and he had two elder brothers and an elder sister. One day, when he was about seven, his eldest brother Kassim took him to the school, which was a hard walk from their home, a mile and a half at least. Their father did not like it. The only thing they will teach him at that school is how to be lazy and how to give himself airs, he said. But Kassim had often seen the children at the school while he waited for the bus to take their coconuts and okra and brinjal to town. He saw how cheerful and clean the children were. He heard their voices reciting and murmuring across the road. Abbas knew that sound because sometimes he accompanied his brother to town, apparently to help and learn, so that one day he too could take produce to the market, but really because his brother knew he enjoyed the bus ride. He was so small that he could get a ride for free, so their father did not mind so much.

They waited for the bus under the tree, and across the road they heard the little children reading and reciting softly to themselves. It was a sound that made Abbas smile, and it was a happiness he would have liked to share. He knew that Kassim would have liked that too, for himself. He told him so. Kassim was then thirteen, nothing but a skinny boy who had been a labourer all his life. He was too stupid by then to go to school. It was too late for him. That was what he said as they stood under the tree across the road from the school, waiting for the bus to town. His brother Kassim. Then in a café in town where they stopped for a bun and a cup of tea, they heard someone on the radio talking about how it was everyone's duty to send their children to school, and how noble it was to seek knowledge even if it took them as far away as China. His brother asked who the speaker was and they were told it was the new qadhi, an enlightened man who wanted to change things, who wanted to make people think about their lives. He did a weekly sermon on the radio, and he talked about how people should look after their health and think about their diet and be charitable to their neighbours, and he said that to take care in these matters was a duty to God. In every sermon he said something about sending children to school.

One day, a meeting was called under the big tree and someone from the government came to speak to them. It was in the afternoon after Friday prayers, which were held right there under the tree, because the mosque nearby was not large enough and the congregation overflowed into the clearing anyway. His father was there, as was Kassim and his other brother Yusuf, who was so quiet that he was nick-named Kimya, silence. Kassim na Kimya and their little brother Abbas who was also kimya, the children of the miser Othman. The man from the government was tall and thin, and dressed in a kanzu and kofia. He prayed with them before he spoke, and when he did speak it was with the same urgency as the qadhi on the radio. He told them that now the war was over, the government was ready to improve the lives of its subjects. The war was news to Abbas, but later he would understand. This was 1947. The man from the government spoke at length about the bene-fits of education and encouraged everyone to send their children to school in the new year that was about to begin. They walked home in silence, their father striding ahead as usual and the three brothers quiet with their own thoughts.

That evening Kassim said in front of the whole family that Abbas should go to school. Their father snorted and threatened and everyone fell silent, but Kassim did not back down. He argued and pleaded and whined at their father for days on end. It was enough that all of them were ignorant beasts of burden, but if the government wanted the young ones to go to school, then it was not right to prevent that, he said. What harm could it do? Their father tried to shut Kassim up with abuse – you don't understand anything, you ignorant little puppy – and when that did not stop the pleading, he just ignored him and looked away. Then on the day the new school year began, two weeks after that meeting under the tree, Kassim took Abbas by the hand and without saying a word to their father, he walked with him to school. When school was over that afternoon, Kassim was waiting to walk home with him, and Abbas saw that he was bruised from the beating his father had given him, but the next morning Kassim took him by the hand again and walked him to school, and that was the end of that. Tears came to Abbas's eyes as he lay silently in the dark remembering that first day, remembering his brother.

That was the first big moment in his life, that school in Mfenesini. For years he had tried not to think of these things, and sometimes he even persuaded himself that he had forgotten many of them. His tears there in the dark were for his brother Kassim as much for himself on that January morning in 1947, nostalgic old man's tears for two people now lost to him in a frenzy of panic and guilt. He tried hard not to think of so many things, and for years he thought he succeeded, even if at times he was taken unawares by something that struck out of nowhere with unexpected ferocity. Perhaps it was like that for many people, ducking and weaving through life, wincing as glancing blows landed now and then and putting up a ragged rearguard against a strengthening adversary. Or perhaps life wasn't really like that for most people, and time brought with it calm and reconciliation, only he had not been so lucky or did not recognise his luck. Despite his evasions, he had known that time was wearing him down, and that it was getting harder to shrug off the matters he should have put right but had avoided. Now he was ill and worn out, unable to busy himself or distract himself, lying in the dark waiting for the pain to arrive.

That school in Mfenesini. Think about the school in Mfenesini. He drew a diagram in his mind. There were three blocks: the central one faced the road and the two smaller ones were at right angles to it, making an open quadrangle. Between the central building and the road were flower beds and shrubs, and from one of the bushes hung a length of metal rail that was the school bell. The timetable teacher, as they called him, kept an alarm clock on his desk, and when a period was over he instructed one of the children in the class he was teaching to run out in the garden and strike the metal bar twice with an iron rod that hung beside it. At morning break and at the end of school, he strolled to the bell himself, and struck out a vigorous and joyful medley, which made the children cry out with pleasure. The walls of the classrooms were three foot high. There were no doors or windows so the children could hear and see what was going on in the other classes, that is, if they dared to look. Behind one of the side blocks was the yard where they played during the break, and beyond that were the latrines. Different classes took turns to clean the latrines at the end of every day. It was good to be made to learn about keeping things clean, their teachers told them. In their homes they lived with filth as if it was their God-given right. Here at the school they would learn the benefits of cleanliness and health. Their teachers were fierce and barked at the children sooner than speak to them. Most of them walked around with a guava cutting or a cane or a ruler, and waved it around threateningly to keep order and distributed strokes when required. The strokes were not really serious and after the first year all the children pretended the ruler or the stick did not hurt. It was all part of school, it was what made you learn.

Whenever he was needed, his father took him out of school for a few days. He did this triumphantly, as if he was making a stand against a cruel law. Abbas was put to work weeding or packing or whatever else he could manage at his age, so their father Othman the miser could gloat to his children that everyone in his house worked for the food they ate. These interruptions slowed him down at school, added a whole year in the end because in addition to the weeks his father kept him home during that class, he also fell ill with fever and had to stay in bed for a long time. His teachers told him off for missing classes, but it was a country school and he was not the only one who had to miss classes now and then. Despite his disregard for school, his father sometimes came to the school on the way to town, and went from class to class until he found his little son, and then looked at what was going on with an amused smile. There was enough reluctant affection in that smile to make Abbas smile to himself as he remembered, or thought he remembered. Maybe that was just an old man's sentimental lie. Maybe there was no reluctant affection at all in his father's smile, just scorn.

Well, then, smile or no smile, there was the huge tree on one side of the road, and on the other was the school. During school hours they were not allowed to cross the road, even during their morning break. He did not remember anyone ever explaining why. School rules were there to be obeyed, not to be quibbled over. It was as if once across the road they would escape into the foliage and disappear, although the classrooms were open to the sun and air, and there was no fence or wall around the school grounds. Perhaps the teachers just wanted to make sure they were safe and within sight. The children watched the hubbub that went on under the tree whenever they could. It was a small country market with people selling and buying: fruit, vegetables, eggs, firewood. There was a kiosk selling tea and snacks. He often thought of that little country market under a tree, no, perhaps not thought, more like the image appeared in his mind as he made ready to sleep or when he drifted into memory. The image that came to him had depth and texture, it was not a picture. He felt the warm breeze and heard the laughter of the people buying and selling. Sometimes a new detail appeared, a face he had forgotten to think about for forty years, or an incident whose significance he suddenly understood after all this time. He had seen places like that on TV, not Mfenesini, but places like it. And when he saw these other places, he also saw Mfenesini better. How did that happen? Once they were watching something on TV about Sudan, and they saw a market under a tree and he said, *Mfenesini.*

'What's that?' Maryam asked.

'That's where I went to school,' he said. She asked him to write it down so she could see how it was spelt. He should have gone on then. They had more time after the children left, and he should have gone on, but he fell silent and she did not make him speak.

It must have been the buses that made the teachers nervous, not that there were so many of them but they were unpredictable. Sometimes nothing went past for an hour or more, and then a bus packed with people hurtled out of nowhere and pulled up by the market. If the bus was on its way to town, it stopped to load up with produce or, if it was on its way back, it stopped to let people off. That market was a small torment for the children. They could not keep their eyes away from all that business across the road. Their teachers were constantly demanding their full attention, and that meant keeping their eyes fixed to the front, even if all they were doing was reciting a multiplication table from memory or listening to the teacher reading a story. Someone was always getting a clip round the ear for letting his eyes wander. It was always boys, girls were not hit, not by the male teachers and all their teachers were male. If a teacher hit a girl, her parents came to school to complain, as if he had done something indecent to her.

When something happened under the tree, like a fight or someone toppling off his bicycle, whoosh, the whole school got on its feet, despite the teachers. Abbas smiled in the dark as he remembered that. The teachers worked so hard to keep them quiet and obedient, like it was a point of honour for them to do so. Sometimes it was as if they failed as teachers if the children so much as twitched or scratched themselves. How their teachers loved that deep submissive silence. But they could not make that silence endure. They could not quite keep the children in check. Something always happened, some small insurrection, irrepressible laughter, an undaunted boy whose cheek could not be suppressed.

They seem such quiet, eventless times after all these years and all the things that happened to him later. He went to school, he worked on the land, and sometimes he roamed with the other boys. The most memorable thing that happened in that time was his sister Fawzia's marriage. She was the eldest of them all, and was becoming rebellious and difficult under their father's regime, complaining in a high-pitched whine the whole day long, storming away from any rebuke and disappearing without explanation for hours on end. She must have been seventeen then, and the disappearances must have hastened her wedding day dramatically. You can't have a girl that age going off for hours like that. What else could she be doing but ruining her reputation and bringing dishonour on her family? At eleven years old, Abbas would have been too young to know how such things were done, but a husband was found for Fawzia and the arrangements were put under way.

Their father never stopped complaining about the cost. The expense of the celebrations used up everything he had put away, he said. No one believed him, although it was true that weddings made families poor. Parents used up their savings or went into debt to provide silver and gold and money for the dowry. Then they laid on a banquet so their relatives and any other loafer who wished to, could come and fill their bellies with biriani and ice cream. They paid up to avoid being shamed by gossip. They would be called mean if they failed to satisfy the greedy stomachs of guests they did not even invite but could not turn away. Their father did not mind being called mean. He already was, and he did not care in the slightest. But he paid up as he was required to do. He had no choice, as his wife told him repeatedly, otherwise he would dishonour their daughter. So a big banquet was held, and cooks came in a team from town, bringing their own cauldrons and serving platters, and their ice-cream churns. There was incredible excitement among the youngsters. A calf was tied up a little distance from the house, bleating and bellowing as if it knew what was coming, and a crowd of boys sat buzzing nearby, waiting for the butcher to come and slaughter it. Only when he came he chased them all away before he started. Then fires of clove wood were built and the air began to fill with the aroma of a biriani. The drummers played and guests began to arrive from town and from other places. The women went to the area screened off with palm fronds while the men mingled under the shade and greeted each other, clapped each other's shoulders and laughed. Their father Othman laid aside his short hoe, and wore a new kanzu especially made for the occasion, and a kofia that the groom's father had given him as a gift. Across his shoulders he wore a silk shawl that smelled of camphor, which he brought out of one of the chests in his room. Somehow he managed to suppress the pain it caused him to waste so much of his money on this frivolity, and even to look a little dignified in his finery. Then later the biriani banquet was perfect, and the drumming and singing went on late into the night, and the boys crept in the undergrowth to peep in on the women dancing behind the palm fronds.

Yes, Fawzia's wedding was the most memorable event of that time, although that was not to say that the rest was intolerable. He loved the rains, and the way the ditches filled up, and the frogs multiplied, and all the trees and bushes dripped long after the rain had stopped. He liked school, and could even tolerate the work on the farm, and sometimes went to town with Kassim, as he had done for years, to take the produce to the man they supplied in the market. Then afterwards they wandered the streets for a while, and stopped at a café for a bun and a mug of sweet milky tea.

In the end, at the age of sixteen, he passed the examinations to go to a teacher training college in town. Well, it was not exactly in town, it was six miles out. He had seen it from the road several times on their bus trips to the market. The buildings were painted white and had long verandas and red roofs. From the road, the college looked like a palace by the sea. Some of the buildings were dormitories for students whose homes were on the other island. Local students took a special college bus every day from town, and took the bus back at the end of the day. When he knew he had been selected to go there, he borrowed a bicycle and went from Mfenesini to the college. It was only about ten miles away. He wandered the grounds and walked on the beach and loved it. But his father would have none of it, the hard-faced bully. He told him that he had had his schooling, more than enough of it to last anyone a lifetime. He had had his fun and games, and now it was time to come back to growing okra and brinjal full-time rather than be thinking about bringing even more expense on them with fees and uniforms and books. The whole family turned against the old man, even his Ma. Kassim called him a miser to his face and said to him that he had ruined their lives with his meanness. Their father chased after Kassim with a stick, shouting at him for his defiance and his disrespect, but his brother did not stop arguing even as he ran. Kassim was then twenty-one, and strong enough to wrest the stick from his father's hand and break it in half with one snap, but you can't do that to your own father, not where he came from. You took a beating or you ran. The argument went on for days, with the brothers and their mother taking turns, trying to wear the mean old man down. They got nowhere.

It was a small place, and even a family quarrel was soon known to everyone, especially as Othman the miser did not mind describing his grievances to other people there under the tree. Eventually his sister Fawzia came to hear of what was going on. The life in town suited his honourably married sister, and after her move she became bold and independent, meeting new people and going out daily to visit with them. She turned out to be naturally gifted at small-town scheming and intriguing, with an ear finely tuned into rumour and gossip, and with a sharp wit that made her popular and daunting at the same time. When she heard about these arguments she came home to find out what could be done. It was she who found the solution that allowed Abbas to go to his college. She pawned some of her dowry gold for the fees, so perhaps the dowry was not such a waste of money after all. Then, because his sister and her husband only lived in one rented room themselves and cooked in the shared yard, and so did not have space to spare, she persuaded her husband's relatives to take Abbas in while he studied. Abbas was not sure what arrangements were made, or if the relatives took him in out of kindness. It was not always polite to enquire into such details, but it meant he went to study in town and lived with the relatives of his sister's husband. They gave him a small storeroom, so he had somewhere to sleep and somewhere to work. A small storeroom with a view of the sea. No, don't go that way, don't go that way. He couldn't think any more about that. He didn't want to think about that any more. Not now, no, not now, go to sleep, you cowardly old man. Picture a brightly lit number: 1. Then picture another, glowing silver: 2. And another in flashing magenta: 3. And out of thin mist emerges another: 4. Mashaallah, keep going.

Maryam worried that Abbas was becoming a stranger to her. He was unpredictable, still for long periods and sometimes staring at her as if he had no idea who she was. Then he was tender, holding on to her hand as if he was afraid of allowing her to move out of sight. Dr Mendez had warned her that he might forget things or appear to lose his memory but this would probably be temporary. She did all the checks the doctor required her to do, and fed him the medicines she had prescribed. Abbas did as Maryam instructed, left it all to her, most of the time. At other times be became abrupt and difficult, sobbing with pain and pushing her away.

She worried about the children, that they should not come to think ill of their father, that they should not see him again until he was calmer. As the days passed, Abbas grew a little stronger, although not strong enough to walk to the library as the doctor asked him to do every week. That doctor! Abbas wouldn't even know the way to the library in his state. She went to the library for him and borrowed audio books that she thought he would be able to listen to. At night she lay on her camp bed, listening to Abbas fidgeting on the bed in the dark, dreading that her children might stumble and lose their way in life, that they might lose their father. Abbas slept better in those early weeks of spring. The doctor had given him something to help him sleep, and perhaps the heaps of warm bedding helped. The sleeping medicine made him confused when he woke up but at least he slept, and the rest was bound to make him stronger.

Moving

2

THE FIRST TIME ANNA saw their neighbour, she was in her garden, moving in and out of sight with an air of someone who was oblivious to everything but her work. Anna caught sight of her from the back upstairs window while she was showing the movers where she wanted the boxes. It was a quick glimpse – or rather several quick glimpses – of a slim woman with long fair hair, in jeans and boots, her shirt sleeves rolled up, digging plants into her garden bed from a tray of little yoghurt pots. After a few moments she rose from her haunches and strode in the direction of her house, hurrying a little, urgent to get those plants in. Anna guessed that she was putting on a performance, as if she was aware that she was being watched and wanted to give an appearance of courteous indifference, just getting on with her work. It went through Anna's mind that they might have a neighbour who was a fusspot. Anna moved away from the window just as she came out again, and she sensed that her neighbour looked up seconds after she had moved out of sight.

That was on the day they moved in. For once it was not raining and was, in fact, a mild and sunny March day. With every other move she had made it had rained all day, making everything messy and awkward, adding to the shambles of it all. This was the first move with Nick, or the second if you counted when they had decided to share a flat. At that time, she had moved out of a room in a housing association flatshare into Nick's flat in Wandsworth. It was more Tooting than Wandsworth, but Wandsworth sounded better. Not just sounded better when anyone asked you, it sounded better to live in. Tooting sounded like a repair yard for trains, or an abattoir or a psychiatric hospital. The room she had moved from was in Tottenham, which if you were naïve and generous, made you think of a glamorous football team. It surprised her, when she made the move that time, how much she had accumulated and squeezed into her one room; when she arrived in Wandsworth the van that Nick had hired for the day was packed and bursting. He was determined to make only one trip, for some reason. He made this into a joke, a kind of dare, but she could see his determination. When they unloaded the van her plants were mutilated, a leg was broken off one of her old chairs, the ironing board was twisted. Fortunately, nothing valuable was damaged. Not that she owned anything valuable, she just said that to tease Nick. The mess was all right, though, even if it was sad to see useful or tender things damaged. It was what you would expect moving to be like, the sweating, the grumbling, the manhandling, and then chaos subsiding into order. She loved that, the moment late in the evening when all that was urgent was done and you could clear a space to have the first meal in the new place. Damp hair and muddied newspapers on the floors only added zest to the baked fish or whatever you might have put together between cleaning the bathroom, or switching on the boiler, or unpacking the essentials. They, this time with

Nick, could then smile over the irritations and laugh about the worst moments, and begin to look around with some satisfaction at what they had done. She guessed that on this occasion, (she felt like that), even the bed, with its tired old mattress and sagging springs, would feel a little bit like a sophisticated adventure when they lay in it in its new location.

Because moving is like starting again, like making something new out of bits and pieces, like having another go at getting it right this time. She had in mind the tame moving from one flat to another, which people do when they are young and not too weighed down: because they know someone who is moving out of a nice place in a better area of town or one that has more space, and which incredibly was charging the same rent or only a little more. A lot of moving is not like that at all, as Jamal was sure to have told her in several of his moments of passion about the injustices heaped on his beloved immigrants and asylum seekers. It was not as if she did not know herself, but Jamal lost himself in his zeal sometimes. For millions of people, she could hear him say with that tremulous intensity of his, moving is a moment of ruin and failure, a defeat that is no longer avoidable, a desperate flight, going from bad to worse, from home to homelessness, from citizen to refugee, from living a tolerable or even contented life to vile horror. She felt sympathy for what he said, but she was not sure what else was expected of her. Everyone got on with things as best they could. It would not do to say anything, of course. She would only come out with clichés that made her sound hard-hearted and smug, but her sympathy could never go out fully to Kosovan sex traffickers and North African body smugglers as his could. So her moving with Nick was not that kind of life-shattering moving, and probably it was not even like starting again, but it was still a big decision, to give up her job and sign up as a supply teacher and follow him here like a partner in waiting.

She had said to him, 'Are sure you know what you're asking me to do?' What she meant was: Do you realise how much you are asking me to give up and what I will take it to imply about you and I?

He said, 'Yes, I do know. This will work out for both of us.'

Their shared smiles made her certain they understood each other.

The reason for moving was because Nick had just taken up his first academic post, taking his first unequivocal step in the career he had coveted for so long. Normally he would not have been expected to start until September, but because of illness and study leave and other shenanigans that she could not fully comprehend, the department was unexpectedly short of staff and had asked him if he would start as soon as possible. He had started immediately, commuting from Wandsworth to Brighton during January and February (right through those early weeks when Ba fell ill) while she went through the formalities of resigning from her job. It was a job that suited her, but she was also curious about what lay ahead, to see how things would turn out. You see, Nick said, it's exciting, isn't it? It was not as if giving up her job was going to leave them penniless. He would be getting a salary right through the summer instead of having to look for a job in a café, and there was plenty of time for her to find a permanent job for September. In the meantime, they began looking for somewhere to rent.

They hired a house removal firm, all paid for by the

university's Human Resources department. It was her first encounter with removal men. They arrived at eight o'clock in the morning and had packed everything in the truck in two hours, the furniture, the boxes, the plant pots. They were courteous and friendly, making just the right amount of conversation without becoming tiresome. It was a surprise. She had expected them to be gruff and resentful at having been reduced to such menial work for a living, instead it was they who politely put her at ease. They graciously accepted cups of tea while they worked, managing to seem pleasantly surprised at this unexpected civility, and they were so efficient that it made her feel sorry that there was not more for them to do, that it was not possible to give them a fuller opportunity to demonstrate their expertise.

She had thought it would be frustrating to have people fussing around their things when they were perfectly capable of moving themselves. She had always moved herself, with a little help from whoever was available, and why did they need to move everything? What was the point of taking that broken-backed old bed? Why not buy another one there? She thought hiring a removal firm was one of those corrupt little habits they had acquired from their betters, who were too lazy to do anything for themselves and would pay someone to do their breathing for them if they could. But it was not frustrating at all, in fact it made her feel good to be deferred to in so many small decisions. That was part of the courtesy of the men, to make it seem that she could instruct them to do whatever she wished and they would do it. It made her appreciate the thrill of being rich enough to pay for deference, even though it was Human Resources that was doing the paying. She knew that Nick was pleased to be the provider of these new perks. The university doesn't treat you too badly, does it? he said. If they had offered you a company car, then I would really have felt that we were moving up in the world, she said, teasing him.

It was a small house, its walls rendered white and its front door painted blue, and she thought their furniture clumsy and bulky, but the sofa and chairs were manoeuvred in with the minimum of fuss. The bed went upstairs like a lamb. The desk, the cooker, and the fridge marched obediently to their allotted places. If she and Nick had been doing it themselves, there would have been talk of taking down doors, passing things through windows, even considering removing banister rails to get the desk upstairs, and certainly plenty of exasperated instructions and irritable debates. Instead Nick was on a stepladder, in noisy good humour, making a comic art out of hanging curtain after curtain, as if it was important they secrete themselves behind carefully arranged cover at the earliest opportunity. When they toured their house in the silence that followed the men's departure, his arm was heavy on her shoulder, and the weight of it aroused her because she knew they would soon make love. She glanced out of the back window into their neighbour's darkening garden and saw the scattering of plants she had been putting in earlier in the afternoon.

'Did you see the neighbour?' she asked, leaning against him, her voice lowered as if she might be overheard. 'She was fussing about in the garden, planting things. She looked so busy.'

His other arm came round her waist, and she was enveloped in him. She shut her eyes for a few seconds and felt herself heating up, drifting into the beginning of lovemaking. He let her go after a moment and walked past her to the window. He glanced out briefly, then drew the curtains as if to keep out the offending view. 'No I didn't see her,' he said, but as if these were words just for the sake of speaking. She knew that his mind was on other matters. 'What did she look like?'

'Slim, fair-haired, self-important,' she said.

He looked at her for a long moment, as if thinking through what she had said. 'Not my type,' he said. She smiled, waiting for him to smile with her, waiting for him to come over to her.

That first evening in their new rented house, Nick cooked a roast lamb that he bought from the butcher round the corner. He had noticed that there was a butcher on the main road when they came to view the house, and a greengrocer and a baker, and spoke about their presence there as a kind of special piece of luck, an unexpected remnant of an extinguished way of life. As soon as he was done with the curtains, even before the movers had left, he had gone to make his first visit and had returned with a joint of lamb and a story of two elderly butchers who looked like brothers, and who served him with old-fashioned charm. She guessed he would have done his best to charm them in return, giving them that hard-to-resist grin of his, and that he would have shown them his almost boyish delight to see them there.

Anna called her mother when she went downstairs, and her mother marvelled at everything she told her, how well everything had gone, what a lovely day, how efficient the movers were, how big the bedroom, how compact their little house, the lovely blue front door, that the phone was already working. She had not wanted to try the new number until she heard from them, her mother said, in case it did something funny to the phone line, or tripped something. Anna supressed her irritation. Her mother said *tripped something* as if it was a technical term for the unpredictable caprices of machines. She came out with strange anxieties like that sometimes, as if she was thinking of somewhere else, of another place where things were done differently and where simple matters were fraught with difficulty.

'What something funny could it have done?' Anna asked.

'I don't know. It might have made something go wrong with your phone line if I called before it was ready,' her mother said.

Tripped something, Anna thought. 'What can a telephone call do to a telephone line to make it go wrong?' Anna asked.

'I'm sorry, I don't know, Hanna, but it is such a bother when machines go wrong,' her mother said. 'Anyway is Nick happy? Does he like it there?'

'Of course he does. We wouldn't have taken it otherwise,' Anna said tetchily. 'Anyway, he's happily cooking our dinner and playing Miles Davis at full blast. Can't you hear it?'

'Yes yes, that's nice,' her mother said, still not convinced, even though Anna told her the world was changing and that cooking could make a man happy.

'How is he?' Anna asked. She tried to resist a feeling of distaste as she asked, not only because she felt forced to do so but because of the answer that she was likely to get. What could her mother say? He's better (he's not worse), he's worse (he's not better). She would not say: Actually that second stroke may have finished him off. He lies there voiceless and incontinent, groaning for sympathy and bullying the life out of me. She could not say that, it would be too shocking, it would make her seem heartless, and perhaps she did not even think it. If it was up to Anna, and

78

she would not admit to thinking this to anyone either, she would let the stubborn man go quietly, or at least leave him alone with his secrets and his silences intact. Jamal worried about what his silences contained, but she had tired of that, not from dislike of him but because of the pointless tedium of whatever it was he would not tell them about himself. She had given up trying to unravel her unknown mongrel origins, and interested herself in what she was in her life, not what she came from. But still she asked the question, for her mother perhaps, or for herself more likely, so she would not seem callous and uncaring in her mother's eyes. 'Is he getting better?'

'Oh yes, he's sleeping better and getting stronger every day,' Maryam said. 'That's the main thing, for him to get stronger. The rest is doing him good, and the physiotherapy, and the medicines. You know, I had no idea what miracles physiotherapy can do. He's very well looked after, really.'

'Of course he is, by you. Can he do anything for himself, or do you still have to do everything for him?' Anna asked, unable to resist a spasm of queasiness at the thought of what that really meant. 'You don't want to make yourself ill as well.'

'Oh no, he looks after himself more and more every day. He's doing well. Stop worrying yourself about me,' Maryam said.

'Can he speak yet?' Anna asked.

'No,' Maryam said after a moment's hesitation. 'But he can make sounds, you know, not words at all, but sounds that are trying to be words. The physio says it's very promising. I get him audio books from the library, and he listens to them a lot. It's funny. He can't bear the voices on the radio, but he listens to the books.'

'What books?' Anna asked. Her father used to read slowly, and the books he liked he read more than once. She used to buy him books sometimes, to broaden his reading, books that had excited her when she was at university, but she was not sure if he read them. She thought he preferred books that gave him information, that told him things he did not know, and did not get up to too many narrative tricks. 'What books is he listening to?'

'Some poems I got for him, classics something,' Maryam said.

'Poems! Why did you get him poems?' Anna replied, unable now to prevent her impatience from showing. 'Why didn't you get him something he would like to listen to? *Huckleberry Finn* or something like that.'

'He likes them,' Maryam said, and despite herself, Anna could hear the smile in her mother's voice. 'He sometimes used to read me poems from books he took out from the library. I looked for those in the audio section and got them for him to listen to this week, and he likes it.'

Anna grinned at the absurd vision of her father reading poems to her Ma. She wondered what his choice would have been: 'If' or 'Daffodils' or something to do with the sea. 'The Lotus Eaters' maybe, that would combine syrupy rhymes with *The Odyssey*, perfect. Once she had bought him a copy of Aimé Césaire's *Cahier d'un retour au pays natal*, in a parallel text, because at that time she had recently come to know the poem herself and had been overwhelmed by it. Perhaps she also wanted to show off to him a little, look, this is the kind of stuff I read these days. She had no idea if her father read the poem, and in any case, she herself came to tire of Césaire's booming self-indulgent language and the theatricality of its emotion. While her mother talked, listing the audio books her father was going to listen to in the coming weeks and the improvements the physio promised, Anna's mind wandered to her and Nick's love-making earlier in the afternoon, and she briefly stroked her left nipple where Nick had nestled for a while. She made encouraging noises to her mother but was not really listening any more.

'I'll come down to see you when we're more settled,' Anna said, getting ready to hang up.

As if sensing that Anna was thinking of going and because she was perhaps not ready to let her go, her mother asked about Jamal. 'Has Jamal got your new number?' she asked. 'Have you heard from him?'

'Oh yes,' Anna said, lying to save herself a lecture on keeping in touch. He preferred emails, and that suited her too, but she got the lecture anyway.

'Well, you must keep in touch with each other,' her mother said. 'There are only the two of you. You have no other family. You must always look after each other because there is no one else to turn to in times of trouble.'

Anna listened and offered comfort as best she could. She did not say that she also had Nick (had had him in full that afternoon).

Maryam heard Hanna's impatience as she hung up, and she shrugged. She had taught herself to make light of these slighting gestures. She went back to the living room and saw from the look in Abbas's eye that he wanted to know.

'Hanna,' she said. 'She was asking after you. They've just moved today, you know.'

Abbas nodded slowly and turned back to the muted television, which was showing a nature programme. He too had learned to retreat from Hanna, who had once been so dear to his life. She turned against him after she went to university, not with anger or rudeness, not at first, but with sullen and withdrawn resistance. Maryam knew how that hurt him, Hanna's withdrawal of affection, and how he had tried to draw her back in ways that had worked before, with teasing and questions and jokes. Only that no longer worked, and one day when Abbas was making one of his blunt jokes about her clothes, Hanna had said to him: Leave me alone, Ba, and had left the room and marched right out of the house to go wherever she was going. It stunned him. She had never spoken to him like that before. Abbas could not get used to that, or to the way she talked about boys she knew at the university, or to the fact that she slept so much of the day and did not disguise her boredom at home. Sometimes he said things. In the end she did not come back during vacations, just visited for a few days and then left. Perhaps that was what happened to everyone, and they all learned to swallow what hurt they felt as their children tired of them.

Maryam returned to the household paperwork she was going through. For the twenty-five years they had lived in the house, it was always Abbas who did that. It had started when she became pregnant with Hanna. Before that they did not bother with bills until the threats arrived, but then they moved to Norwich for his new job and she became pregnant. As soon as she told him, he insisted they get married. He was appalled by the thought that someone might call his child a bastard one day. He became a saver, he scrutinised every bill and they had to give up all frivolous spending. They seemed to live like that for years, but one day, when they had saved enough, they bought this house in Hector Street. She remembered the day they moved in as if it was yesterday, and the memory made her smile. A friend from work drove the van for them because neither of them could drive. Abbas said they should hire a wheelbarrow and walk their few possessions round from their rented flat, but she said it was too far away, and Hanna was two years old and Jamal was already on the way. He said he was only joking, but she wasn't sure. She looked up at Abbas, a smile on her face, and watched him for a moment as he stared woodenly at the TV. Her swaggering sailor man turned inspired householder. Because he was inspired. He wallpapered, retiled the bathroom, repaired what needed repairing, and turned out to be a tireless gardener. He planted vegetables and flowers and a plum tree. He built a paved terrace outside the back door. In time, that garden was full to bursting with roses and tomatoes and plums and fennel and jasmine and redcurrants, all growing anyhow as if they just found themselves there. It's natural growth, Abbas said, not an army of plants marching in a line. One day she saw him building a small wooden house and asked him what that was. He said it was a chicken house for the run he was planning. She talked him out of that, and they bought a rabbit instead. The children will like that, she said. But the rabbit didn't and very soon escaped. The house made its way into the garage as so many things had done, and it was still there. Neither of them liked to throw things away.

Jamal loved playing with all that junk in the garage. He was such a quiet boy and so often played alone that Maryam worried, but Abbas said no, let him be. That is what he is like, kimya. Some people are just like that.

He must have moved into the studio flat by now but she guessed he would not ring to tell them his address for a few days yet. He hardly ever called, and sometimes just appeared. They would be sitting down in the evening and would hear his key in the door and in he would walk. Hello

Ma, hello Ba, how are you all? I thought I would come and visit for a few days. Abbas loved that, that he could just come *home* like that. She loved it too. Only she wished he would call and tell her where he was living and that all was well.

The studio flat was roomy. It had what the letting agent's details described as a kitchenette: a small fridge, a sink, and a short counter on which stood a toaster and a microwave oven. What else did a student need? A corner of the room was walled off for the shower and the toilet. A bed and a wardrobe occupied the other side of the room. The desk was under the window with a reading chair beside it. It was a compact, nicely organised student room, and its sparseness and the orderly disposition of the furniture pleased Jamal. The window overlooked the back garden, and out of it Jamal saw their neighbour painting his garden shed. It was just a quick glimpse of a white-haired man seen from behind, sleeves rolled up, standing beside a metal garden table on which stood a large tin of paint. He was leaning back from the side-panel he had almost completed painting. Jamal could see from the patch that remained that the original colour of the panel was green, and he was painting it cream. He had never seen anyone paint a garden shed before.

The walls of his room were also newly painted, and bare. He would have to get some pictures to hang there, some new ones, not the ones he had in his previous room, which were clippings from magazines and newspapers he had accumulated over the years for their mischief and wit. Among them was a cutting of Junior Wells doing the cakewalk dressed in black silk. Wells looked as if he was loving it so much it made Jamal happy just to look at it.

Another was a picture of Nelson Mandela and Thabo Mbeki in their expensive suits doing the toitoi on the viewing platform as the South African Air Force flew over to mark the handing over of power to the rulers of the new South Africa; doing that same mocking jig that the terror state had tried to stamp out with its guns and Caspir armoured cars. Then he had a print of an Inuit carving of a wounded and starving man, made out of whalebone. It was the most moving picture he had ever seen. He would put those pictures away now so that one day he would find them and remember how things looked to him at one time. Instead he would get a picture of a landscape, one with water and hills, and perhaps a distant tree, a view that was enigmatic and open, and which promised to yield something unexpected to the persistent observer. He felt that he was at an important moment in his life, although he was not sure of the source of this feeling. Perhaps it was a sense of impending decisions, that for the first time in his life he would be able to choose what he would do with himself. He considered this and decided that he did not think it was that. Perhaps it was to do with approaching the end of his PhD, a sense of completing a job, and it was this which made him feel grown-up, an adult, an agent in the world. He did feel that sense, but that was a plodder's delight, satisfaction at (nearly) getting a job done, not any expectation of having arrived at transforming knowledge. Or perhaps it was sitting beside Ba while he lay slowly dying in a hospital bed, perhaps it was that which had given him this sense of imminence, of an approaching illumination he must attend to. In this frame of mind, he was drawn to austerity, and when he lay in the dark he pictured a landscape that was empty but not without meaning, whose clarity was deceptive and compelling and inviting investigation. It was not troubling, this sense of imminence, just present like a steady pulse when he allowed himself to feel it, and maybe it was nothing more than an illusory self-importance.

Later, when he looked out of the window again he saw that the neighbour's shed was fully painted, and he saw how tenderly it glowed in the twilight. He had noticed, in that passing glimpse of him earlier in the afternoon, that the man was dark-skinned. Was that why he was painting the shed, a cultural impulse that was still unlearned? He tried to remember if his neighbour's front door was painted. They were always splashing paint on everything, his uncles, always trying to brighten up England's gloomy stone walls. They did not realise how much their hosts loved their stone walls. A slim white-haired man in a checked shirt and grey corduroy trousers. His garden was neat and planted with bushes and some kind of a climber, none of which had yet opened. In the border, some daffodils and snowdrops were flowering. He wondered where he was from. Always, when he saw someone like him, someone dark, someone as old as his neighbour, he wanted to ask, where are you from? Have you come a long way? How can you bear to be so far away? Was it so intolerable there, wherever it was? It must have been, for you to choose to live in this ugly northern city. How has it been here in all these years? Have you come through?

He knew the answers to some of these questions. It was what he studied, migration trends and policies in the European Union. He could describe the patterns and provide the historical context, locate this wave from the Maghreb and its destination and that one from Zimbabwe and how it dispersed. He could construct tables and draw

86

graphs, yet he knew that each one of those dots on his chart had a story that the graphs could not illustrate. He knew that from his Ba, and he knew that from the faces he saw in the streets, and from the silent spaces in the reports he read. He knew that it was a clutter of ambition and fear and desperation and incomprehension that brought people so far and enabled them to put up with so much. And that they could no more resist the coming than they could the tide or the electric storm. So much had to be given up for life to go on. That was not science though. To be scientific, you must first give the trend a name and then study it, never mind the aches. You can leave that to some-one else.

But perhaps he was maligning his white-haired neighbour, turning him into a tragedy before his time, or wishing him ill when he was content, growing his garden and living with his family, painting his shed and feeling proud of his achievements away from his home. South Asian, he guessed from that quick glimpse, or South Arabian, Yemeni maybe. There are millions of them like that, millions of us, who do not fully belong in the places in which they live but who also do in many complicated ways. You could find happiness in that.

Their own back garden was the usual student house patch of overgrown lawn, with little mounds of debris scattered about, a broken chair, empty bottles and rotting piles of weeds. The mess of it made Jamal smile, made him feel comfortable. He imagined the pain with which his Ba would look on that neglect. One of these days, when it was not so cold and the sun was out, he'd see if the people in the flat below would give him a hand clearing up the rubbish. He had met them already. They had come to introduce themselves, Lisa and Jim. He was a student in statistics, modelling avian migration patterns for his research, and she was working in the library. He guessed they would be willing to help. They looked like that kind: people who would love to join in and share a feeling of community. They might even plant a few flowers, something fast-growing and colourful, petunias and daisies and marigolds. The person occupying the flat across the landing had not yet come back from the Easter vacation, but she was nice, Lisa said. When she came a few days later, Jamal found out her name was Lena, short for Magdalena, and that she was a beauty. She had dark-blue eyes, which were bright and smiling in the excitement of meeting. Her complexion was deep, like a light tan under the skin, and her dark hair had a hint of red in it. She was writing on nineteenth-century Irish women's poetry. It cheered him to be sharing a house with such attractive people, like living in a landscape that pleased the eye.

The dream came back to Anna for the first two nights in their new house. She had not had it for a while, not for two or three weeks. Before that, it came every night for days on end and lasted for hours. After some days it stopped, then started again following an unpredictable pause. The dream was of a house. She lived in part of the house and the rest of it was derelict, with sagging roof beams and creaking, half-rotten wooden windows. There was someone else in the house, not someone she saw but who was there in the vicinity, just out of the frame. It was not Nick, or it wasn't most of the time. Sometimes, after she woke up, she thought it must have been Nick, and at other times that it was one or other of the several men she had known. It was not a house she recognised, even as a picture. Everything about it was unfamiliar. The ruined part was barnlike and empty, and visible from every part of the rest of the house. In a strange, unsettling way, she felt she was always visible to the dereliction as well, as if it was something living. That part of the house was brown, not a real colour but more like a colour of exhaustion. The paintwork was peeling, and its beams and bannisters leaned slightly from age and fatigue. Its dereliction was malign, watchful, accusing.

The dream sprawled for hours, and in it she was ridden with guilt. She climbed narrow stairs and forced open dusty doors on rusty hinges to have a look at the work that needed to be done. She explained their plans to someone who remained invisible, who listened without reply. She explained what was needed to be done, when they might be able to do it, about a builder she knew who would do a good job, or a carpenter who would offer them a good price. It was all lies, for she knew no builders or carpenters, and even in the dream she was aware of that, that she was lying to whoever was there listening to her. And even if she did know builders and carpenters and could have them for a good price, she knew that they would not be able to rid the house of its malign decay or relieve her of her guilt. In the dream she knew the cause of her guilt and pain, when awake she was not sure. She imagined it was to do with the repair of the house, that it was her responsibility to see to it and she had failed to. But she could not be sure if this was the reason for the insistent feeling of wrongness she felt in the dream. She could not be sure that some suffering or pain had not occurred in that derelict house, or was not even occurring at that moment. Nick never fully appeared in the dream, although he was there sometimes, she was sure of that, maybe. Nor was Nick the invisible person she sought to explain herself to. She did not know who that was, or why she had to explain herself to her or him.

Nick was distressed by the dream when she first told him. She did not tell him at once but only when the dream became recurrent. She was not sure why she delayed telling him, if it was simply that the right moment did not come up, or if the feeling of the dream was too painful, the sense of guilt too real, or if she thought he would laugh at her concern about its meaning. It was how they were together, laughing at each other whenever one of them became solemn about *life's tragedies* (the words spoken with a comically downcast face). They liked to keep things light between them, and it gave Anna a mature sense of proportion that she could refuse to see her pain as exceptional. She laughed at *life's tragedies* to avoid the lure of solemn self-importance, which is what she thought a sense of the tragic implied. She thought Nick's laughter was similar but with its own difference. His was to do with wanting to seem relaxed, to seem a man of sophisticated temperament who had no need for self-pity, officer class, although that did not stop him from being full of himself about his *work*.

Anyway, she did not tell him about the dream immediately. The dream was both sinister and squalid, both threatening to her and implicating her in a nameless wrongdoing, and while she was in it she was frightened in some place deep inside her, and felt smothered by a darkening stench that was slowly filling up the house. Perhaps she did not tell Nick at once because she wanted to have a better understanding of all these feelings before she recounted it, because she feared he would make light of it all, or even mock it, refusing to take it seriously.

It was her feeling of guilt that most troubled him. 'What's

it all about?' he asked. 'What do you have to feel guilty about? Is it about your dad? And why a house? Why do you feel bad about a house?'

'I don't know if dreams work like that,' she said, letting his question about Ba pass. 'I don't think you dream about things that bother you as themselves. Or that dreams are always about things that bother you in some concrete way. You know, that if you're worrying about a house, you dream about a house.'

Nick made a scorning face. 'Thank you for clearing that up for me,' he said.

That was the end of that conversation. She had wanted to go on to say something about the uncanniness of the dream, its extreme unlikeliness and how disturbing its menace was, but she had seen that her quibble had irritated him and she did not pursue the subject. He could be a pig when the mood was on him. So she was not sure now if she would tell him that the dream had come back since they moved. It was probably to do with the move anyway, and would go away of its own accord, and take whatever it meant with it.

Nick had gone to work first thing, to take the books they had brought down to his office. In the weeks he had been commuting he had only taken a few essential books, and had often found himself short of a text or two when he needed it. It would be good to have all his books within reach again. He said he would not be long, but she thought he would. It didn't matter, she wanted to unpack the boxes. She hated having her things hidden away. Back by lunchtime, he said, but she thought not. He liked that kind of thing – organising his space for maximum effect. She imagined that the books would be arranged to a system, by theme, then alphabetical by author within the theme, century by century. Then a couple of journals would be thrown on the desk, and the pens would be left like that, and the right pictures would be pinned on the board. So that when you walked into his office you would think, here is a serious academic. He did that with his study space at home, when there was only her to impress. But then maybe it was more than a desire to impress, that it was his idea of himself, so that even if there was no one to see he would still want to sustain the air of a scholar.

Just before he left in the morning he said he had received a text from his mother, inviting them to spend the Easter weekend with them. Anna did not say anything, but the thought made her wince inside. He did not like it when she said anything critical of visits to his parents', but what she thought and did not say was *oh fuck no, not Easter weekend again.* The first time she went visiting Nick's parents was an Easter weekend, soon after she met him, which was just before the school vacation. She was then in her third year of teaching, working in a school in King's Lane, which because of the quirks of zoning boundaries fell in Wandsworth Borough even though it was a stone's throw away from Brixton. As a result it was popular with parents because its catchment area excluded the black rowdies from the high-rise estates, who had to go to school in the neighbouring Lambeth Borough. She went to a party given by one of the teachers she worked with who lived in Wandsworth. Nick, who lived in the same apartment block, was a friend. He was tall but not very, strong-looking but not huge, athletic, his light-brown eyes shining with intelligence. His smile was so full that it seemed as if he was about to burst into laughter. When they were introduced, she saw the interest in those eyes. It was not something she could miss. Then when they began to talk, they sparked each other off and everything they said seemed unbelievably funny and witty. She was seduced and could not wait to have him, and she knew from the way their bodies swayed towards each other and their hands hovered that she would not have to wait for long. She was unattached and he was getting over a relationship, so there were no complications. In fact, everything happened so fast that after a few days she was more or less living in his flat every weekend. He wanted her to move in straight away, but she said no, let's not rush.

He was planning to spend the Easter weekend with his parents, and he said to Anna, 'Why not come? There's room. Shall I ring and ask?'

'I've promised to go and see my mum and dad in Norwich, and I was thinking of doing that over Easter,' she said, (making the effort to say *mum and dad* rather than *Ma and Ba*). But Anna knew that Nick wanted her to go, and she herself was curious, so she said, 'I suppose I could go to Norwich before the weekend and come over to you afterwards.'

Perfect, he said. When he rang his parents and told them about Anna, they said bring her too. We'd love to meet her. They were to arrive on Saturday in time for dinner and then go to the service on Sunday morning, which if Anna wished to attend she was welcome, then go home for lunch afterwards. Nick's sister and her partner would also be there, although they would only come for the day.

That was more than two years ago, long before Ba's collapse and illness. When she arrived in Norwich a couple of days before Easter, as she had promised her mother, she was wearing a low-cut top and she saw a shade of disapproval pass over her father's eyes. She had known he would do that, but she was determined not to be forced to dress like a prude just because he preferred that. It had been a battle between them ever since she started university. When she wore anything tight, or short or revealing, he disapproved. In the early days he just ordered her back upstairs to change, and she did that a few times to avoid a fight. *What will anybody think if they see you like that?* he said. *That we have not brought you up to have self-respect.* In the end he got tired of the bad feeling these encounters aroused and he tried to ignore her, looking hurt that she took no notice of his instruction. It had been different when she was younger. She could do no wrong then. But when she grew into a young woman, he became a tyrant about self-respect, or tried to but she always fought back. Finally he retreated from her and tried not to see the things he disapproved of.

She remembered how her mother kissed her and held her out at arm's length, praising her appearance and complimenting her clothes, good old Ma. Somehow, Ba steeled himself and came over to kiss her as well. She put her arm in his and led him back to the living room, knowing he would be unable to resist her affection. She talked with him about her teaching work and about her plans, and about the children and how precocious some of them were. He listened without saying much, smiling, and after a while seemed to forget about her top. When she had persuaded him (and herself) that she was taking life seriously and was working hard at her career, she went to the kitchen where her mother was preparing dinner and told her about Nick. She did not tell her father about her boyfriends any more. He thought she had too many of them. Why not wait until you find the right one? Then he always asked: Is the boy English? What did he expect? A Greek god? She had never let him meet any of her boyfriends after the first one. His name was Martin, that first one, and Ba met him when they came to collect her after her first term at university. As they parted, she had kissed him, and Ba had not spoken a word all the way home. Then when Martin phoned her over the holidays, he came out to the hallway every few minutes to try and hurry her off the phone. Is this what we sent you to university for? To turn you into a proper English girl? Well, they didn't send her to university, she sent herself, with her own efforts and talent. After that she just made sure he never got to meet any of her boyfriends, and after a while she did not bother to tell him about them either.

Her mother made no comment about Nick; she wanted to tell Anna about her latest feud with Dr Mendez concerning some digestive difficulties she was having. Anna herself was in perfect health and nothing about her body surprised her or caused her unexpected distress. When she felt unwell, she knew why, more or less. She could not really take the difficulties her mother was having with her bowels seriously and she listened out of politeness. Dr Mendez was dismissive about her mother's problems and Ma was distraught that she could not persuade the doctor.

'What a foul bitch that woman is! You should ask for a second opinion,' Anna said.

'I don't know how you get a second opinion,' Maryam said. 'She says there is nothing to have an opinion about.'

'It's your body,' Anna said, uttering one of the wisdoms of the time. She thought her mother Maryam looked perplexed at this idea. She could not understand why her mother allowed herself to be intimidated by the doctor. She could see her sitting quietly while the bitch doctor said to her, *Women of your age are absurd hypochondriacs. Go home and make yourself a cup of tea.* Or maybe that was not what was really happening, and her mother just got the wrong end of the stick, or did not explain herself properly or just needed to protest a little more, to be more stubborn. She sat with her parents for a while after dinner, Ma chatting and Ba listening without saying much, gathered together in some place of his own. She used to feel excluded by their intimacy at times, but now she understood it for what it was. They were adrift, out of their depth, lonely together. They had done this deliberately, she thought, cut themselves off, living timorous lives, expecting slights and disregard. She could not wait to leave the next day. She remembered how when they came home for the vacation, Jamal and she used to whisper to each other: Welcome back to the morgue. The next day, she took the train from Norwich to Chichester, where Nick's parents lived, feeling like a traitor.

That miserly gene surfaced quite unexpectedly. She said that to him once and he looked so surprised and then so pensive that she thought she may have hurt him. She only meant to tease him, but she had forgotten that he had once told her that his father was a mean man. She knew he had turned miserly to help them save because Hanna was coming, and he had turned out to be better at it than she had expected. She was only pretending pique and irritation, because she too took to their frugal style. It made her feel grown-up, capable of denying herself, and made their life together seem purposeful.

When Hanna was a baby, he treated her like an object

that could easily break, cupping her whole tiny body in his hands as he lifted her. When they put her on a mat on the floor, he made a nest for her with cushions and blankets so she would not roll over. When she made an irritated noise, he looked alarmed, and sometimes repeated the noise as if to tell her that he felt it too, whatever it was. As soon as he came home from work, he asked if she was awake and if he could hold her. Then he lay her on his thighs, and rocked his legs from side to side while he twittered and sang to her, and she gurgled and chuckled as if she had never seen the like. If she cried at night, he said bring her here, and he lay her down between them on the bed. Maryam could not suppress the feeling that this was wrong, that they were spoiling her. She remembered being told in the antenatal clinic that you should let babies cry, but he would not have that. Let the poor thing cry on its own as if there was no one here who wanted her? He rocked her and tutted at her and made silly noises until she stopped. And if she did not, he fretted and tried one thing after another until she gave up and whimpered and fell asleep. Hanna drew a tenderness and patience out of him that she could not have guessed at. By the time Jamal came, the overwhelming astonishment of their first baby's perfection had diminished a little but then Jamal came with surprises of his own. He turned out to be such a silent and accommodating baby that Maryam became concerned. It took him a long time to learn to walk or to speak. *Leave him alone*, Abbas said. *He's thinking. Look at that frown, that's a thinker's frown.* Hanna had learned to speak at an early age, and she chattered at Jamal for hours and made him part of her games while he lay on a mat or in his rocker and frowned contentedly. Forbearing. That was the word Abbas gave her for him. A forbearing little man.

As they grew older, Abbas tried to be a little more firm, less chuckles and kisses and more direction and instruction. You have to learn to look after yourselves. You don't want people to make fun of you. Life here is not a holiday. It made her laugh, some of it, because to her it seemed so transparently a pretence, an exaggeration. He could not keep up his strict act all the time and there were many moments when he could not resist his old mischief. He took too many things as his responsibility, his duty by them, and she wanted to say to him: play with them, laugh with them, do not fear for them so much. Then they grew older and became teenagers and wanted to do things their own way, which was not always his. But even before then, she knew that Abbas was retreating more and more to solitary places where he could not be reached. Sometimes his face turned sour and his eyes glowed with what she could only think of as pain. It was as if the children brought something back to him that he had learned not to think about. When she asked him, he looked surprised or pretended to look surprised, and said that there was so much to worry about with children. He smiled apologetically as he said that, and she did not press him. The children found his silences daunting, she knew that. The silences made them afraid of him. She did not think he always understood that, and he was hurt by their withdrawal and took it to be a kind of rejection. Yes, perhaps he was right, there was so much to worry about with children.

She was just in her twenties when she had them, and to her, for the first time in her life, it seemed that there was nothing to worry about. In a way, she felt herself growing up with them and did not have to force herself to enjoy their endless games. She felt the difference in their ages, hers and Abbas's, through the children. How irritated he sometimes was by their chatter. How he could not always throw himself into their hilarities. He did his best, hid his smiles when he felt he had to be stern, and bought them unpredictable and unexpected presents. But sometimes he seemed to her like someone who had grown older than his years.

Anna was in slight trepidation when she arrived in Chichester that first Easter weekend. She had never been invited to stay the night with any of her previous boyfriends' families. She had known Nick for only just over a month, and from all the things he had said she expected his parents to be stiff and patronising, prosperous people who knew their worth and who were exacting in their judgement of others. Perhaps they would be frosty towards her for intruding into their family festivities, and she wondered how enthusiastic they really were about inviting her. Without intending to, Nick had made them sound difficult to please and censorious, describing moments of tension with them and some of the things they disapproved of in him. She felt as if she was heading towards the kind of scrutiny in which she would inevitably fail to impress, and yet she would have no option but to try to please, and defer and play the fool. But when she arrived, Nick's mother embraced her and kissed her lightly on both cheeks, smiling at her with her whole face. She was a slim woman with a lean face and short fair hair, dressed in a light-grey blouse and a patterned skirt, blue eyes smiling. She held on to Anna for a moment, leaning back to have a good look at her.

'I am so glad you could come and see us, Anna,' she said. 'We have heard so much about you.'

The courtesy was practised but Anna liked it anyway, for

its own sake, and because the words and the hint of warmth in her voice were a relief after what she had been dreading. She thought that kind of warmth was a gift that some women of a certain age had, an unforced kindness that she knew her own mother had too, a studied mildness, which was intended to reassure and reconcile, and with it came a civil inflection of the body that conveyed something affectionate and sympathetic. She had not met many women in whom she saw those gifts. 'I am Jill,' she said, 'and this is Ralph.'

Nick's father stepped forward from where he was hovering and held out his hand. He was a tall man of about sixty or so, with grey hair receding at the temples. As he shook hands he bowed slightly from the hips, a jaunty and satirical gesture at gallantry. He was wearing a light-blue jacket and an open-necked shirt, and somehow managed to look formal in his attempt at informality. 'How do you do? Do come in,' he said, smiling, and then stepped aside to usher her and his wife ahead of him into the sitting room. As soon as she entered she saw what the outside of the house and the hallway had already hinted at. There was wealth here. It was a large room, furnished with old-looking furniture she could not have named, all of it in exquisite condition. The windows overlooked a large garden with a lawn and some trees in blossom. It was too late in the evening to see clearly, but she thought she saw a summer house or a pergola towards the bottom of the garden and a glint of water nearby in the gloom.

Nick sat beside her on the sofa, and Jill and Ralph were attentive to her, asking about her journey, offering her a drink. *You must be starving*, Jill said. *Dinner won't be long.* There were flowers on the dining table and the light was muted, and when they sat down to eat Anna was struck by the elegant simplicity of the meal and the intimacy of the room. By then, Ralph was in charge of the conversation, orchestrating and prompting mildly, glancing at Jill every few minutes as if to seek her agreement. Now and then she repeated the last phrase or two he had said, but there was no deference in this echo. Anna sensed her self-assurance even though she ate silently while her husband talked. It made her think of her mother Maryam and how so much intimidated her, neighbours, teachers, doctors. She guessed that the very stubborn Spanish lady doctor would behave differently if she were dealing with Nick's mother. It was historical, she guessed. All those centuries of overlordship of the world must have made some impact on self-esteem, even as they corrupted generosity and understanding. But also from her own achievements. She knew from Nick that Jill *ran* a hospital, (while her mother used to clean one), so she had a powerful, professional position, a huge salary, independence. As she thought this, Anna imagined how courteously Jill would be able to intimidate her mother Maryam if she ever felt the need, and how, if that necessity arose, she would do it without hesitation. She felt a slight shiver of dislike, as if Jill really had done that to her mother. Jill must have sensed something because she glanced up and caught Anna's eye with a look of enquiry, her head slightly tilted, ready to oblige. Anna shook her head, smiling, and turned back to listen to Ralph, feeling as if she had slandered Jill who had been so friendly and easy in her welcome.

Moments before, while she was engaged with these thoughts about Jill, Ralph had been talking about Zimbabwe, and she came back into the middle of what he was saying. He was worrying about the government campaign that was then just beginning, to expropriate land owned by farmers descended from European settlers and give it to African peasants. She heard him say that whatever the rights and wrongs of such situations, you cannot make anything better by turning the clock back, especially as the enterprise of these farmers is now the mainstay of the economy.

'I know it sounds like victors' logic,' he said, and she saw Nick nod, 'but you have to think cleverer than just reversing a historical injustice, otherwise you end up committing another one and making everyone poorer into the bargain.'

'There is one word you are leaving out there, Dad,' Nick said. 'To give the land *back* to African peasants. It's only two or three generations ago that that land was taken away. People still remember what belonged to them.'

Ralph smiled, nodding in return. When he spoke, his voice was warm, friendly. There was no rancour in these exchanges: 'There is feasible evidence that sooner or later it is the political barons who really acquire the land, which is exactly what you would expect in any society, so I am not sure how much goes *back* to the peasants in this situation or in any situation like this. But in any case, think of the legal problems, the compensation, the break-up of complex modern farms into allotments, aside from the abuse of constitutional rights. Why, it would be like trying to make up for the Clearances by bringing all those Highlanders back. It might fulfil some ideal of justice, but it would create absurd difficulties and new injustices. You have to take the long view in these matters and not dwell on the cruelties of the present moment or the recent past. That only leads to a paralysing sense of grievance and then to an irrational extremism.'

'Maybe we can think so calmly because we are spared the daily consequences of those cruelties,' Nick said. 'I doubt you would think quite so calmly if you were made poor as a result of such an injustice.'

Ralph shrugged apologetically. Anna thought there was something theatrical about that gesture of uncertainty when she guessed that he was expressing firmly held views. They sounded like firmly held views. 'That seems all the more reason why we have to maintain a rational and intelligent attitude to what at first sight looks like intolerable injustice,' he said. 'We have to look far in the distance when we try to put right what is wrong at the moment. We should worry about what new problems we create when we try to solve a problem, and that is what Mugabe is not worrying about.'

Nick shrugged in his turn, and Anna guessed that they had had this conversation before and had now arrived at a familiar impasse. Father and son smiled at each other, silently agreeing to leave the matter there, and Anna felt some dissatisfaction at the disinterested manner they could debate injustice and then just lay it aside, but she also felt a stab of envy at their ease with each other.

Ralph started talking about a recent trip to Tunis, where he had gone on business. He did that skilfully, putting down one topic and taking up another, as if he had a whole shelf of them and he could pull down one or the other as the need arose. He was not an oppressive talker, and spoke unhurriedly as if what he was saying was of no great significance, just telling a story or offering an opinion, which he had a good idea would prove interesting. He leaned forward at times, eager to convince or persuade, and Anna thought it was a likeable mannerism, expressing a kind of modesty as if he was not certain if his case could stand on its own.

'To an ignorant visitor like me,' he said, 'the city seemed relaxed and at peace and prosperous. The shops were full of merchandise, the cafés and restaurants were crowded. People were hurrying everywhere, going about their business. I stayed in a smart and elegant hotel that was full of guests, who to my eye looked Tunisian rather than tourists or wealthy foreigners. On the Sunday I went for a stroll in the park, and it was crowded with families doing all the very things you would expect to see on a Sunday afternoon in the park. In the streets everyone was well dressed, especially the women, whether they were wearing smart fashions or their national dress. So it was a surprise when my host – a Tunisian himself – told me not to point to the ramparts of a seaside villa, or not to look too directly at the armed policeman walking beside the sea wall, or turned me away from staring at a building that had caught my eye. He turned his face nervously away from the villa and from the policeman as he gave me this warning, as if concerned that his words might carry, or someone might read his lips. This was on an outing to Carthage, yes the same Carthage that belongs to all of us. The President has a seaside villa there, the very one I was pointing a finger at. Apparently the security apparatus is nervous and brutal, and is very suspicious of the slightest interest in the Big Man, yet you would have no idea of this from looking at the way people were quietly going about their business. What do you think of that?'

'What do you think of that?' Jill echoed, with an enthusiam that made Anna start. Her repetition was so blatantly unnecessary that it made Anna wonder if, despite her appearance of self-assurance, Jill was struggling against shyness. And blurting out Ralph's last words like that was like announcing that she was there too, and not to be ignored.

They were silent for a few seconds while Ralph gave them the opportunity to say what they thought, but since no one spoke, he continued: 'I could not imagine British citizens living with that kind of intimidation with the same equanimity, I really could not. Do you suppose,' and here he turned towards Anna, whom she assumed he imagined to be an expert on the subject, 'you can become so habituated to oppression that you cease to feel it as oppression? Or do you think it is a matter of national character? I don't mean biological character or the renowned British phlegm or the bloody-minded island people myth, or not that altogether, but something to do with the culture of a nation, how citizens of a nation see themselves.'

He paused again, as if allowing room for objection, as if inviting comment, but perhaps just seeking reassurance that he was not alienating his listeners. He glanced again at Anna, who reached for her glass of wine to evade his scrutiny and saw that it was empty. In that instant, before turning back to Ralph, she caught the look in Jill's eyes, which were also resting on him. Her eyes were expressionless, as if she had taken herself away, or perhaps deliberately blanked them in disapproval, and even from that brief glance Anna was struck by how different that look in her eyes was from the friendly way she had seemed earlier on. Anna looked away quickly and realised that she herself was as intimidated by this stern self-absorbed woman as her mother would doubtless be. As Jill filled up her glass and she turned to thank her, she saw that the look in her eyes had changed again. Her eyes were now smiling, waiting for Anna to turn, watching her greedily. She lifted her own glass slightly in a silent toast.

'Some peoples just will not put up with injustice,' Ralph

continued, and she thought she heard Nick grunt in agreement, and guessed that the chorus of freedom-loving people was about to begin. 'They will march and commit arson and throw up barricades if pushed too far. Massacres, executions, imprisonment will not extinguish this stubborn refusal of tyranny. Other peoples are cowed and obedient. It may even be that they do not recognise their oppression as injustice but as the order of existence. Is it something in their cultures that incline them to be that way? Is it religion? Is it a historical conditioning of brutal misuse?'

Is this what happened every mealtime? She thought Nick might speak, might even start to feel embarrassed, but he seemed absorbed in his food and glanced at his father between mouthfuls. Jill also seemed to have recovered her poise and seemed ready for more. She found out later, when she knew him better, that Ralph liked to make these comparisons of national character, whose real point was to observe that, at its best, British steadiness was a force for decency and a quality to admire. No, he not only liked to make these comparisons, it was an obsession of his; a way of understanding the world. He made his comparisons without insistence, without enthusiasm, but as if they were calm observations of civil truths. She wondered that Ralph did not seem to notice the abrasive underside of his comparisons, which was a smug suspicion of everyone else's unsteadiness. On that first meeting, she could not help thinking that Ralph was talking so much out of awkwardness about her presence, that he did not like her there but was too polite to let it show.

After a moment's rest, Ralph spoke of when he was a policeman in Northern Nigeria, a brief spell of imperial duty before Nigeria's independence forced him back home to make money.

'You know, it was reading Orwell and that essay of his, "Shooting an Elephant", that made police work seem something decent to do. Isn't that curious? When what he was intending to show was the unworthiness of our imperial enterprise?

'Do you like Orwell, Anna?' Ralph asked, turning to her at last with a look of prostrate attention. 'Nick said you studied literature. Do they ask you to read Orwell these days?'

Anna was drawn into the conversation, and she found herself gradually soothed by Ralph's blatant flattery and impressed by his wide reading and his intelligent observations. He seemed to have read most of Orwell and Forster and Conrad and Kipling and was able to move easily between these writers, drawing comparisons, inviting her opinion, listening. It was like a seminar, gently steered by Ralph, and Anna was completely absorbed. It was Jill who broke the spell, rising to clear the dishes. A short while later Anna found herself in the kitchen, helping Jill and telling her about her school and the children she taught and how she liked working there.

That was her first meeting with Nick's parents: Ralph who could not be ruffled in his self-satisfaction, and Jill who seemed first kind and then complicated, and then withdrawn and apologetic. Anna felt a discomfort on that first meeting, which she still could not fully lose. She did not say this to Nick, because it made her sound like a wimp, but she did not think they liked her.

Maryam was forty-eight years old when Abbas had the second stroke, and when they let him out of hospital she gave up work so she could look after him. There was not much choice in the matter. It was either that or have a carer in the house, and she knew how much he would hate that, and anyway, it was not as if she was giving up being the Governor of the Bank of England. She had to learn to think differently about money when she had hardly thought about it at all. She had left everything to him. She had to learn about allowances and how to claim them, how to access his pension, how to do everything without his help. She had to learn how to care for him. It took a while for her to absorb and understand these new arrangements, to know them with as little resentment or disgust as she thought she should. Abbas could not speak or laugh or feed himself, or clean himself properly after using the toilet. She minded that last one most of all, however hard she tried. She could not help herself. She could not hide it from him although she did her best. He always shut his eyes when she cleaned him, but sometimes she saw tears coming out of his clenched eyelids.

After the early weeks passed, and Abbas was receiving regular therapy and beginning to make progress, she thought it was time she shook herself awake and found something to do. She went to the hairdressers to have the grey banished from her hair, and if Abbas's therapy sessions allowed, she went to the gym one afternoon a week. She took to the young woman instructor there immediately. She was a thin blonde-haired woman who wore large glasses and spoke in a rapid and unusual way, as if she was pretending to be someone else. Maryam liked her friendly bossiness because it allowed her to disguise her ignorance about what happened in a gym. She also liked her unstinting flattery and her cries of joy for every new little exercise Maryam completed successfully.

One day she read in the local free newspaper about a Refugee Centre in Norwich, which, among other things, offered legal advice and information to refugees and asylum seekers. It helped them to trace families and relatives, and just generally helped them to settle. There were some stories in the feature, stories of real people and what had befallen them and where they were now. It was work that would have special meaning for her because of Abbas and because of her own confused beginnings, and because of Jamal who was studying the subject. She saw that some of the staff were volunteers, and she thought that was something she would like to do. It would be a bit like joining a family business. On the afternoon that Abbas had his physio session, Maryam went to the Centre and offered her services. Abbas would probably not like her to do it. If he could speak, he would probably say she was just going to bother people who had their own lives to sort out, interfering and asking questions that nobody wanted asked, offering advice, which helped no one. And she was not sure when she would find the time from looking after him, but she went to the Centre that Thursday afternoon and offered her services anyway. Is there anything I can do to help?

Maryam turned up at the Refugee Centre looking elegant and relaxed, more so than she realised because inside she was tensed with the expectation of being refused, not needed, superfluous. But her offer was accepted, and she hurried back to the Health Centre to collect Abbas, wondering how she could now fit it in. On the drive home she could not help herself and told Abbas what she had done. She glanced towards him to see if he had heard her, and she saw the beginnings of a tight little smile on his face. It was a tiny grotesque grimace, but it was a smile, his first since the stroke.

'Abbas, you are smiling,' she said quietly, smiling herself.

'You can smile. It's about time you did, Mr Boots. So you don't think the Refugee Centre is a bad idea?'

She rang Jamal later that evening (after she had tried Hanna first) and told him about the smile first of all. *It was a tiny little thing but it was a smile all right.* Then she told him about the Refugee Centre.

'What will you do there?' he asked.

'I can help in a lot of ways,' she said. 'In the crèche, with the literacy classes, or with community events at the Centre.' She wanted Jamal to be impressed but she could not be sure from his voice if he was holding something back. 'It was what made your Ba smile, so he thinks it's all right. Don't you think it's a good idea?'

'If you want to do it . . . I mean if you want to do that kind of work. It might be quite ordinary, boring. Cleaning, making tea, skivvying work, not much different from what you did at the hospital or at home,' he said.

'So you don't think it's a good idea,' she said, disappointed.

'Yes, of course it's a good idea,' Jamal replied. 'Especially if it made the invalid smile. It will be good for you to do something different, get a break from the caring, do something that you want to do. I just worry that they might not let you do anything interesting. You know, that it would just be more chores for you to do.'

'Oh no, I don't think it will be like that. I think there will be a lot to do,' Maryam said, and she made sure that he heard the smile in her voice.

The next day of their visit Nick borrowed Jill's car and took Anna out to the country. They had slept in separate rooms, and Anna had not expected the luxury of a large comfortable bedroom with its own bathroom. When she shut the bedroom door, the carpet, the curtains, the wallpaper and the furniture absorbed all sound, and the room felt unattached to the rest of the house. It was like a hushed, sealed capsule floating free. When she opened the curtains in the morning, she looked over a large garden, which was so full and neat that she guessed it was looked after by a team of gardeners. The structure she had seen in the gloom was a pergola with a vine growing on it. Nick drove to a nearby village he wanted her to see, and they strolled through it while he told her about the ancient church, and about stories of the English Civil War in which it featured. He told the stories as if they belonged to him, as if he was present at their unfolding, standing at the edge of a nearby lane looking on these events happening in the open. They saw no one in the village until they entered the pottery, where the potter smiled at them without stopping work on his wheel. Nick explained in a whisper that the pottery was famous, and people came from far and wide to buy pots here. It was a small village, and soon they were out in a country lane where daffodils were still in bloom and which was shaded by huge budding trees.

'Your mother does not talk very much,' Anna said.

Nick laughed: 'You mean my father talks a lot. No one gets to say much when Dad is in the mood, which is when he is relaxed and comfortable with the company. I must say, he seemed very much in the mood last night. So that means he likes you. You'll get used to it, you'll have no choice,' he said, laughing again at the thought. 'Anyway, I heard you and Mum chattering away in the kitchen, so it looks as if everything is going well.'

Late in the morning Nick said they would have to go back so he could attend the Easter service. Anna said she would like to go too. Nick said she should not feel she had to. He went because he did not know how to get out of it after all these years. The vicar of the church they went to was his Dad's brother, his Uncle Digby, and for as long as he could remember, his parents had said that the Easter service was the most important ceremony in the Christian calendar. According to them you did not have the right to call yourself a Christian if you did not attend the service to rejoice in the saviour's resurrection – even though they did not trouble themselves too much to exercise this right at other times of the year. Besides, the service and the late family lunch afterwards had become their own pleasant family tradition. 'I'll come,' Anna said. 'I'd like to.' She wanted to feel that she had been invited into their warmth and intimacy, and she wanted to share it fully. She did not want to hold back and quibble.

She told him that she wanted to go to the Easter service because she had never been to one before, or been to any kind of church service for that matter.

'No!' he said, gratifying her with his disbelieving surprise.

It was true: not a service, nor a christening, nor a church wedding, nor any of those things. She had seen these events in films and on TV, that's all. Everything she knew about Christianity was entirely theoretical, mostly things she had read when she was doing her literature degree and bits and pieces you cannot avoid picking up.

Nick said his lineage teemed with vicars and lay preachers. Hearing Anna say that about the Church was like meeting someone who said he had never seen the moon.

It was another one of those things her Ba had made sure they were ignorant about. When Anna started school, some of the Muslim parents began a campaign to have their children excluded from events that had anything to do with Christian practices. The parents were staff and postgraduate students at the university in Norwich, not many, but they knew how to campaign. It was a Church of England school, although that had nothing to do with her and her brother being there. It just happened to be near them and had a good reputation. When the exclusion campaign started, the headmaster thought a principle was involved, namely that children attending a school such as his had to participate in all its practices otherwise the school's *esprit de corps* would be in jeopardy. In addition, he did not like having the school's style cramped and tempered with in this way by a handful of people who did not value the ethos it held dear. But the parents organised petitions, threatened appeals and in the end the headmaster agreed to allow the children of Muslim parents to exclude themselves from certain school events. He would much rather they had taken their children elsewhere, but the local council office advised him not to allow the protest to become a scandal. And because her name was Hanna Abbas and her record said she was a Muslim, her parents were offered the option of excluding her and they took it. Hanna was excused from any Christian events, and so was her brother Jamal when his turn came. The teachers did little to make it easy for the Muslim children, keeping them together in one class while the Nativity play or the harvest festival went on in the hall. They were the awkward squad, and the school did not mind them knowing that they were.

It was her father who was the Muslim, although there was nothing particularly Muslim about what he did or the way they lived. Sometimes he told them what it meant to be a Muslim, the Pillars of Islam, as he called them, praying, fasting, giving alms, going on the pilgrimage to Mecca, although he never did any of those things himself. He told them the story of Muhammad, and of Muslim conquests of most of the known world, from China to the gates of Vienna, and of its scholarship and learning. The stories were like great adventures, that was how he told them, tales of when men were giants and it was still possible to stumble on a treasure chest of emeralds and diamonds when searching for firewood in the forest. What their mother Maryam knew about religion was what she had picked up along the way, and it was the lightest of burdens. She probably would not have thought to exclude her children from anything, but their father saw it as a small reprieve from the overwhelming corruption of his children, so he insisted they be excluded. The campaigning parents, of whom he was not one, kept a watchful eye on the school, and her dad did not want it said that he had neglected to care for his children. Then after a while Hanna and Jamal became used to being excused from any Christian activity, and insisted on it themselves, because they knew that was what they were expected to do. That it was what their dad wanted them to do. That was how she could grow up in England and not go to a church once. If their dad was a proper Muslim, he would have committed a great sin by keeping them in ignorance about their religion, instead of which he kept them in ignorance about everything, or tried to anyway. There was so much more he should have told them, a great deal more about a great many things.

Nick did not say anything when Anna told him this, but Anna could see the look of distaste on his face, and she assumed it was distaste for her Ba. She felt a moment's brief regret, but nothing that she had said was untrue. It was sad if her description made him sound like a bigoted immigrant, but that was what he had laid himself open to, and she resisted the impulse to say something in his defence.

Anna was surprised by the service. It seemed such a fake. She so much wanted to be moved by the evocation of the drama of the resurrection, to witness an affirmation of faith, to feel the solemnity of the moment, but Nick's Uncle Digby made the words seem exaggerated, and his delivery had a practised piety that gave them a hectoring tone. Anna even wondered if Uncle Digby was a believer, despite his pious words and his clerical costume. She thought a believer would have a certain stare – ardent, manic, furious, or even just kindly – but Uncle Digby's eyes, even from a distance, were blank and irritably preoccupied. She did not think Uncle Digby was a good advertisement for his vocation.

It was nearly three by the time they all sat down to eat lunch. Anna sat with Nick on one side of her and Anthony, the boyfriend of Nick's sister Laura, on the other, silently chewing his food for the most part. Laura, who had met them at the church, and Anthony, who had pointedly spent the service in the pub, had both greeted Anna with the same hard, unabashed look, as if weighing up a judgement for later. It made her shiver. They both worked in an architect's practice where Anthony was a senior partner. Anthony spoke in a loud impatient voice, his manner that of someone who would not hesitate to lose his temper if things did not go his way.

Uncle Digby the vicar, when she met him at close quarters, was a soft-looking man with lush dark hair sprinkled with grey. He no longer looked irritable, and was already a little mellow. Initially Uncle Digby and Ralph shared command of the conversation, but Uncle Digby soon gained the upper hand, especially as his wife Florence seemed in the middle of a long story, which she was telling to Ralph in a lowered voice. Uncle Digby asked, in his

ceremonially kindly voice, to hear more about what everyone was doing, and how remarkable that was, and just the
other day he had heard something interesting about that
on the radio. It was clear that he had frequently refilled
his wine glass while waiting for lunch. Anna caught Jill's
eye, and Jill, her face shiny with rushing to get the food on
the table, smiled with just a touch of mischief, as if something slightly comic was going on, and she guessed that
Uncle Digby was going to make a fool of himself before
too long.

At some point Uncle Digby, who was sitting across from
her, turned towards her with a pungently benign smile and
asked her, 'And where do *you* come from?'

'Anna's British,' Nick said curtly, answering for her.
Anthony made a soft snorting noise.

'Yes, of course Anna's British,' Uncle Digby said. 'But
what was she before she was British?'

They were all looking at her, waiting for her to speak, to
tell them what her real nation was. She wished she could
get up and leave, and walk quickly to the train station and
travel to wherever her real nation was. She wished she had
more panache and knew how to charm people she did not
like.

'Where are your parents from, Anna?' Uncle Digby asked,
still kindly but smiling less fully, perhaps made suspicious
by Anna's silence.

'My father is from East Africa,' Anna said, hating Uncle
Digby for being an oily old fake and hating herself for being
intimidated into a disclosure that she had no faith in. She
had almost said *I think* but she had managed to suppress
that. It turned out that Uncle Digby had lived in Kenya for
several years, and that Anthony had been born there, and
everyone perked up to engage in this new development.

They had a beach house on the south coast, Anthony said, smiling and suddenly eager to talk. He had an old photo of the beach house at home.

'To look at you, I'd say your father was from the coast,' Uncle Digby said, announcing her origins with authority.

'We left when I was quite young, but I still remember it,' Anthony said, cheered by his childhood memories, his clean-shaven head glowing.

'Where on the coast was he from?' Uncle Digby asked, raising his voice a little to force Anthony into retreat.

She noticed that the tempo and the drift of the conversation was making everyone smile, anticipating a little biographical sketch of distant but not unfamiliar origins. 'I don't know,' Anna said.

After a puzzled silence, Uncle Digby said, 'You don't know where your father comes from! Well, I find this hard to believe.'

'I don't know,' Anna repeated, unable to think of anything else to say.

'I'm shocked. Do you mean you don't know, or you don't want to know? It makes me sad to hear you speak with such little interest about your home, Anna,' Uncle Digby said, his eyes lowered and his mouth turned down wretchedly.

'I am British,' Anna said, and heard the strain in her own voice as she spoke.

'Please stop bothering her, Digby,' Jill said.

Uncle Digby waved her words away. 'We see families falling apart because children do not want to know about the world their parents came from. To keep communities together, host and stranger need to know each other, but we cannot know each other if we don't know ourselves. We who care for the welfare of immigrants work as hard as we know how to get that message across, to encourage people to know. Those words *I am British* feel like a cold tragic blast to me sometimes.'

'Hold on, Digby,' Anthony said, grinning. 'You are about to make our jungle bunny cry.' Anna looked at him with a kind of wonder, taking in his grinning, thick-skinned muscular face and the mockery in his eyes. She could not think of anything to say and was afraid she was going to do something abject. She could already feel her eyes stinging. 'It's all right,' he said, leaning forward, grinning and lightly touching her hand. 'Digby didn't mean anything. It's all just words to him. He gets sanctimonious when he hits the bottle.'

'Anna, please come and give a hand for a moment,' Jill said, rising to her feet.

Anna stood up and followed, but she walked past the kitchen door and into the bathroom instead. She stood at the sink for some seconds, staring at herself in the mirror, until she felt the stinging in her eyes recede. When she came out, she saw Jill standing by the kitchen door, waiting for her. She nodded at Anna and they went back to the table.

She stopped her unpacking and stood suddenly still at the thought that she had been unkind to her father in what she had said to Nick that weekend. How could she speak about him like that? She knew that he struggled with the lives they lived, that not all of it was to his liking. Sometimes he talked bitterly about the ignorance of the people they lived among, about their wilful content with the wrong that was done and was being done in their name. He spoke about events at work, and the abuse he had to put up with there, but he was a tough, stubborn man and had somehow kept his balance and advanced himself. If his love was clumsy, it was also devoted. And he was not even the tragedy that she described. She should have remembered that and not spoken of him so slightingly. She wondered if it was to make Nick see that she was unlike them, that she was not one of those immigrants. At times she thought she understood how difficult it must be for her father, still a stranger after all these years, coping with that strangeness all his life, so much older than Ma and unable to share the enthusiasms of his children or to make them truly share in his. She stood still for a long moment, thinking about him and begging pardon.

Anna sat down at the computer she had just switched on and typed: I am British. She waited for the Digby cold tragic blast to blow, and it did as always. A dog in breeches.

On Wednesday evenings, Jamal stayed late at the university to attend an Islam Reading Group. On his way home, he stopped at the corner grocery store to get some milk. The store was poorly lit and cramped with shelves and merchandise. It was empty except for its owner, who remarkably enough was not a Pakistani but an Englishman of European ancestry. He was leaning against the counter, reading something he had there. He had a small Union Jack pennant beside him on the counter and another one on the notice board for messages and advertisements. When Jamal came in, the store owner twisted his upper body ostentatiously to look at the clock on the wall behind him. It was a few minutes before eight, and he usually shut at eight. Whenever he came to the store and was met by its owner's hostility, Jamal was reminded in a small way how dangerous every day was. But he came anyway because the nearest other shop was some distance away, and he did not mind that pulse of danger. Lena from the flat across the landing had come with him once and was so surprised by the man's silent rage at her that she swore never to return. He smiled at the angry man as he paid for the milk in silence, and left.

Jamal had started attending the Islam Reading Group meetings soon after he began his PhD, to fulfil the need to understand more about a religion he was nominally part of. One of the students he shared a house with at the time persuaded him to attend. He was not sure what to expect when he went to the first seminar: prayers, sermons, prohibitions. He feared that there would be communal prayers and he would be shamed by his ignorance. He did not know the words and only had a vague idea of the sequence of the gestures. Ba never prayed, nor taught them anything about prayers. But when he went to his first group meeting, there were no prayers, and no one exposed him or hectored him. Several of the reading group were not even Muslims. Instead they listened to a paper on the inadmissability of apostasy in Islam. Jamal did not even know what apostasy meant, let alone its inadmissability in any religion.

His then housemate, Monzoor, who was doing an MA in Law, must have thought he had launched Jamal on the road to safety, and pressed him to come to the mosque with him for Friday prayers. Jamal said maybe, but first he would learn a little more. Manzoor was disappointed, but determined. 'It is not learning that comes first, but recognition of God's oneness and completion. We are Muslims. God has favoured us with the gift of this knowledge and He has promised us many wonderful things. He has required obedience and submission in return. You have not been obedient and you have not submitted. There isn't much time,' he said. 'Your sins have been mounting for years. Ignorance is no excuse. You must begin putting your account right otherwise you will be denied all the good things God has promised us. Come to prayers with me, and you will please God and He will reward you.'

Maybe, Jamal said, and managed to resist salvation. He would first learn a little more.

Then not so long after that first meeting came the 9/11 bombings in New York, and the wars that followed, which made knowing more imperative. He would have attended the group anyway, but now he did so with the need to hear different voices on what was happening in the world. He went diffidently, and he thought the others did too, not to find solutions or to hold forth against the hatreds released by these events, but to understand what little it was possible to understand. The Islam Reading Group, despite the anxiety it no doubt caused the university authorities, was just another academic seminar, a talking shop. Their subject that Wednesday evening was the Zaydis Shia in Yemen and their doctrinal differences with other Shia sects, the Ithnaasheri and the Ismaili.

Jamal's first thought before he knew anything about the casualties, was: Let it not be the Palestinians. All they had at first were the deceptively familiar images of a plane flying serenely across the New York sky before ramming into one of the towers and bursting into flames. Moments later they saw the other plane, flying unhurriedly, so it seemed, into the other tower. And his first thought was let it not be the Palestinians who have done this, because if it is, they will now lose everything as the Americans turn their wrath on them. Then he thought, let the buildings be empty. Let it not be Muslims who have done this. Let it be maddened drug barons or crazed criminals. But of course it was Muslims, and they were proud of what they had done. And the towers were not empty but crowded with people.

In the days that followed came the stories of senseless deaths and terrifying near misses, of people hurling themselves from the burning towers, of heroic rescues and anguished loved ones waiting for news. The images of the planes exploding into the towers played again and again on television, and he felt that he had witnessed them before they happened, and in a way he had, in all the disaster movies that had rehearsed these moments like a foul prophecy. What those movie images had not foretold was how unpredictably dangerous and fragile the world they lived in had suddenly become, how they all felt in danger of attack now. It had not occurred to him before to imagine what living in danger of attack felt like, as thousands of people must feel in many parts of the world. He had thought of the rights and wrongs of what they endured: in Palestine, Chechnya, the Congo, but he had not even tried to imagine what living in that danger felt like. Perhaps it did not feel like much after a while but became something pervasive and crushing, and you trusted to instinct and luck, just hopping from one near miss to another, resigned to terror. It made him realise how safe he had believed the world they lived in to be.

Those planes exploding into the towers, the hard-headed brutality of that act of terror, whatever its rationale, changed that. He understood that such desperate acts of violence were the response of the weak against the strong, and that what made them repulsive was also part of their impact, their unpredictability, their indiscriminate destruction. Those planes exploding into the towers, and the death of three thousand people and near deaths of many others, released a rage and panic that would lead to the deaths of hundreds of thousands of other people, to the destruction of countries, to mass arrests, to torture, to assassinations and to more acts of terror. He did not know this as he watched the images and listened to the stories, but he knew that retribution would follow because that was what it meant to be a powerful state, and that what was to come would be worse than what they were looking at.

For some reason, he feared for his father. He thought of him and how agitated he became about the killings in Bosnia, how he shouted at the reporters and especially at Douglas Hurd, the British Foreign Minister at that time. *Would they allow this if these people were not Muslims? In Europe? In this day and age?* When Hurd appeared on the screen, his father would listen for a few seconds as the leather-backed *statesman* went through his mollifying patter, and then start accusing him of murderous cynicism. *You don't believe a word you are saying, you liar. What you really mean is I don't care what happens to these people because they are not like us.* His father did not think of Bosnians as Europeans, really, but thought of them as more dark-skinned, like *us*. They were Muslims, after all. Even though the nightly evidence on television when Muslim Bosnian spokesmen were interviewed demonstrated that they looked nothing like us, he was unable, or perhaps never tried, to give up his ambivalence in demanding that they should be treated as Europeans while still believing that they were like us, and it was because they were like us that they were not protected against Serb bloodlust.

Jamal worried how the images of the destruction of the towers would agitate his father. He could imagine his irritation with the knowing analyses of the world, which every news report seemed unable to resist, but he feared he would get impatient with the solemn self-righteousness of the politicians when he knew, when they all knew, that war was being planned. He feared his father would say hard-hearted things about the dead.

He heard people saying that the Americans had brought it upon themselves with their bullying and manipulation. But it could have been any of them in there. Even if you think that the American military were arrogant and swaggering bullies, this act was indiscriminate mass murder. He saw people dancing for joy in some parts of the world. Maybe they thought that what they were seeing was a clever television trick. Maybe they didn't believe what they were being told. Maybe they thought the numbers dead were untrue. Maybe they could not feel sympathy for the dead because they could only gloat over the violence against America and so could not take in the murder of the innocent.

He thought of the march that tried to prevent the war. There were hundreds of thousands of them demonstrating all over the world. He had never been on a march before, except for the noisy exhibitions they sometimes put on at university about the parochial concerns of student life: campaigning for lectures to be made available online, or protesting against a pay strike by academics at examination time. The era of the demo had long since passed, and to him those events were like distant myths of self-indulgent times, the wild music, the crazy sex, the sit-ins, the demo itself, the heroics of the Grosvenor Square anti-Vietnam War rally in 1968. That rally was eight years before he was born, but he had seen a film about it and heard about it, and it made him wonder where those marchers found the audacity to do what they did. Perhaps they suspected that nothing much was really going to happen to them. It was true that the leaders of those mobs had long since burned their waistcoats and cut their hair, and become headmasters and MPs and government ministers and business executives, but they had a bit of spark then, a bit of loud-mouthed daring.

He had a clear memory of the anti-capitalism riots in 1999, but that seemed more like organised combat than a demonstration, both sides uniformed and masked and dementedly violent. The march on 15 February 2003 was peaceful, a mass coming together made up of people who doubted the wisdom or justice of inflicting war on Iraq. Most of them would have trembled at the idea that they were activists or even political. Most of them were not there to exhibit their anti-social prowess or their political radicalism, but their outrage at what they suspected was their government's deception. Many of them were marching for the first time, as was Anna, as was Nick, as was Jamal, and were there to say no, to add their own little bit to the wide-spread scepticism that this war was necessary. For Jamal, in any case, it was a desperate yell of protest at the swell of ugly rhetoric that required him to be mute, that required his compliance with the violent designs of people whose goodwill he thoroughly doubted. Compliance, that was the vogue word of the time, and he did not want to comply. Somehow, they expected that if enough of them turned out, their government would be forced to pause and listen, although Jamal had his doubts that the military machine could be halted.

Bush and Blair took no notice, of course. They took no notice of those who marched, or of others who did not march but raised their objections in other ways, and went right ahead with their war. It made Jamal wonder what it meant to be a citizen: how millions of them listened to what they were told, and thought about it and were not persuaded, how so many people, all over the world, spoke their reluctance and outrage and disagreement, and yet how all this made no difference.

Hanna said he was naïve to have expected the protests to make any difference, although he had not really expected that, and had joined the march without much hope. He heard a man on the radio spitting with restrained rage: 'There are real terrorists in the world,' he said, 'and they have to be destroyed or kept penned in their own wild lands. You can't expect the government to take any risks with that. The march was fine but it is an image of a fantasy world, as if you can deal with terror by giving the terrorists a sermon.'

The war had started by then, and havoc had descended on Iraq. They saw repeated images of Iraqis cheering the arrival of Americans and the joyous toppling of statues of the tyrant, and the hard men who understood realities declared that the Iraqis themselves wanted this war. Their army did not even bother to fight. They wanted the Americans to win. And look, the war is all over, and we are witnessing the barbarian encampment burning. It will be messy for a while and then get better.

What an irony it was that when this war that Ba had dreaded began he was lost in his own deep fog and these new horrors hardly penetrated through his confusing pain.

In the middle of the night, which sometimes came early and sometimes came late, in those hours before dawn, when the world was silent around him, he lay awake and felt his body rotting inside him. He ran a hand down the bony carapace that was holding everything together and thought that one day soon it would collapse into the melting rot inside him.

It was such a long time ago, more than forty years and in real time even longer ago, yet in the silence of the midnight hours those days of his life came back to him with absurd clarity. Even where a thin mist obscured past events, he sensed and felt the meaning of what his memory was trying to recall. It was unrelenting, this labour his mind was engaged in despite his desire to forget. Everything seemed so close, however long ago it happened. He felt those times like a thud in his chest, and he felt the heat of the breathing bodies that appeared to him.

Words were coming back to him, and he was eager for them when at first he had not cared. Now he wanted the words back so he could talk, so he could tell her about his years of silence, so he could describe to her his wretched cowardice. At times he was confused about the things she told him and the names she mentioned. Who were these people? But he remembered so much, everything it seemed, about the other life he abandoned.

He remembered his years as a college student, that was the happiest time. He had never told her about that. It was like a new life, moving to town with Fawzia's relatives, moving away from the tyrannous parsimony of his father's house. Perhaps he should have stayed and found what happiness he could there. Maybe he would have done some good if he had stayed instead of spending his life stranded in a place where he could do nothing of any use to anyone, only aching with guilt now his body was too frail to resist. Perhaps he should have stayed and shared in the calamities that befell them. No good thinking like that now he was fit for nothing. At times he felt he had done everything wrong, at other times, not everything. There were times when he felt that he could rest. For years that had seemed a mercy, that some things he had done were well done, but now it was a struggle to hang on to that reprieve.

He had a good time at the college, though. He remembered how he went to the college the week before the start of term, to pay his fees and collect his papers, and how afterwards he walked the tiled corridors and the shaded paths in the grounds with a feeling of incredulity. That he should be allowed here. When term started, he found out that he knew no one, but the instructions were so clear that he just had to follow the herd and obey the rules. That was what was new, the discipline, first of all. There were so many new rules, but no one shouted or waved a stick, or stood arms akimbo glaring at the students as if looking to pre-empt a stampede. The teachers were polite and patient, and the students followed the rules to the last detail and were polite themselves. Perhaps some of the teachers sneered at their ignorance, but even that they did politely.

They played games. There had been no games in his old school, but at the college they did athletics and cricket and badminton and volleyball, some of them games he had never even known existed. These were English games, and it might have been excusable not knowing about them if the British had not colonised them. It was less excusable that he had never heard of algebra or geometry or physics or logarithm tables in his country school, when this was knowledge it had taken the whole world to bring into being. Even the subjects he had studied before were taught differently in the college. There was a library, with hundreds of books that he could take home to read if he wished. It was like all his schooling until then had taken place in a small room, a small empty shut-away room. Then someone had opened the door and he found out that the room was a tiny little cell in a huge building. There were wide corridors and verandas on all sides, and he was free to walk around if he wanted, or more likely if he dared, because his ignorance was so complete that he was intimidated by everything and was pleased enough with the little steps he was taking.

That was the picture of his college that still came back to him, those early days of starting there, the extent of his ignorance, the incredible content of learning. He was sixteen years old when he started and he was there for three years. It was the happiest time and he yearned for that time always. He made friends, he learned to swim and he went home to his little room with Fawzia's relatives and did what work he was given to do every day. At first he went back to Mfenesini every Friday afternoon and came back on Sunday evening. He wanted to lessen the burden on the relatives who kept him, but after a while he went home less often. His brothers treated him like a hero, wanting to hear about what he learned and flattering him for every little triumph he recounted, but his father laughed at his college uniform. Look at this poor stooge, look at this karagosi, he said, look at the airs he gives himself. Go and say your prayers. After prayers, he made him get into his old rags and gave him dirty work to do, just so he would not forget to be humble. Nobody eats for nothing in this house.

Othman the miser, his great bully of a father. And yet once, he had seen him sob like someone who had lost his mind. He would never have thought him capable of such tears. They heard cries coming from the road at the other end of the lane, a man shouting and a donkey braying in fright. His father ran down the lane to investigate and he followed. Both his brothers were working at the other end of the farm and did not hear the cries at first. When Abbas and his father reached the road, they found a man beating an exhausted donkey with a thick stick. He stopped for a moment when they appeared, surprised to see them. His head must have been pounding so hard with fury that he had not heard their noisy rush through the tangled lane. He was frothing at the mouth with rage. The donkey was lying on the road, too exhausted to rise or struggle, twitching involuntarily with terror. After the briefest hesitation, the man resumed his work, lining himself up to deliver blows to the tenderest parts he could reach, the mouth, the belly, the meat of the donkey's haunches. His father, Othman the miser, yelled again and again for the man to stop, in the end falling on his knees and covering the donkey's head with his body to prevent the blows landing there. The man pulled his father off angrily and threatened him with his stick. His father sat on the ground a few feet away, weeping and sobbing uncontrollably, his glasses smeared with tears. In the end, his brothers Kassim and Yusuf Kimya came, and the three of them dragged their father away. He wept for hours, rocking and holding his head, so that they began to fear that he had lost his mind. Perhaps he did for a while, but in the light of day he was back to his mean old self, standing in the yard with his short hoe, yelling for his sons to get to work. The brothers went to the road to look, but there was nothing there, just a small pile of dung, which insects were busily carting away.

During his second year at the college, he did not go to Mfenesini every Friday afternoon but occasionally stayed in town. He expected rebuke from his father for shirking and was anxious that his brothers would think he was learning to forget them, but his absences somehow meant that his father treated him less angrily when he did go. The occasions of his visits home grew less frequent as the year passed. The aura of town, and college and study must have made his life seem complicated and busy, while theirs was weeding and digging and labouring. He could feel the difference growing between them. When he went home for the vacations, he was even allowed to sit in the shade with his books for an hour or two now and then, so long as he did not abuse this great privilege. By the end of the second year, he was staying in town all week. He did not do anything very exciting. He went to college, did his work, strolled by the sea with his friends or went to watch a football game. On Fridays he went for prayers at Msikiti Jumaa in Forodhani and was now and then invited to eat with the family of one of his school friends. Sometimes he attended the rallies, which were then happening as politics was building up.

Then one night he saw her. It was not that he had not seen her before, but that was the night he really saw her. She was a young woman who lived next door to the relatives he was living with. He caught sight of her from his window and thought her attractive. He was just looking, eyeing up the daughter of the grand family that lived next door, that was all. Her father was a businessman, a merchant, a man of means and some eminence in the neighbourhood. He owned an electrical-goods shop and a butcher's stall in the market. One of his sons ran the electrical shop and the other the butcher's business, and they were wealthy enough for each of the sons to own a car. He had never seen the young woman in the street, because when she went out she was covered from head to toe in her buibui. He only guessed that it was her because he saw her coming out of the door. But on her terrace she walked about uncovered, unaware of his gaze.

It was at the beginning of his third year at the college, and his life of quiet outward content had no knowledge of girls or women. He listened to some of the other boys talking of their adventures and affairs with envy, and he was not sure if he should believe them, but he did not think such excitements were likely to befall him. He liked to look at the beautiful women he passed in the streets. Not all of them covered up as his neighbour did, and some of them knew how to wear the buibui so that it did not conceal anything of importance. Later he fantasised and guiltily sinned on his own. He did not know how to take matters beyond that, and did not even think of that on that first night he really saw her. He thought she was beautiful, that was all, and started to look out for her on her terrace. It wasn't a crime. He was just taking a look, not even thinking of anything, not even interested in anything, just enjoying how she looked.

He used to watch her from his little slit of a window. The relatives of his sister's husband lived on the third floor of a tall narrow building. They had two rooms to themselves and he had a small storeroom, a tiny cell, which he fitted into tightly. There were no shutters and no glass in the window, just a hole in the wall about nine inches wide and two feet high. A cool breeze blew through it at twilight, and sometimes when it rained he felt the lightest sprinkling on his feet. When it rained hard and the wind was blowing in the wrong direction, he rolled up his thin mattress and moved his books to the top end of the bed. He had glimpses of the sea over the top of the neem trees alongside the dockyard warehouses, and he looked down on the terrace of the house next door with its potted shrubs and washing lines.

If he thought about how snugly he fitted into that room,

he sometimes found it difficult to breathe. When he raised his head from his books there was nowhere to look but out of the window. He was very happy in that room even though he was anxious and felt unworthy about many things. He was eighteen. He was poor, a charity case. He was shy. He had no confidence. That was how he thought of himself. He had no skills apart from his diligence in studying. But he remembered that it was a happy time in that room. He was in his last year at the college, which had been like a new world to him. He was doing well there, and soon he would be offered a job as a teacher and would have a respectable living for the rest of his life.

The relatives he lived with were poor; there was no electricity in the house and no running water. The water had to be fetched from the standpipe in the street every day and carried in buckets up those three flights of stairs to the storage tank in the kitchen. The bathroom was shared by everyone in the house, and was on the ground floor, a dark frightening room, which he only visited out of utter necessity. Their meals were humble, but his relatives were kind. He was courteous and grateful, and they were pleased with his gratitude. They treated him like a son of the house, sending him on errands or to fetch a bucket of water from the standpipe, telling him off for oversleeping or for working too hard, or for missing a reading for a neighbour at the mosque.

He watched the girl from the window because she was there in front of him. That night, as he sat there at his window looking out on the dark, ready to go to bed, she came on the terrace with a candle. She put the candle down and pulled off her shift in one movement. She stood naked in the candlelight for a few seconds and then reached for a cloth that was on the clothes line and wrapped herself in it.

She could not have known he was there because he had not lit a lamp in his room. She never took her shift off again like that, but after that first time he had his own picture of her in his mind. Even after all these years he could still see her, that unexpected movement when she reached to the back of her shoulders and pulled off her shift, and revealed her slim naked body to the candlelight. He had nowhere to sit in his room but on the bed and that was next to the window. It did not require any planning for him to be watching her whenever she came out while he was in the room. Perhaps he became infatuated with the sight of her but he did not intend anything more than to look. Where would he have got the daring for that?

Then one day she saw him looking and did not seem to mind. After that he often sat by the tiny window, reading his books and looking at her as she sat with her chores or leaned against the terrace wall, looking out towards the sea. He watched her as she hung out the washing, or as she sat in the shade picking stones out of rice, or as she watered the plant pots in the late afternoon or even as she just sat there in the evenings. Sometimes at night, as he lay in bed by the window, he heard voices coming from the terrace, and he thought that was the family catching the breeze at the end of a hot day. Just a little harmless flirtation, he said to himself, teenagers making eyes at each other from the safety of their homes. But her father caught them out in their little game. He came out one twilight evening and found his daughter sitting on a mat, and turned round quickly enough to see Abbas at his window with the lamp glowing beside him. Abbas did not think anything serious would come of it. The merchant was a man of means, and he was just a boy living next door with his penniless relatives, taking a peep at his daughter. For a while, he would have to cross the street when he saw the father but if he kept out of the way, the memory of him at the window would soon fade. After all, he was only just looking out, maybe not even looking at his daughter. If she happened to be sitting on the terrace when he was looking out, how was that his business? But that was not how it was to be.

The girl's aunt lived with them, and had lived with them since the death of the girl's mother many years before. The girl's father told the aunt about what he had seen and she raised the alarm. She said if the girl was sitting there uncovered instead of running inside as soon as she spotted the boy, then the harm was already done. The aunt was someone who knew about things, and knew how a story can change as it passes from hand to hand and how it can grow into a different shape, especially where it concerned a young woman's reputation. She went in search of Abbas's sister, Fawzia, whom she knew from weddings and funerals that they both regularly attended.

One day Fawzia came and told Abbas that he had been summoned home to Mfenesini. She would not tell him what it was about, and when they got there he saw that there had not been any summons, that it was all her doing. She made a big show out of it. She gathered everyone together, their father, their mother, his two brothers, who all came together nervously, expecting her to announce a tragedy, that she had been divorced by her husband or he had been jailed for smuggling or for pilfering at the Public Works Department where he worked. She told them that Abbas had dishonoured the daughter of the rich merchant who lived next door. Abbas was frightened by the announcement, and felt a sudden leap in his chest as if he had lost his footing on the edge of a high wall. That's complete rubbish, he said, but

Fawzia ignored him and provided more details of the outrage the merchant felt and how she had been called in to convey it to the family. Abbas could not understand what she was doing or what it meant. Their father did a lot of shouting, which he did happily enough whenever he had the chance, but now there was dishonour to consider as well.

I knew it would end like this, he shouted. I knew it, I just knew it. Those European teachers and their school have turned your head. Their books have taught you to give yourself such airs that you think you can go and fuck a rich man's daughter. Now they'll beat you in the streets like a dog, you don't know these Yemeni merchants. That's what happens to a poor boy whose head gets too big. Someone knocks it off. Like this, he said, slapping him hard across the back of his head, and then he gave him another slap to make his point clear.

His mother sobbed as his father ranted, and his sister interrupted him whenever he tried to speak. She told everyone that the only honourable thing to do was to propose marriage, and that she was going back to town that same afternoon to do that in the name of the family. Nobody had better try to stop her because she could not hold her head up if her family did not behave honourably in this matter. His father and his brothers gave Abbas sly grins and his mother's sobs died down. They had expected beatings and abuse from the merchant and his powerful friends, not talk of a good marriage. After a day or two Abbas began to grin slyly himself too, even though at first he had been alarmed at the way things were going. He had no objections to marriage. He was old enough by their practices and he would soon have a job, and he already knew that the girl was beautiful, and that the family was wealthy. Within two weeks, which passed in an exhilarating blur, the marriage was arranged and consummated, and he had moved in with her family. Fawzia was very pleased with her work and told Abbas several times how grateful he should be to her for saving his life.

In the hours before dawn, he lay humbled in his defeated body, trembling with weakness and the anguish that he felt about the young woman he so unexpectedly married when he was eighteen. A shiver of revulsion and self-hatred ran through him. The first few weeks were wonderful. His wife, Sharifa, was as beautiful as that first sight of her in candlelight promised. He had no idea of the pleasures the body was capable of, and how easy it was to rid himself of anxieties and inhibitions about what to do as a husband. After the wedding he moved into Sharifa's family home because the room he lived in was only a store, hardly big enough for him on his own. He moved in with her father, her aunt, and two elder brothers and their wives and children in their large two-floor apartment above the row of shops. They were given a room on the top floor, next to the aunt and the kitchen and the bathroom and the terrace on which he had first seen Sharifa. The rest of them lived on the floor below, the father in a big room that looked out over the street, and the brothers and their families in two rooms at the back of the house. There was also a reception room on that floor, a place where the women of the house received visitors. He stood on the terrace in the evenings, sometimes, and looked up at the little window to see if he could catch sight of his old self brooding there.

No, he was happy. He could not believe that such luck had come his way. He had never known so much space and privacy before. They had a room all to themselves with many small comforts he was enjoying for the first time in his life. They had a spring bed and a radio, and a rug on the floor. He spent all the hours he could spare in that room. He talked with his new wife when she was not busy with her duties. He revised for his final examinations, which were coming very soon. He listened to the small radio her father had given them as a present from the shop. It was like a retreat from the world. They had eggs and maandazi for breakfast. They ate meat *and* fish every day, all of them except the father eating the afternoon meal together under the awning in front of the kitchen, crowded on the mat that was rolled out and rolled up before and after each meal every day. The father ate alone from a tray sent to his room. Every Friday they had pilau made with mutton. It was a life of luxury, alhamdulillah. All that was required of him was to do his schoolwork, eat until he was full and wait for his wife to finish her chores.

That room he shared with Sharifa was like a deep shade under a tree, like a gentle sea breeze blowing at evening. It was like one of those blessings in a story, he thought, except that the joy of it was real. A shy, hard-working and faithful youngster is showered with good fortune and builds a house with a garden for his beloved and his long-suffering parents. He did not build a garden and did not want to live with his parents ever again, but he had his beloved. Yes it would have been like one of those blessings, except those things don't happen in real life, and every blessing has a poisonous thorn hidden in it. As he became used to the excitement of his new life, he could not miss how poorly and disrespect-fully her family treated him. After a while he began to see that Sharifa did so as well, at least in front of the others. Every day it seemed to get worse.

He fidgeted in his sick bed, trying to evade the host that

crowded him. I can't be bothered with remembering all that now, those arrogant little pharaohs. I can't be bothered with all this.

The brothers were always teasing him and laughing at him in their worldly way, treating him like a stumbling innocent blundering through life. They were notorious men. Every evening, in their separate cars, they parked in discreet places to wait for women who came in search of them. They were both married. Their wives were from Aden, and preferred the dust of Yemen to that of the little black island with its incomprehensible yabber, which they hardly bothered to speak properly. They went visiting in Aden every year or two with their children and stayed away for months. If they gave any thought to what their husbands did to amuse themselves while they were away, they never spoke these thoughts, and he did not think even Sharifa knew her brothers' reputations in the town. He did not think it would have mattered to the brothers if she knew, or if the wives were absent or present. None of it would have made much difference to their prowling.

When the brothers made fun of him, he laughed too, because everyone else did and he did not want it to seem that he minded, and perhaps the laughter was not meant unkindly. They had been hospitable, they had given him affection, and he was a lot younger than they were. They laughed at his youth and his innocence, and he told himself not to mind, but still, he felt silly about almost everything when they were around. Their wives covered their heads when he walked into the room, and spoke in a coded language of their own invention (they were sisters), but he was sure that what they said was mockery of him. Sharifa's father gave him money in front of every-one, as if he was an employee, as if he served him. He did not give him the money at a regular time, but randomly. Sometimes he gave him coins and sometimes he gave him notes. It was like he was giving money to a charity. When the aunt thought he had got something wrong she rebuked him like a child, snapping at him and raising her voice so the whole house would hear, and even his wife laughed at him then. It seemed to him that people in the street could hear her shrieking at him. There were times when he wondered if the aunt was deranged. Her outbursts were so violent and out of proportion. He could not help but feel the humiliation even though he tried to talk himself out of it.

They would get used to him, he said to himself, especially after they began to see that he deserved their respect. They frightened him, and he thought they knew they did. He hated them. After a while it made him suspicious that they treated him with so little respect. Once he began to think like that he could not get the thought out of his mind. He thought they laughed at him to mock him, and laughed at his father and brothers, who had acted like starving freeloaders at the wedding. He thought they were mocking him for his poverty and for their country ways.

All the happiness and contentment he had felt about his future receded from him. The first thought in his head when he woke up in the morning was that he would have to bear their contempt. The thought filled him with an anguish so deep that he found it incredible to think of it now. He was young, deferential, used to having little in his life, and had no understanding of the unrelenting arrogance of the rich and the self-regarding. His stumbling inadequacy in the face of these circumstances made him feel hateful even to himself.

One night, late at night, after they had made love and

were talking softly – he shut his eyes and could feel her beside him – Sharifa told him that she was not a blood daughter to the merchant. She told him she had never known her real father, who died suddenly in his twenties, when she was a year old. She did not remember anything about him. No, she did not know what he had died of. No one talked about such things. You don't ask what people died of. They died because their time had come. Her mother then moved in with her brother, the merchant, but she too died soon after that, of fever. No she didn't know what fever, just fever. Why was he asking ridiculous questions? Was she a doctor? She was three years old when her mother died, so she did have a memory of her, only one very power-ful memory and almost nothing else. She remembered playing near her while she was cooking on a seredani, prob-ably just out there in the kitchen or under the awning. She stumbled and knocked the pot off the fire. She would have fallen into the fire if her mother, by some miracle, had not plucked her up into safety. Her hands were scalded by the pot but that was all, otherwise she was unhurt. That was all she remembered of her, how she plucked her out of the fire and then was so frightened that she slapped her for her clumsiness. After her mother died, she grew up as a child of the household, and the merchant and his wife, may God have mercy on her soul, treated her like a daughter. He had always treated her like a daughter. Abbas asked what the merchant's wife died of, and Sharifa slapped him hard on the thigh.

Then he found out that Sharifa was pregnant and at first he was overjoyed about that. The very idea that a child he had made was on its way! Only as the weeks passed and her date grew nearer, he began to think that the baby was coming too soon after the wedding. Once he began to think like this he could not stop. After his examinations were over and he had so much time on his hands, these thoughts would not leave him alone. He began to fear that the child was not his. That there was some trick, some plot, that they had trapped him to save her from dishonour, that the child was someone else's, and that something vile had happened that they were trying to hide. That the wedding had been arranged hastily to save her and the family from embarrassment. That after the child was born and his wife had been saved from dishonour, he would be forced to divorce her. He was sure his sister had known about this, and had received a gift from the family to arrange it. There was nothing easier to do than divorce a wife. Just one little word will do it. Was that why the brothers were treating him with such mockery?

He tried to persuade himself that he would cope with the meaning of all these thoughts when it was necessary. Why worry himself with suspicions when what he needed to do was to harden himself, to grow into a man and learn to plot? He had passed his examinations, had been allocated a school where he would begin teaching in the new school year and he would have a job for life. But he could not convince himself. He could not make his body uncoil from a tense knot of anticipation, could not look at his image in the mirror. He began to hear things in what his wife said and thought that she had been forced to marry him to hide her shame when she had known another. He was convinced that something vile had happened in this house. He dared not find the words for it. He was convinced that many other people knew about what had happened and were getting ready to have a good laugh at the skinny cuckold. The place he lived in was like that. They would laugh at him for the rest of his life, pointing him out as he walked past and tell the story of his stupidity. He believed this, and became afraid. After six months of marriage, his wife looked as if she would deliver any day. He was certain that there were many people in the town who were already counting. They had nothing better to do. So in early December 1959, when he was nineteen years old, he ran away from her and from his country and from everything and everyone he knew. That was the courageous and admirable thing he did. He ran away.

He lay in the dark and felt the trickle of tears running out of the corners of his eyes. No good now, weeping like a baby after all that time. He must have made a noise because he heard Maryam stirring, and then she called out his name. Abbas. After a moment, he said to her: Mfenesini.

Flight

3

MFENESINI, HE SAID. SHE sat up in the dark and asked what that was. Then when he said it again and it still made no sense, she switched on the torch that she kept beside her camp bed, pointing it away from him. He too was sitting up in bed, looking towards her. In the middle of the night. She went over to him and put the bedside lamp on. He said the word for the third time. She thought he was rambling, just woken from a dream about that faraway place in Africa where he came from. 'Mfenesini,' he said for the fourth time, smiling. 'My school . . . where I went to school. I told you before.'

She gave him the notebook that she kept beside the bed, for him to write something down when he could not say it, and he wrote Mfenesini. He could not write for long, the muscles in his right arm and leg were still weak, but he could write a few words. He was talking more now and attended speech therapy four times a week, eager to get the words back. He walked to the health centre himself, for the exercise, timing himself each time. It was only a short distance away. When he was well it would have taken ten minutes, to the bottom of their street and left, straight down the road. Maryam walked with him the first two times, but then she had to do her voluntary afternoon at the Refugee Centre, so on the third time he went on his own and he was fine. He went on his own after that, taking his time. It was late summer and the weather was kind, and he walked slowly, using a stick to take the weight off his right leg. She watched him go sometimes, her brave Mr Boots. The doctor told him that the latest scan showed that the damage to the left side of his brain was not as bad as it had first seemed and he was making excellent progress with the aphasia. What he needed to do now was to build up his strength, attend all his therapy sessions and be cheerful. Fat chance about being cheerful, but he was obedient about therapy and exercises, and the words were coming back. It was not always easy to understand him, but the words were coming back, and his mind was clear. Each time he said more, his happiness brought tears to her eyes.

She looked at the word he had written in the notebook and then spoke it, looking at him. He nodded, smiling. 'This was the name of your school,' she said, and he nodded again. 'Where is that?' she asked.

When she asked him this *where* question before, he replied *back home* or something like that and then changed the subject. The monkey from Africa. This time he said Zanzibar without any hesitation. She gave him the note-book again and he wrote down the word. The word was not a surprise to her, for despite his caution, it had slipped out of him a few times. 'Tell me about Zanzibar,' she said, but he shook his head and began to weep. He cried so easily these days. She sat beside him on the bed, holding the notebook in her hand, and watched as his weeping turned into sobs. When his sobs subsided, and he had wiped his eyes and calmed himself, she went downstairs and brought back the atlas and made him show her where

Zanzibar was. Then he began to talk, a little bit at a time, from a long time ago, before he came here. She sighed silently to herself, wishing that there had not been so many years of secret hesitations. Why did Zanzibar have to be such a secret? Whenever she had asked him where his home was, he said East Africa. Then he said he only went back once, when his ship docked in Mombasa for a few hours. There was no time to go ashore and all he had was a view of the town. So she guessed that home was Mombasa.

The night was beginning to lighten, and she saw that he was tiring. He had probably been awake for hours, thinking about Mfenesini, so she said she would make them some tea. When she came back upstairs he was asleep.

Later that night he told her more. She waited for him to start when he was ready, but when evening came and they were upstairs in the bedroom and he still had not returned to what he had started in the middle of the previous night, she prompted him. She did not trust her knowledge or her memory, so she made him write the difficult names down in the notebook or made him spell them. He told her that he grew up in the country, near Mfenesini, that place where he said he went to school. On the second night he only talked about that: his father, Othman the miser; his brothers Kassim and Yusuf Kimya; his mother, she was always just Ma; his sister Fawzia (write the names down). Then he told her about the day Kassim took him to the school in Mfenesini. It was called Mfenesini because a huge tree grew by the roadside, and its fruit is called fenesi. She tried to say the word, and he made her say it several times until she got it right. Fenesi. She liked saying that word, fenesi, it made her feel as if she had something hidden under her tongue. He described the fruit to her but she could not picture it.

Like a rubbery green bag with sweet, soft sticky flesh inside, he said. He drew a picture, but she had never seen a fruit like that before. In the end she found out that fenesi was called jackfruit in English, because the next day she got a book from the library, one of those large botanical books with lots of pictures, and they went through it until they found the fruit. It was not an attractive fruit but it made both of them happy to find it. He did not know it was such a well-loved fruit, and that it was found in so many places in the world, although he had seen it in his travels here and there. When she read him what it said about it he was surprised, and really shocked to find out that it had been written about by historians and kings and philosophers. Our ugly stupid fenesi, he said, who would have thought there was all this science and poetry dedicated to it. Then after that she had to go back to the library and find more books about the jackfruit. They found out that the emperor Akbar did not like the fruit, and she never even knew there had been an emperor Akbar in the world or what he had done that was so grand. It was the Jesuit mission to China that first described it to Europeans. Did he know there was a Jesuit mission to China? It was all new to her. Yes he did, he said, but not much more than that. So then she had to go to the library and ask them to find him a book about the Jesuit mission. That was how he was when he found a story that interested him, off to the library to get them to find him more books. They knew him there.

In the days that followed he told her more, and she took the notebook from him and wrote the names herself because the writing slowed him down. She made him check the spelling to make sure she had written the word right. That was at the beginning, when he first started to talk. Then later she had to be patient because sometimes he was not himself, pained by his memories or just distraught because she was there and he could be distraught with her. He became angry, fidgeting and gesticulating at her when she wrote something down, accusing her of plotting against him, speaking in a language she did not understand. Utanifanyia fitna, he said. Can you spell that for me? she asked. After a moment, he did and she wrote the words down in the notebook. When he was deeper into what he was telling her, when he was neck-deep in his shame, he did not seem to mind whether she wrote anything down or not. He came out with things, and sometimes went backwards and forwards as if he could not stop. Or as if he was circling away from what lay ahead.

One night he told her about the college and his happiness there. He described the buildings, the sea, walked her down the corridors and the long country lane that led to the main road. He wanted her to see it, to be there in the afternoon with him when they played football, to feel the breeze blowing from the sea. He hesitated and stuttered, struggling with words, but he did not seem to want to stop talking about that college. How could he keep quiet for so long with the memory of such happiness? But she did not ask him. From the beginning she had determined that she would not ask him anything that might seem like a challenge, in case he lost courage and stopped.

They only talked at night at first, but after a few days, he began to talk in the afternoon, no longer able to contain his eagerness to tell. She saw his growing excitement in the telling, waiting for her to be available to him and only frustrated by his struggle with words. She bought him a small recording machine so he could speak into it when he wanted, even when she was not around. He looked at it in surprise and put it down beside his chair in the living room. Then one afternoon he began to talk about the girl on the terrace. She was surprised at first because he never talked about women he knew before, but then she thought it would be another one of the memories he was displaying to her, a flirtation, a teenage escapade. Quite quickly, his eyes and his voice told her that they were approaching the reason for his silence for all these years. It did not take him long. He did not hesitate except when his tongue failed him, and he did not digress or elaborate, not on this first telling. When he had finished telling her about the woman he married and abandoned when she was pregnant, they sat without speaking for a while. They were sitting in the back room, looking out on the garden, and through the open terrace door she could hear the blackbirds singing. She tried not to think of the word, but it forced itself into her mind. Bigamist. She felt suddenly weary about the complications that lay ahead. He sat in front of her, thin and tortured, staring at the floor.

'You wait thirty years to tell me that you were already married when you married me,' she said, gently. 'That you are not really married to me.'

He looked surprised. 'Of course I'm married to you,' he said, incredulous.

'Not according to the law,' she said, incredulous herself, thinking that perhaps it had never occurred to him that he was a bigamist.

'What law?' he said. 'You're my wife. What are you talking about?'

After a while, she asked: 'Will you tell the children?' He looked helpless for a moment and then nodded. 'Later,' he said.

It must have all been much more complicated than the way he told it but that is what he was keeping to himself for all those years, that he ran away and abandoned a wife and child. He did not mention her name but she would get him to say it. She would not allow him to go back into hiding again. Her mind produced an image, imprecise and vague, composed from a jumble of other images. It was the figure of a mother and child in an unfamiliar landscape, just a shadow or a silhouette of a woman and a child passing down a lane. She was not sure exactly why it caused her such pain. Will he tell the children? Should he tell the children? What will he tell them? Should they just keep quiet, for an easy life? The world is probably choking with bigamists.

He would have been nineteen years old when he did that, abandoned his wife and unborn child. He never sent word to anyone afterwards, and never ever met anyone who knew him before. That was what he said. He did not have a photograph or a single scrap of anything that connected him to that place, he made sure of that, and she certainly had not seen anything like that in all their lives together. She tried to work it out for herself, to understand what could have made him so frightened, what exactly could have panicked him into doing such a thing. They went back to it several times. He told her her name, and her brothers' names, who were not really her brothers and who were obsessed with their lusts. He told her how they mocked him and intimidated him. He no longer knew whether the marriage was a trap or not. He no longer knew what to believe. He did not know how he had managed to do it, to run away, but that was what he did.

How could he have made himself believe that miserable old excuse that the child was not his? She did not say that to him because she did not want him to stop talking. Instead she asked: Why could he not speak about what had happened? Why could he not even speak to her after all these years of their lives?

Could she not see why he could not? He was frightened of what he had done, and for so long there was no one to tell anyway.

No one? she asked.

He shrugged. By the time he met her he was well set in his ways, and thought of himself as someone who roamed the world without responsibility or connection. When he said to her that they should leave Exeter, he did not realise what he was doing. At that time, if he was in a place and he did not like what was going on, he just left. He could come and go as he pleased. When he said to her, let's go, he was treating her as if she was like him, someone who could just leave. He did not think it would be for life, he thought it would be a pretty fling then they would get on with what they wanted to do. But after that he could not bear to lose her.

She was trying to understand why he was so frightened.

He laughed. She did not understand how tiny the place he came from was, how tiny their lives felt there. He was frightened of the world, that was what he was frightened of. Or maybe he was just fearful by nature. And he was acting shamefully, he knew that. There are things that are unacceptable to everyone, and that people will despise you for doing. He knew this was one of them, and that he would be despised by everyone for doing what he had done. And yet he had still done it, terrified as he was. Only afterwards he was ashamed. Only afterwards he learned to supress his terror and his shame and to live his life like a hooligan.

She was also trying to understand the shame he felt for what he had done, what kind of shame it was that made him choose to live with that guilt in silence, when he could have told her and found some relief, as he had now in the end. Or he could have told all of them, and found some sympathy for his act of stupidity, as he surely would have done. How could he manage to keep silent? She was trying to understand that.

They sat quietly for a while, and in that silence she felt the beginnings of nausea. She was getting tired of listening to him. His story was wearying something inside her, making her want to retreat from his pleading eyes. She was feeling worn out now, she said to him. Maybe later he can tell her *how* he ran away. She'd like to hear something about how that happened. Or was he tired of talking about this whole subject for now?

He was tired of *not* talking about these things, of not saying so much, and she must be too, he said. She saw that his brow was running with sweat, and she passed her hand over it to wipe away the moisture. She saw that he too was exhausted, and she said they should leave it for now. Why don't you cool off in the garden for a while and then we can continue later. He protested, his face beginning to pucker with rage, but she told him that he was just being stubborn. She rose to her feet as she spoke, making it clear that she was not interested in a discussion. She knew that he wanted to talk on but she did not want to hear any more, not just then. She did not want to listen to his voice, or hear about his grief. She wanted to hear nothing, no more words. He would not speak to her for days now, she knew.

From the kitchen she heard him talking to himself, whispering. He did that sometimes and when she went near to hear what he was saying, he stopped. She thought he was talking in his own language but she could not be sure. It could just be his own gibberish. He groaned at any time of day or night, all of a sudden, out of nowhere, hideous agonized groans, sometimes in the depths of the night, and could not be silenced for minutes on end. There were times when she stood in front of him while he sat in his chair in the living room, his eyes open and unseeing, groaning with an anguish like sobs, while tears ran down his face.

'What is it, Abbas? What is it that hurts?'

But he could not be reached when he was like that, and she held him and tried to rock him or shake him out of his trance. At times he allowed this and at other times he shook her off. Then he became abusive, calling her names: you moron, you whore. A lot of the time he sat by himself, doing nothing, looking out of the window, or reading a newspaper or doing the crossword. A few days ago she heard him rambling softly about Regents Park and Tutankhamun, chuckling and smiling, hectoring someone and whispering for minutes on end. She thought it was the medication confusing him.

She went upstairs to put the washing away and to air the bedroom, and she saw that he had gone out in the garden and was sitting on the terrace. The sun was behind the house that late in the afternoon, and the terrace was in the shade. He was bent forward, elbows on the arms of the chair, sitting in his profound stillness, although she thought she could see his neck shiver even from that distance. Will it occur to him that he had not only been silent about his shame, but that he had been lying to them, to her, for thirty years? What will she have done, that woman he left behind? She will have given him up for lost and divorced him for abandonment. Can you do that in Zanzibar? Divorce an absent husband? Or will she still be waiting for him to return, trapped by his absence? Perhaps in his eyes he was not even a bigamist since he was allowed four wives in his Islam, and he married her under those rules, probably. Why four? Why not three or five or six? In his favour, it has to be said that after taking one in this system he has not taken another. What will he tell his children? Their children. Will he tell them that they are the children of a bigamist?

Jamal rang home one evening a few days later. He was on his own in the house: Lisa and Jim had gone for a week's break in Berlin where they had a friend. You'll love Berlin, they told him, you must go there one day. Lena had gone home to Dublin for a few days, and was then going camping or boating on the Shannon or something like that with her boyfriend. Both Jim and Lena were on the same submission deadline as him, and he could not understand where they found the audacity to take a break. He was at his desk whenever he had the strength, writing, checking details, revising, with the internet as a bit of a break when he got weary and blocked. He rang his Ma because he felt perpetually guilty about not calling her. He did not think she enjoyed speaking on the phone; she was always eager to end the conversation and never delayed him when he said he had to go. Ba was the legendary hater of the telephone who winced when it began to ring and scowled furiously while anyone was speaking on it. Yet even though they were perhaps happy enough not being rung, Jamal still felt bad for not ringing. He should call to ask after them, and for them to know that he cared how they were. Yes, he had good reason to feel at fault. The last time he called was two weeks or so ago, and it must be more than a month since he had been down to see them. The news then was of improvement, but he should show his face, be a caring son at a time when his father was ill and his mother in distress. So he rang that night, alone and feeling the loneliness, but feeling good about the progress he was making with writing up his thesis; almost there, for what it was worth. That was what he told her, almost there.

When he asked about Ba, she said he was doing fine, able to say and do more every day. He thought she was being careful and guessed that all was not well, or that he was within earshot and she could not speak freely. She did not suggest passing the phone to Ba. He asked if she was all right, and she said yes, yes, what could be wrong with her? So he said that he was thinking of coming to see them at the weekend, and after a moment he heard the smile in her voice as she said, that will be lovely.

He was contemplating emailing Hanna, to see if she was free to come as well (he knew that Nick would somehow be too busy), when his heart jumped from a noise downstairs and he knew at once that it was someone trying to force the front door. He had put the chain on before he came up, as he always did when he was on his own, and sometimes he went down in the middle of the night to check that he had done so. His first thought was that it was the young people who bothered the neighbour next door, the one he saw painting his garden shed the day he moved in. Sometimes when they were sitting in their dining room, they heard banging noises and shouts and then young people running away laughing. That old man was the only dark-skinned person who lived in the street, apart from Jamal, who obviously lived in a house shared with other students and was not as vulnerable alone. He had often thought he should speak to the old man, show him courtesy, say some words of condolence to him about his persecution, but he did not. He did not know what to say. He just smiled to him now and then when they passed.

So Jamal's first thought when he heard the noise at the door was that the youngsters, whom he had never seen but could picture in his mind, boys and girls between fifteen and seventeen, tightly fleshed and grinning, had somehow found out that his housemates were away for a few days and he was on his own, and decided this would be a good time to give him a bit of a scare. He thought himself cowardly about confrontations and did his best to avoid them. It was not only fear of pain that made him avoid them, but of being browbeaten and mocked by loud voices, of being made to look foolish by cruel laughter. Now he trembled a little as he ran downstairs, his mind racing with what he should do. The bell rang before he reached the door, which he saw was unlocked but was held tightly ajar by the chain. They should put a bolt on the door.

'Who's that?' he asked, barking to disguise his terror.

He recognised Lena's voice as soon as she spoke. She sounded worried and out of breath. He hurriedly unhooked the chain and let her in. In those few seconds while he struggled with the chain, he pictured her on the pavement, anxious, glancing over her shoulder at someone who had followed her down the street. When he opened the door, he expected to see eyes glittering in the dark behind her, but there were no terrors at her heels. His imagination was panicking him as usual. She looked weary, though, and as she walked in, she gave him a fragile relieved smile. Their front door opened straight into the dining area, and Lena put her bag down on a chair and stood there, looking uncertain. After a moment, she stepped forward and hugged him, and he held her, his arms fully around her, grateful for her embrace.

Two weeks ago they had danced at a party given by one

of her friends. It was a happy party, the friend had just been awarded his PhD, and there was laughter and hugging and noisy music. Before they left, they danced more intimately and ended up kissing on the way home. Jamal could not believe this was really happening. He thought her beautiful, which was also a way of thinking that she was too beautiful for him. He was surprised when she asked him to the party. Living in the same house, they talked in the way of housemates, and sometimes all four of them went out for a drink together, but their friendship was businesslike. They talked about their work, their parents and friends, the gas bill, and when Lena was talking, Jamal looked at her with pleasure while he could do so without seeming to stare like someone besotted. Sometimes he watched her when she was in the garden. It turned out she loved the garden, and they cleared it up and planted bright flowers just as he had imagined when he moved in. When she was out there and he was reading at his desk by the window, it was hard work to keep his eyes on the page. But he had to be careful to respect housemate rules, not to seem to be staring at her. He had gone to the party with her in this frame of mind, going out with a housemate, and was joyfully surprised by the kisses on the way home.

When they had reached the front door, she pulled away from him a little and put the flat of her palm on his chest. He understood this as a signal to stop and tried to see if her eyes would tell him more clearly what she meant, but she would not make eye contact with him. He took his time downstairs to calm himself and then went up to his own room. He felt strangely rebuked by what had happened, as if he had misunderstood or was trying to take advantage or was forcing the issue. He knew that she had a long-term boyfriend in Dublin because she sometimes talked about him. His name was Ronnie and he was a journalist on one of the Dublin papers, and every few weeks Lena went back to spend some time with him. So Jamal did not expect anything to come of their kisses and nothing did. It was just a snog after a party, a little bit of fun, and after that he slipped back into housemate mode as if nothing had happened. But now here she was in his arms again. He thought of that evening as he held her (he had thought about it several times) but he also sensed an unexpected tension in her arms and in her back, a surprising firmness in the way she held him, a need. Her grip on him eased a little after a while and she stepped back.

'Is everything all right?' he asked.

She shook her head. 'No,' she said. 'I must eat something.'

He sat waiting at the table while she went to the kitchen to make herself a cheese sandwich. She took a few bites and then began to talk. She went on a boating holiday with Ronnie on the Shannon for a few days, she said, and got back to Dublin to find that there had almost been a catastrophe. 'My parents were going to Galway for the weekend, and they left my younger brother Marco on his own at home. It was the first time they were doing that, leaving him for the weekend. He is seventeen, though, not a baby. It's just that they've never left him like that before. They asked him if he wanted to come along. It was some kind of reunion with university friends and Marco did not fancy that. They asked him if he wanted to have a friend round, but he said no, he was all right. They set off late on Friday afternoon, and after driving for about an hour and a half they turned back. My mum said that something did not feel right and Dad turned round and headed straight back. They found Marco in the garage with the engine of

Mum's car running. They got there in time, but can you imagine?

'He has never done anything like that before. He's just like everyone else. He listens to music, knows what's fashionable, watches football on TV. Maybe he likes to be pampered more than he should. Mum gives him a lift to school every morning and indulges all his whims about food, and lets him watch TV until all hours. All of them bearable adolescent vices, I suppose. For boys. I tell him he's a spoiled brat. Then he does something like that. It was incredible. It was the last thing I would have imagined Marco doing. I don't even know if he did it it deliberately or if he just lost himself. He couldn't give any reason for what he did, just that suddenly he felt incredibly lonely and depressed. That was what he said. How can you live with someone for years and not know what's going on in their heads? God knows how Mum guessed. I've just been sitting with them these last few days while they have been going round and round what happened, what they feel about it and what we are all going to do. The psychiatrist wants them all to go into some kind of family therapy, me too, but I said you start and see how it goes. I couldn't bear the thought of that, some smug stranger who was going to sit there asking probing questions and then piecing us all together again. Can you imagine your brother doing a stupid thing like that, though?'

'How is he now?' Jamal asked.

'He is completely shaken about what he has done,' Lena said. 'Of course. He is appalled at what he tried to do, but Mum and Dad will never be able to stop being anxious about him, nor will Marco himself. If he doesn't know what made him do it, what's to stop him doing it another time?'

Then, after he made them tea and she had time to sit on her own for a few minutes, she talked about her parents. Jamal knew that her father was Italian, which was not hard to guess because her name was Lena Salvati. Her parents had met when he came to Trinity College Dublin, on a year abroad for his language degree, she said.

'Why Dublin?' he asked.

'Why not?' she replied. 'Does that seem to you a strange place to learn English? What about Joyce then? And Yeats? And Jonathan Swift? Not to mention Oscar Wilde.'

'Sorry,' he said.

When her father finished his studies in Venice, he returned to Dublin to be with her mum. They are both translators and do all kinds of work, translating scholarly essays, fiction, poetry. After the incident, her dad reminded them that one of his nephews had done something just like that, running a car engine in a closed garage, but he too was found in time. Marco was not around when he said this, and her dad looked at them without saying what was in his mind, which was probably that Marco was trying it on to see what a suicide attempt felt like. Then after a moment, he made a face to dismiss this thought.

Jamal and Lena sat at the dining table long after her urgency had diminished, drinking tea and talking, and as they talked Jamal felt a charge slowly building up. When the moment came he was not taken by surprise as he had been the night of the party. She reached for his hand across the table and he held it between both of his. Then she said, Can I stay with you tonight?

Later, lying in the dark with the curtains open, she told him that she had been thinking about him a lot while she was away. He could hear her smile in the dark as she spoke, lying close to him. She had written him a postcard while they were camping along the Shannon but had not found a moment to post it. Or perhaps she had not dared, or was not sure if she should. She posted the one to her parents but when it came to the moment, she left the one to him in her handbag. Then Ronnie rummaged in her handbag while she was not there, looking for something, she never found out what, because he found the card. He was hurt, furious, you can imagine. What is this, you fucking tart? He was that furious. There was not that much in the card, really, just hello we're having a nice time, but then thinking of you at the end and love Lena xxx. Ronnie did not like that, thinking of you and love Lena xxx.

'Have I told you about Ronnie?' she asked him.

He nodded in the dark and then said: 'Yes, a little bit.'

It was over between them really, but she just did not know how to tell him, how to talk to him about it. They had been together for a couple of years but as that time passed she found him increasingly exhausting. She had liked that at first, his intensity, and that he always wanted to do things, walking, camping, a racing car exhibition, an arts festival. Come on, let's have a bit of light and joy in our lives. It forced her out of her natural sloth, and some of that hiking and camping made her body ache in an unexpected and pleasurable way. But as time passed she found it exhausting, and his enthusiasm began to feel like frenzy. To be honest, she began to find *him* tiresome but felt disloyal for thinking that. He was a generous man, even to complete strangers. She did not want to think ill of him but she did not really feel she had a taste for some of these things he wanted them to do. She tried to tell him that, but he laughed at her and said she was a lazy bitch who wanted to spend the whole weekend in a chair reading a book. Well, not the whole weekend, she told him, but maybe not so much bustle. There was so much he wanted to do, so much he wanted to experience, he said. He didn't want to spend his life sitting on his backside. He loved Ireland and wanted to see all of it and never wanted to go anywhere else, not even for a visit.

'And it's true,' she said. 'I was thinking of you a lot. I was thinking of you when I might have been thinking of him, ever since that night at the party but before that as well.'

Jamal made a humming noise, which signified pleasure, agreement, encouragement, please go on. He caressed her and waited for her to hum in return. The simple talk of lovers.

'He found the postcard on the second day of our holiday,' she continued after a moment, her voice more subdued now, the smile in it gone. 'He came to find me with the postcard in his hand, holding it out like evidence. What is this, you fucking tart? Then he tore it to pieces and flung them away, littering his beloved Ireland. We went through the rest of the week like that, arguing about everything. Every night in our tent he insisted on making love and at times it felt like he wanted to hurt me. You should have heard the names Ronnie called you. I had not expected that of him, that kind of poison. I had not expected to hear what he said about me, let alone nigger this and paki that and big cocks. Maybe that was the angry boyfriend speaking, and later he will be ashamed of what he said. The more he said, the more sure I became about him but for some reason I thought I would hang on until the end of the holiday. I don't know why I didn't walk to the nearest bus stop and make my way to Dublin. Maybe I was afraid of getting lost, or getting into trouble or because I thought he would make a scene. For sure, by the end of the week I knew what

I wanted, and I could not wait to hurry back here and break the news to you.'

Only she got back to Dublin to find that Marco had tried to kill himself. It took a few days to absorb the shock of that, and she saw that it would take her parents and Marco himself a lot longer to muddle through the meaning of what had happened. So after those few days she grew impatient to leave before they dragged her into the endless circuit of their regrets. She wanted to get back here, to her work, to him, to see him and to tell him about what had happened. To tell him how she felt.

Then it was his turn to tell her how beautiful she was, and how he loved her dark-blue eyes, and how incomparably sweet was her voice. Wasn't it strange that he lived across a landing from her for months and did not know how she felt about him, when all the time he was aching for her?

'I knew,' she said. 'I knew how you felt. I couldn't miss it, and then I began to think I liked the idea. When that happened after the party, I thought that would be the start for us, but you went shy or reserved and I couldn't work it out.'

'You put the palm of your hand on my chest,' he said. 'I thought you were saying that's enough.'

'The semiotics of the flat palm. It was a moment of conscience. I wish you had brushed the hand aside,' she replied.

'You talked about your boyfriend,' he said. 'I thought you were saying don't get any ideas.'

'I wanted you to say forget about him, that's all over,' she said, smiling in the dark.

'I was badly brought up, not enough experience in such matters, not enough daring. My Ba did not much like the idea of boyfriends and girlfriends, and I suppose I'm still backward on the subject,' he told her.

'Well anyway, while I was away I thought when I get back I'll just tell you that your time is up,' she said.

They talked until the hours before the dawn, and he told her about his Ba and the illness that had overtaken him, and how he was going to Norwich for the weekend to see them. She said she had just found him at last and he was already talking of leaving her, and he said only for a couple of days and then he would hurry back. It was light by the time they fell asleep.

Anna also rang home that evening, and she too was on her own. She sensed as Jamal had done that something in her mother's voice was not right. It made her think that her mother was about to cry, but she did not cry, at least not so that Anna heard anything. She persisted with her questions until her mother said sharply that nothing was the matter, that her Ba was doing fine, improving every day. He does his exercises, he goes for walks, he has therapy sessions several times a week. He is getting better all the time.

'Then why do you sound miserable?' Anna asked.

'Me? I don't sound miserable,' Maryam said. 'Just a long day. When you come to see us you will make us brighter again. It has been months—'

'Yes I know,' Anna interrupted. 'Is he still talking about the old times?'

Maryam had told her that Ba was talking about the times they did not know about, and Anna had wanted to be told straight away what he was saying. But Maryam said he would tell them himself when they came down. From that, Anna assumed there was nothing much to tell, otherwise her mother would have blurted it out. Anna did not think

165

her mother could resist pressure when she was inclined to apply it.

'The therapy has helped him. He is talking all the time. I can hardly cope with his stories,' her mother said, but she had paused for a good moment before replying. Then her voice dropped to a whisper, 'He gets upset about this war in Iraq, like he has just realised what is going on in the world. I suppose that means he is getting better, doesn't it? Now he's sitting in there shouting abuse at the TV. He does that whenever the news is on, these insane murderers and so on. That's how improved he is. I can't talk for long, he'll make a fuss about the phone. Never mind about his fuss, how are you? Tell me about what you've been doing. Jamal is coming to see us this weekend.'

So Anna decided she would go as well. She had not been for nearly five months, not since they moved to Brighton, although she rang regularly and was in daily (almost) email touch with Jamal. Nothing important could have slipped by her. But five months was a long time. It had never been that long before. She had been busy with teaching, of course, but school had shut for a month and she had been delaying plans to go visiting in Norwich. She knew that Nick would not be coming, and she would rather he didn't anyway, especially if Ba was playing up. In any case, Nick would get bored and frustrated about not being able to work. He had to work at least one day of the weekend to feel that he was coping. He was in London that evening, going out to dinner with a conference crowd and then staying over with friends. She wondered if that counted as work. Anna had never been to an academic conference, and did not know if dinner among academics was like a seminar, with the clever ones talking and the dull ones listening, or pretending to listen. Nick made conferences sound arduous and wearing, and made the dinners sound like torture and the other delegates dull and half-baked (which was exactly his description). Why did he go to so many then? It was his work. Anna hesitated over whether she should worry about this staying over with unnamed friends and decided not to. There were going to be many more events like that, and if she worried about them, she was going to drive herself mad. Something was coming to the boil between them, she sensed that. There was something going on that she could not be sure about.

She supposed that sooner or later Nick would start having affairs, if he had not started already. He had always had a roving eye, and whenever he saw an attractive woman, he took a long surreptitious look at her breasts while Anna pretended not to notice. Perhaps all men were like that. Now that he was going to so many conferences and events in the name of work, she guessed that the affairs would start. Perhaps that is what the partner left at home always thinks. It was not really a decision she could make, not to worry, but she was not sure how to anticipate her reaction to this outcome that she was imagining to be inevitable. What was she going to do when she found out, if she found out? She could imagine that – you could live with someone like Nick and have a good idea that he was up to things when he went away, but have no knowledge of what he did. What would you do then? Confront him with hollow accusations? Ignore him and turn bitter inside? Take lovers yourself? Maybe what she would do was not the kind of thing she could anticipate, and she'd just have to go along with it and see how she felt. But it was bound to happen, sooner or later. Nick was a flirt. He carried on a major flirt with Beverley next door, and although they treated it as a joke, Anna thought they got a frisson out of it, teasing and flattering, and hugging and kissing at the end of it all. One of these days . . . how long had she been thinking like this?

Beverley was the woman they had seen working in her garden the day they moved in, and a few days later Anna caught up with her on the pavement outside their houses and they got into conversation. She looked in her late thirties or so, had heavily permed blonde hair, and on that Saturday morning, she was wearing tight jeans and a baggy wide-necked jumper, which had slipped off her right shoulder as it was intended to. She worked for the City Council in the town planning office, approving domestic conversions of properties, extensions, lofts, French doors, that kind of thing. Beverley quickly told her about the other neighbours either side and across the road from them. Tony and Beth, she's a doctor. She works in the practice round the corner and he is a teacher. Shaun and Robyn, he's an estate agent and she's at home now with the kids. That house there, he's a painter. You can go in there and take a look during Art Week, when all the painters open their houses to visitors. I don't know what his partner does. In that house is Sophie, she lives on benefit. She rushes around all day as if she's busy but she does bugger all, just living off the rest of us. And that at number 26 is Edwina, she's ninety-eight years old and deaf as a doorknob but she goes for her ramble along the street and around the shops on the main road every day, rain or shine. My daughter Billie sometimes plays her music loud, especially if I'm not in. Take no notice of her. She makes an unbearable fuss if you ask her to turn it down. If you need anything just come round, any time. Tell that to your gorgeous man as well. So where have you moved from then? Beverley asked, prompting a little disclosure on Anna's part in return for all the information she had been freely offered.

They heard raised voices from her house on some evenings, mostly Beverley shouting and snarling, and the lower rumble of a man's voice. Anna had seen a man calling at her house on more than one occasion. He was a dark-haired man in a smart suit, and the first time she saw him he double-parked his sleek new-looking Saab and crossed the street without so much as glancing either right or left. He was carrying a picture frame in one hand, the back of it was turned towards her, and from its ornate look Anna guessed it was a painting. She assumed that he was the man Beverley was shouting at and barging into furniture about in the night. She imagined that he would not have shouted back, but would have talked with sinister self-assurance while waiting for Beverley to finish ranting.

On another of those occasions she had seen him stop at the door for a few moments, dressed in a dinner jacket with a white silk scarf around his neck, like a gangster on the way to an event to which she was not invited. For someone with a training in literature, it was impossible for Anna not to sketch in the rest of the story for herself, in which Beverley was the powerless mistress of a wealthy art dealer with dubious connections. Anna had not heard much of the daughter's loud music that she had been warned about, a couple of times on a Sunday morning maybe. She heard Beverley when she was in a hectoring frame of mind or when she was talking on the phone late at night, when she heard not so much the words but the lover's tone and the loud brazen laughter. One night just recently, the shouting had reached a new pitch, and the rumble of the man's voice rose to a roar. Then Anna heard the daughter shouting, *Stop it! Stop it!* and a little while later the front door slamming and someone sobbing loudly. It sounded like Beverley.

She was not sure exactly why she was wary of Beverley, perhaps because of the frantic way she flirted with Nick, or perhaps because she could stand unabashed at her window and watch what went on in the street, and later, when the moment came, did not hesitate to provide a summary of what she had compiled from her observations. She thought that in times of trouble Beverley would be a denouncer.

Nick did not see that at all. He thought she was good fun but maybe a bit nosy. 'She's all right,' he said.

When they decided to move to Brighton, Anna had seen it as a big decision, a commitment, like saying that they planned to be together for a long time. The thought of having a child had been in her mind for a while, and after they moved, after the gesture of permanence that they had made, the thought became more pressing than it had been before. They had been together for nearly three years, their lives were good, and Nick was beginning to make his way in his career. It was a good time to think about a child. When she said this to Nick, he looked interested but sceptical. What's the rush, he said. It made her think. Having a child had seemed the next thing to do, perhaps prompted by expectations she had internalised without question, as well as by an instinct she had not reflected on. When she did reflect, she began to consider what it was that was good about their lives. Nick was attractive and intelligent, and he made her feel beautiful and desirable. The sex was good. She loved sex, had loved it since she went to university and discovered its absorbing pleasure and its easy availability. The experience liberated her from the fears she had absorbed from her parents, from her Ba and his immigrant anxieties, his obsessive desire to escape notice, his secretiveness. Her pleasure in sex made her feel sophisticated and worldly, and somehow that she belonged here. Nick was also good company, he knew how to move in the world, how to charm. He wasn't tense, or violent, or too domineering. He wasn't.

As she considered this summary of his virtues, she began to feel the emergence of a rebellious reluctance in her. She was tempted to suppress the thought but she did not, and it took time for the thought to emerge fully, which was that she did not want to have a child with Nick. One minute she was considering having a child with him and the next she was having serious doubts about him. What an idiot she was! She did not want to be tied to him for good, as she would be if she had a child with him. She did not want Ralph and Jill to be part of her life for ever. Or Laura, or Uncle Digby. She did not want to live with their particular brand of knowingness and self-assurance for the rest of her days. It was a frightening thought at first, this anticipation of the end between them, but she became used to it, and with his increasing distraction Nick helped her to become used to his absence. Perhaps it was intentional, to get her used to the end without acknowledging to her that that was what he was doing. No, she did not think that likely. He had too much ego for that kind of thoughtfulness. So there, she was beginning to allow herself to think cruelly about him.

He was happier since starting his academic job, flippant in a new way. She could feel the confidence growing in him. He did not always explain himself as he used to, and did not always listen when she talked, interrupting her when he had tired of listening to her. He did not interrupt her often, but she felt it every time he did, because the bluntness of it was something new in the way they were together. It did not happen at once, this new casualness, because if it had done she would have been unable to suppress the hurt and they would have argued. It happened slowly, and she was able to tolerate his off-handedness as part of his distraction, coping with a new job, the pressure of new routines. She too was busy with her supply teaching job, and the bustle in their lives disguised the worst of his patronising airs, as she came to think of them in time. She could not believe that he was not aware of his manner, and assumed that quite quickly since their move, in the few months since they left London, she had begun to bore him. Was she exaggerating? It might be a phase that might pass, but it depressed her, and made something sour inside her, and it was then that her reluctance about having a child with Nick began to emerge. Sometimes they went for a day or two without touching, which had never happened before between them, and she wondered what it was exactly that made the distance between them. Was it also her doing?

When he first told her about this conference in London, he said he would probably come back in the evening. Then just as he was leaving in the morning, he told her he was staying the night with some of his old university friends, but would call her if plans changed. There was nothing much in all that, but she did not like it that he did not feel it necessary to ask or explain. It was a sign of something, she was sure. She hated that these pathetic grievances occupied her mind, she hated that she felt she was turning petty and watchful, like a neglected wife who had no option but to endure.

Jamal neglected his desk the next day, spending the morning sleeping off the night before. Every time he surfaced he could not believe that Lena was lying there beside him. Then finally he woke up and saw that she had gone, but he could hear the slight hiss of the plumbing and guessed she was in her room showering. In the afternoon they walked to Sainsbury's to buy supplies for a celebration dinner. As they were leaving, they saw a man walking on the pavement give way at the knees and fall slowly to the ground. His face hit the pavement with a dull thud. Lena gasped and put out a hand as if to restrain Jamal from rushing forward. It was a momentary gesture and she withdrew her hand when she saw the look of surprise in his eyes. He hurried to the fallen man, oranges and vegetables scattered around him, and knelt on the pavement beside him. He saw at once who it was. His eyes were shut and blood seeped out from under his head.

'It's our neighbour. Get help,' he said to Lena, pointing towards the store. He saw that the man's face was screwed up in pain, and that the grimace made his face more lined than it had seemed from a distance. He asked him: 'Can you hear me?' and the man nodded slightly, with some difficulty, his neck twisted on the ground. After a moment he opened his eyes, and Jamal was not sure if he should move him or leave him as he was until someone who knew what to do came along. He might have had a stroke and the worst thing might be to move him. Or perhaps he was drunk. A thin line of dark liquid was running out of the corner of his mouth and he could not tell if it was blood or vomited wine. 'Can you turn over on your side?' he asked, remembering from somewhere that this was the best position if he were to vomit. 'I'll help you, see if you can turn over on your side.' The man did as he was told and turned his body so that he was lying on his side. Jamal thought he looked very uncomfortable and did not know whether he should ask him to move back the way he had been. Just then two female staff came running out of the store with Lena behind them. They turned the man over on his back, then lifted his head off the ground and rested it on a rolled-up Sainsbury's jacket. Blood was running down the side of his face and out of his mouth, and he had a deep cut on his temple. He looked at Jamal and his eyes moved fractionally. When the ambulance arrived, one of the paramedics sniffed near the old man's mouth to see if he was drunk and then shook his head at his colleague. They hustled the man on to a stretcher and fitted him with an oxygen mask in the van.

The ambulance woman looked at Jamal briefly, flicking her hand towards the van. Are you coming? Jamal shook his head to mean no, he's nothing to do with me. He felt treacherous as he did so, as if he was abandoning him. After the ambulance drove away, the two Sainsbury's staff started gathering the scattered shopping and put it back in the shopping bag. Lena picked up a cloth cap and said to them that she could take the shopping for him. He was their next-door neighbour. The two women looked at each other, unsure what to do.

'Perhaps it'll be better just to leave the groceries for now,' one of the women said, frowning.

Lena shrugged and the woman nodded. Yes, that will be best, she said.

It was while they were walking home in silence that Lena realised that she still had his cap. She held it up to Jamal, smiling. 'I forgot to give it back,' she said.

It was an old cap, the band worn smooth by age. He had seen the man wearing it many times. His Ba had one like it, which he wore now and then as a stylish accoutrement when he was taking a walk. Who did it belong to, the flat cap? To the working man or to the landed gentry? He had seen pictures of it on both their heads. And how did it end up on the heads of immigrants? It had been mean to deny him. As he thought about the man's collapse, he remembered how his Ba came home and collapsed inside the front door. Imagine if he had not reached home but had fallen face down on the pavement instead, some long distance from home, and a neighbour who happened by chance to be passing by had cringed at the thought of becoming involved, and said that he did not know him. When it came to his turn, he had done no better than that shameful imagined neighbour. He had been living there for months now and had not once spoken to the old man, not even a few words of greeting. He knew that young people tormented him and had not gone round to see if there was any way of offering sympathy at least.

'We'll take the cap to him when they bring him back,' Jamal said.

The ambulance brought him home the following morning. Lena saw it arrive and called out to Jamal, and they watched from her bedroom window as the ambulance man took their neighbour by the elbow and started to move forward. Their neighbour stopped and carefully disentangled his elbow from the ambulance man's grip and then said something to him. They saw him smile and then saw him move forward slowly and shakily with the ambulance man a few inches behind him. The ambulance was there for a few minutes, which Lena said was reassuring, that it did not just drop him off and roar away. Jamal guessed that other people down the street were standing at their windows, looking at the ambulance that had delivered one of their neighbours home. No one came out to enquire or to offer help. Just like them.

Jamal said: 'He looked a bit shaky, didn't he? Should we

175

offer to help, in case he needs anything? Shall we take something? Do we have anything? Maybe some fruit, he seemed to like oranges. And his cap, we should take that back to him in case he decides to go for a walk or something tomorrow.'

'Let him sort himself out,' Lena said. 'Then we'll go round later.'

'I have to go to Norwich tomorrow, so we should do it this afternoon,' Jamal said, and Lena made a sad face about his going.

Later in the afternoon they went to call on their neighbour. The front door had a large brass knocker with a head of a spiky flower, a thistle or a daisy perhaps, and Jamal tapped it twice. He thought he saw a movement in the unlit front room, and a moment later the door opened and the man stood in front of them. The side of his face and his lower lip were bruised and swollen, the flesh around his left eye had puffed up and there was a large dressing on his temple. He looked at them calmly, unsurprised, and Jamal thought perhaps he had caught sight of them at the door and had had time to compose himself. He was dressed in a checked shirt and corduroy trousers, as he had been the first time he had seen him in the garden, and now that he was nearer he saw how slight he was. His eyes were grey and still, not yet friendly.

'We're from next door,' Jamal said, pointing towards their house, and he nodded.

'You dropped your cap,' Lena said, and stepped forward to give it back to him. He smiled then and took a step towards her to collect it. 'We were there when you fell yesterday and saw that the cap was left behind . . .'

'So it was you,' he said, his voice rising with pleasure and his face opening into a smile. He winced and clutched his

176

face as the smile stretched his swollen lip. 'Please excuse me,' he said, as he waited for the pain to recede. After a moment, he smiled more carefully, apologising. 'I was very confused but I remember your face now. Thank you for coming to my help.'

'Are you all right?' Lena asked. 'We just wanted to say if you need anything we'd be happy to assist. My name is Lena and this is Jamal. We brought you some oranges. Do you need anything? Food? Medicine?'

'This is very kind of you,' he said, smiling through his injured face and looking thoroughly surprised. 'Thank you, Lena and Jamal. I am all right. I had some kind of blackout but it is nothing serious, the infirmities of age, that's all. Thank you, but I have everything I need, and tomorrow the nurse will come to check on me, so I'm in good hands. You must come and have a cup of tea with me sometime so we can talk properly.'

'Yes that will be nice,' Lena said.

'Well, we won't bother you now. You must need to get some rest after that shock,' Jamal said. 'But we are next door if you need help.'

'I will be quite all right, Jamal, but thank you,' the man said.

Jamal noticed that he did not tell them his name, and that he did not offer his hand. Was he just a private man or unfriendly? His smile was friendly. He spoke in an educated voice, the infirmities of age. He said all that to Lena when they got back to their house.

'He's probably still shaken. Those bruises look quite bad,' Lena said. 'He looked quite sprightly, I thought, and we did take him by surprise.'

That night Lena spoke about her brother Marco, and how every summer their parents took them to Italy, to

Verona, to stay with their dad's family. They wanted them to speak Italian, and when they were children they only spoke Italian at home.

'Can you speak?' Jamal asked.

'Oh yes, it really worked. Only I hate my name. I don't know why they had to call me Magdalena. Why not Susan or Marie or something like that? Dad's name is Carlo and mum's name is Anne, and Marco is Marco. Why do I have to be Magdalena?'

'Lena is a lovely name,' Jamal said.

'Here is the delphinium,' her Ba said when Anna arrived on Friday afternoon, and then he subsided into a happy smile. It made her laugh out loud to hear him use that old name. He made up names for them when they were younger, unexpected names that did not always make sense to her. Delphinium was the one that lasted the longest for her, and which she liked, while Jamal had to put up with being Giant Pacific Prawn or Ziggurat. It made her happy that he remembered the name, that he was smiling.

She sat with him in the garden, asking routine questions to which he replied briefly. She did not see any signs of his shouting, and she wondered if Ma and Ba were struggling to cope on their own. He felt so weak, he said. It was ridiculous. Anna thought he looked better although a little restless, perhaps just trying too hard to seem all right. Her mother came out with the tea, and the three of them sat in the breezy August sunshine, while she brought Anna up to date on the medical drama of her father's life. Instead of arguing with the doctor about Ba's medication, Maryam simply reduced the dose, especially the sleeping drugs. She could see for herself that this treatment made Ba better, he could do more things for himself, he could concentrate better, he could read. He did not feel so much nausea as he did before. When she saw all this, she confessed to Dr Mendez what she had done. The doctor did not make a big fuss, although she was not amused. She said it's not what the doctor ordered but we'll try it your way for a while. That was the doctor making a joke, which was unlike her, Ma explained. He has already had the benefit of the rest, the doctor said, and she then reduced the prescription as if it was her idea all along. Ba sat there grinning at them, wagging a finger at his wife for her audacity. She thinks she's a doctor now, he said.

From the bedroom window upstairs, Anna watched him as he sat on his own on the terrace, his eyes rapt on the leaves falling in the summer sunshine. He was so silent and still, that she imagined he would be able to hear a sparrow building its nest. She could not imagine why Ma had sounded so upset on the phone a few days ago, maybe it was a quarrel that was now forgotten. Later they went for a walk while it was still light, and then her mother took Ba upstairs for his exercises. There had been no shouting, no whisperings, no suspicious stares. He was weak and a little edgy, perhaps even slightly irritable, but he was also gentle and listened with a smile. After their dinner, when the news came on television and it was all about raids and explosions and tormented children, he listened without a word, leaning back in the chair to reduce the heartburn that now troubled him. Both Anna and Maryam glanced at him at moments when they would have expected him to react, but he watched wearily without a word, his eyes hidden behind a blank stare. It had been a long day for him, and although he had wanted to wait up for Jamal, who was coming on the late train, he was very tired and could not stay up any longer.

After he went to bed, Anna talked about her work, how she had been offered a permanent post and some new responsibilities at the school where she was doing supply teaching. She did not say anything about Nick, that he had still not rung when she left that morning, and she had not called him to see if he was back. She could see her mother was not really listening to the stories of her thriving career, but she kept going anyway. Perhaps she was distracted by Jamal's imminent arrival, or perhaps her mind was on whatever it was that had been troubling her a few days before, on the maybe-quarrel Anna had declared forgotten. She would have to find a way to ask about that. Her mother's face was made solemn by her thoughts, and as Anna talked, with eyes on her mother, it occurred to her how unlike her that look was. How whenever her mother turned towards her, she expected her face to be open and readable: concerned or content or resolute as the situation demanded, not this distant inward gaze that made her seem so unexpectedly sad. She understood then how much work it must take to sustain that face of concern and attention that she was used to.

Anna was looking for a way to move the conversation in her mother's direction when Maryam looked her directly in the eye and then held her gaze. Anna stopped speaking and waited, suddenly tense from the unaccustomed intensity in her mother's face. Maryam began to speak, at times looking at Anna, at times looking away. After a few moments, she was lost in her story, uncaring, captive to the feelings that now seemed to have overtaken her. Anna knew that she should keep quiet, should not ask any questions. This is what they have been talking about, Anna thought, the dirty secrets. That is the meaning of the tension and the long looks in both of them. She wished Jamal was there because the thought of the ugliness she was going to be forced to listen to was making her queasy. But as her mother continued to talk, Anna realised it was not what she expected at all.

'I was sixteen years old when I left school,' her mother said, 'knowing nothing or next to nothing.'

She had enough sense to know that she was someone without any worth. They used this word a lot at school then. Was it worth it? Staying on? No, not for her. There was no point, she was too far behind. She was living with Ferooz and Vijay then. When she started to live with Ferooz, she wanted to be a psychiatric nurse, like her. It made Ferooz happy to hear Maryam say that, and she laughed and said if that was what she wanted to do, then there was nothing to stop her. Ferooz was good to her, kinder to her than anyone had ever been. She talked to her all the time, hugging her and kissing her, encouraging her to do the school work, to catch up. She had gone to several schools by the time they took her, but even with Ferooz's help, she could not settle. She had missed her moment. All the moving from school to school was not the best thing for a child and she had fallen too far behind and had become used to not making any effort to understand. It was not worth it. She was not a bright enough child, that was what she thought of herself, and another child with more determination would have coped somehow and done well. Someone like that would have found pleasure in the struggle against those troubles. There had been too much anxiety in her life. She could not make her mind quiet enough to take things in at school.

Ferooz told her stories about how her future life was going to turn out if she worked really hard. Ferooz was a good woman, but life was too complicated for all of them and none were exempted. There are so many opportunities in this country, Ferooz used to say. If you work hard, you can make your way even if life has given you an unkind start. Look at Vijay. After the accident, they thought all he would be any good for would be weaving baskets or begging in the streets, a burden to everyone all his life. But he pleaded and fought to be allowed to stay on at school, then he found dirty work in the town and attended night classes and learned to be an electrician. Then a friend who was back for a visit told him there was work here in England, so he saved and borrowed and along he came. Look at him – and if Vijay was within earshot he would clown at this, holding himself up and flexing his biceps like a champion on TV – he worked hard and he got his rewards.

That was Vijay's constant advice. Work hard, work hard, nothing is impossible. He was so determined, not like a hero, but like a small stubborn man who knew he was not worthless. He was always occupied, not as if he was forced or stressed, but as if he always had something waiting to be done. He left for work at seven in the morning and came home at seven in the evening. After his dinner, he sat at the small table in a corner of the living room and did his study-ing. He had started a correspondence course in accountancy and was hoping to learn enough to get a job in an account-ancy office, and then build up his knowledge in that way. That's the kind of man Vijay was, silent and hard-working about almost everything he did, even eating. Maybe cricket got him excited, when India were playing, otherwise he was quietly busy and let the world get on with it.

By the time she was a teenager, she thought it was strange, being driven like that, like being a captive to little ambitions for success or wealth. It seemed a joyless life, working all the time. She thought it was a mean way to live, mean in spirit and without any interest in anyone else. But Ferooz did not seem to mind. She talked to him whether he was studying or eating, if that was what she felt like doing. Sometimes he replied and sometimes he went on with what he was doing. Neither seemed to mind. She worked hard too, cooking and cleaning and carrying and fetching so that Vijay could continue to be a miracle of perseverance. Ferooz liked to say that about him, a miracle of perseverance. She heard someone say it on the radio, Lady so and so was a miracle of perseverance in the campaign for children's rights. She thought it was a lovely way to describe Vijay.

A car stopped outside and after a moment Anna heard a car door slam. She guessed it was Jamal arriving in a taxi, and she hurried to the front door before he rang the bell. Somehow it seemed important that he should not ring the bell, that he should not agitate the fiends that were abroad in their house at this hour. When they came back into the room, Maryam tried to rise to her feet but Jamal smothered her in a hug and forced her back into the chair. Anna had said something to him. He sat in a chair, no he was not hungry, not tired, yes a good journey, sorry he was late. Yes it was good to see her too. They waited in silence until their mother was ready to begin again.

'Go on, Ma,' Anna said.

'I was telling Hanna about Ferooz and Vijay,' Maryam said, and for some reason her eyes wandered to the photograph of Abbas that was still on the shelf and had not made it back upstairs since all the months ago when he was in hospital and she talked to Jamal about their early days together.

Things became complicated when she first went to live

with them, at least for a while, and Ferooz had to make arrangements at work. Then, when they got used to her – and she tried very hard to make them get used to her – she was given a key. Ferooz did not come home until six, so Maryam had an hour or two of TV before she arrived. It was the happiest time for her, that hour or two after school, sitting quietly in the upstairs flat, feeling safe from everything, watching the excited children on TV. She loved living with them, a room to herself, fussing and kindness from Ferooz, a bit of worldly wisdom from Vijay when he remembered, and time to herself when she could do what she liked. It may seem strange for a child to think like that, to want to be alone at the age of nine, but everything had been such a bustle and confusion in her life that those afternoon hours were a comfort she had not known was coming. She always switched off a good while before six. When she was first given a key, Vijay asked her what she did when she came home from school and she said she watched TV. He did not like that. He frowned and shook his head sadly and told her she should catch up with schoolwork, not waste her time with TV. After that when he came home he put his hand on the TV to see if it had been in recent use. Then Ferooz started to do the same when she came home, so to show that she was obedient and as hard-working as they wanted her to be, she switched off in good time and sat down with a book or with crayons or something like that. She tried to like doing the schoolwork, but her mind could not settle to it.

Then as she grew older, she became the skivvy of the household. It started slowly. When Ferooz came home from work Maryam helped in the kitchen. Ferooz gave her a stool to stand on so she could reach the pots. She was teaching her to find her way round a kitchen, which she told her was something every woman should know, even if later she was lucky enough to marry a prince. Ferooz was surprised how quickly Maryam took to it, because she was still so small. Neither of them knew at the time that it was what fate had in store for her, a lifetime of pots and pans. That was how it started, helping out in the kitchen. Then Ferooz started to leave things for Maryam to do when she got back from school, peeling vegetables, getting pots ready, laying the table. Then making the dough for the chapatis, putting the dhal on the fire, until finally she was cooking the whole meal for all of them.

They were careful with money, and the food they ate was simple. It was a skinflint house. That was how they lived, saving everything for the future. When Ferooz came in from work, she checked the bin to see that Maryam had not thrown away vegetables that could have been used. She did that at first, when she could not trust her to be as careful about waste as she was.

In another year or two, Maryam could not remember exactly how long because time moved differently when your life was like that, she was also doing the cleaning and the washing. Ferooz did not talk so often about her future career as a psychiatric nurse, but she kissed her when she came home and found the washing folded away and the table laid for dinner. And Vijay was happy enough to have Maryam sitting with them, fetching something for him when he needed it, and having her around as someone they treated kindly. Because they did treat her kindly, they told her so, and they told her what they had rescued her from. She did not always understand their meaning at the time. Perhaps that was what they had in mind all along when they took her, to exercise their kindness and save her from a degraded life. To teach her to find some dignity in living with sober people and doing honest work. She had been confused at first by Ferooz and her talk of family.

The work she did in the house was not hard. She even liked it, to prepare a meal and cook it, and then clean up and put everything away and wipe the kitchen down. It felt like it was an achievement. Something she could do and complete with satisfaction. Even Vijay did not tell her to work harder any more because he could see she was. Her school work improved too. She was in a secondary school by this time, a noisy and crowded school where teachers and pupils kept each other on the run all the time. She was so far behind that she was put in with the thick ones. That was what they called themselves. The work they did there was easy. Some of the teachers brought them comics to read and let them play board games in class. She started to get good grades for the first time. She also made some new friends. Their teacher was pleased with her and she liked being in his class, Mr Thwaite. He had a big ginger beard. He even called her Maryam instead of Mary, which no one else at school did. He told them some very unexpected things, Mr Thwaite, drifting away from his lessons into improbable stories that they never wanted to hear the end of. One day he told Maryam a story about her name. After the Muslims conquered Mecca, he said, they went to the Kaaba to remove all the idols and paintings that pagan worshippers had put there. Do you know what the Kaaba is? It is the great stone towards which Muslims face when they say their prayers. There was only one God for the Muslims, and the idols of other gods made the Kaaba unclean for them, so they had to remove them. But among the paintings was a small icon of the Madonna and child. Mohammad, the Prophet of the Muslims, put out his hand to cover the icon and ordered that everything else should be painted over. The name of the Redeemer's mother is beloved by all people, Mr Thwaite said. He had to explain many parts of the story to her before she understood it, and years later when she understood even more, she wondered what happened to the icon.

Anyway, after school she went home to all her chores. When they were done she went to her room and listened to music on the cassette recorder Ferooz and Vijay had bought her for her birthday. She could listen to music all day then.

She told herself that she was happy, but of course she wasn't really. Nobody of that age really is, with all the things that are happening to you, and your confidence is low, and you are afraid to look the fool. So what she was telling herself was that in spite of those things that make everyone unhappy at that age, she was a happy teenager. She wished she was cleverer and had something to look forward to, something to do with her life, but she was not unhappy. She was used to the watchful way Ferooz and Vijay lived, counting everything, even the spoons. She thought of them as kind people who let her live with them and looked after her. She was grateful to them, and she did not mind doing the chores for them, or if she did mind it was only now and then. She began to understand why they worked so hard and watched everything. They were determined not to fail, not to be defeated, not after coming such a long way and putting up with so much. She thought it was all that struggle that sometimes made them gloomy.

Then Vijay's nephew came to live with them. She was sixteen and in her final year at school when he came. Vijay now worked as an accountant in a firm owned by two Indian brothers from the same area he himself came from.

His main work was to do the accounts of several small local businesses. He wore a suit to work and it was easy to see that he thought of himself as someone who had achieved something in life. Well, he had, he had, although this did not stop him studying as hard as ever for the next stage of his professional qualifications. The nephew, whom Maryam was told to call cousin, was Vijay's sister's son. Vijay sent for him and arranged for him to study accountancy at a college in Exeter. It was Vijay's offer of reconciliation with his family, but also he had thought of starting his own firm once his nephew had enough training, a proper family firm of accountants. So the nephew came to live with them.

She had not spoken about him before but he had something to do with what happened to her, with how she left Ferooz and Vijay. They had to know these things. Well, they didn't have to know, but it might help them to understand something of how things have turned out. And she did not want to keep this to herself any more.

The nephew was older than she expected, about twenty-three or so, full of smiles and namastes when he arrived from the airport with Vijay. He slept on a quilt on the floor of the living room because there was nowhere else, but Vijay said that would be no problem because Indians can sleep anywhere and are used to hardship. He was no trouble at first. In the morning he rolled up his quilt, had a cup of tea and a slice of bread, and left for his college. He did not come back until it was time to eat in the evening. He spent all his time in classes or in the library, and did not even stop for lunch. Vijay thoroughly approved of his dedication. She didn't think he went anywhere on his own in the city, and when he came home he did not say much except to Vijay. He was a bit shy about his English, with very good reason. She could not understand him most of the time, and even when she did, his words came out in a jumble, as if he was speaking his sentences backwards. Then after he settled down, Maryam sometimes came home from school and found him there in the flat. All along he knew that she was not the daughter of the house, not even adopted, just a wastrel taken in by his relatives and now the household skivvy, Maryam Riggs. All the daughter talk was slowly forgotten as time passed, except as a kind of scolding. It had taken so long for her to understand, but when she saw the way Vijay was with his nephew, she understood something about family, the responsibility, the affection and a little pride, and knew that Ferooz and Vijay had not felt like this about her.

The nephew grew to be a nuisance to Maryam. When she came back from school and he was there, he followed her around, speaking in words she did not always understand but whose meaning she grasped from the gestures that accompanied them. When Ferooz and Vijay were around his eyes followed her like he was touching her. She knew already from the arguments she had overheard between Ferooz and Vijay that he was complaining about sleeping in the living room when the girl had the room. Dinesh needs to study and to get a good rest so he can concentrate at college, Vijay said. If he can't sleep, he can't study. That was his name, Dinesh. She had not said his name aloud for a long time. Ferooz argued with Vijay and said, Maryam is like our daughter. Maryam smiled when she heard her say that. Vijay said, yes of course she is, which is why she will understand that this is for the good of the whole family. Maryam knew that sooner or later she was going to have to give up the room, and then there would be nowhere to hide from cousin Dinesh when they were alone in the flat.

She got into trouble with Ferooz because she stayed out longer to avoid the cousin and she could not do all her chores properly. They thought she was beginning to turn wild, wasting time in the streets and seeing boys. In this country, a girl will be spoiled sooner or later, however carefully you look after her, Vijay said. She had thought to say something to Ferooz because cousin Dinesh was now a menace to her, making her frightened of what he might do. So when Ferooz got annoyed with her again for staying out too long, scolding her for neglecting her duties when they had looked after her like a daughter all these years, Maryam became upset. She said that cousin Dinesh was bothering her, that was why she was staying away. Bothering her how? Ferooz asked. You know how, Maryam said. Ferooz made a disgusted face and slapped her. That's what she did, she slapped her on the face when she had never hit her once in all the years. Then she told her that she was a filthy girl and never to say such a thing again. Maryam couldn't tell her that he came into her room and looked through her things. She couldn't say that he followed her around and put himself in her way. She couldn't say that he put his hand on her waist and on her hips, and that she knew that one day he was going to do something worse to her. But after Ferooz slapped her . . . It was such a shock to be hit on the face like that. After that she could not tell her what was happening and what she was afraid of.

After the school examinations, they told her to move out of her room so that cousin Dinesh could have a proper space to do his studying. It was as if the nephew had been promoted to nobility. He called for Maryam to fetch a drink for him, he told her off for not ironing his clothes properly, he complained about the food. He even treated Ferooz in a different way, smiling at her as if she was foolish, sometimes ignoring her when she spoke to him. That summer after her last year at school, Maryam got a job in a café and thought if she could earn enough she would move into lodgings. But the money was not enough and the work was such a drudge, although she liked her mates there. Later she got a better job in a factory, which is where she was working when she met Abbas. She still went to the café sometimes to have a cup of tea and meet with the people she used to work with, and always got a cream cake on the house. That was where she saw Abbas the second time. He glanced at her and recognised her. He hesitated for a moment and then came to say hello. She couldn't remember what he said but after a while he sat down and they chatted and then he said good-bye, see you again some time.

That evening cousin Dinesh came into the kitchen and grabbed her and groped her and tried to kiss her. He kept saying things, you smell beautiful, you are shining. He was shorter than her but strongly built. He was older than her. She hit him with the spoon she was stirring the dhal with but he just laughed and would not let go. She struggled away from him in the end but he stood in front of her, laughing, wagging a finger as if everything was just a bit of fun, groping the servant girl for a bit of a lark. That was how things became: whenever he found her on her own he tried again, each time more horrible than the last. She fought as hard as she could and landed many blows with spoons and the rolling pin but she knew that one day, when he had built up enough courage, he would force her, and the thought sickened and terrified her. She thought Ferooz knew too. She thought Ferooz looked at her as if she knew.

Then they found out about Abbas. She said his name, casually, describing him as someone she had met at the factory, but her tone must have given her away. They interrogated her until she no choice but to come clean. She could not have imagined the fuss they made, as if she had done something obscene. For two days it went on like that, with threats to lock her in the flat so she could not meet him, and warnings that if she did not obey they would throw her out. Cousin Dinesh joined in too. You have no respect for yourself, he said, curling his lip like a jinn in one of those Indian movie magazines he liked to read. On the third evening, when she came home from work, he forced her hands against a wall in the kitchen, pulled her jumper over her face, blinding her, and forced her into his room. She fought him off as hard as she could but he was stronger than her, and he dragged her to her old bed.

This is so vile, Anna thought. Why are you telling us this? Why are you telling us now? I don't want to hear any more of this vile story.

'Somehow, while he struggled to release himself from his clothes, I wriggled out of his grasp and ran to Ferooz and Vijay's room and bolted the door,' Maryam said, her voice sober and unaccustomed to their ears, giving an account of a mild horror she had witnessed, playing the moment down. 'I stayed there until Ferooz came home. I heard cousin Dinesh begin on her as soon as she arrived, and by the time I opened the door for her she had the whole story of how I had exposed myself to him and he had admonished me and I had run away to hide in their room.'

They shouted at her and threatened her, and she thought Vijay would have thrown her out or locked her in a cellar if he had one. It was in the blood, this corruption, he said. Ferooz warned her repeatedly that if she did not show more respect they would have no option but to throw her out, after all the kindness they had shown her. It was a Friday night, she remembered that very clearly. Abbas had asked her to go to the cinema and she had agreed but of course she couldn't go. The next morning, before anyone was up, she collected a few clothes in a carrier bag and went to him, to Abbas, and they ran away from that town.

Abbas said let's get out of this place, and she thought fine. She did not tell him about the attempt to rape her. She was happy to go far away from the mess, get away, leave it behind. She didn't know if she had any rights, or if they could have her brought back to be their skivvy again. So when Abbas said: *Yallah, let's get out of here*, she said hurray.

'I did not tell you about the cousin before,' Maryam said. 'And I don't know why it feels important to tell you now. It is only a man forcing himself on me, and after all these years I should have forgotten about it, like an old scar that fades. But I still feel the humiliation of it, the injustice. I could not even tell Abbas at first, but now I feel it is important to tell you. It did not feel right to tell you before, to have you think of your mother like that, as someone who could be menaced in that way. It did not feel right to tell you those things when you were younger, to have you think that the world was that unsafe. But now I want you to know, so that you don't think there is a dirty secret I am keeping from you. I wanted to explain to you fully why I ran away from Ferooz and Vijay, and why for so long I could not bear the thought of getting in touch with them.'

'It's all right, Ma,' Anna said, wanting her to stop now, not wanting to hear any more stories about her ugly life. 'It's all right. It was a long time ago. Don't distress yourself any more about it.'

Maryam looked steadily at her daughter, and she understood her desire to stop her talking. 'It is also because I have been listening to Abbas telling me things I did not know. It made me realise how sad it is to live with these things on your own, to let them poison your life.'

'Oh God,' Anna said. 'What has he been saying?'

Maryam stared at them for a moment, looking for words, then she said: 'He has another wife. He abandoned her and her child in Zanzibar many years ago.'

Jamal sighed and leaned back in the chair. Anna glared at her mother.

'I can't bear this,' she said angrily. 'I can't bear these shitty, vile immigrant tragedies of yours. I can't bear the tyranny of your ugly lives. I've had enough, I'm leaving.'

'Shut up, Hanna,' Jamal said. 'Let Ma speak.'

'My name is Anna, you moron,' Anna said, but she did not leave.

Then briefly and as brutally as before, Maryam told them how Abbas ran away because he thought the child was not his, and since then had not spoken of his flight to anyone. For forty years he has lived with his shame, Maryam said, unable to speak about it to anyone. Now he wants to talk about it because he thinks he's dying. Let him tell you himself, she said.

'I don't want to hear it,' Anna said. 'I don't want to know. I'm leaving. I'm going to call a cab and catch the next train to London. Or to anywhere.'

Jamal left the room and went upstairs. The upstairs landing was dark but he did not need a light to know his way around. He opened the door to his parents' bedroom and slipped silently inside. He steadied his breathing and after a few moments of standing there in the dark, he knew that his father was awake.

'Ba,' he said.

'Jamal,' Abbas said. Then he began to whisper, and when

Jamal drew near he realised that he could not understand anything his father was saying. He sat on the floor in the dark and listened to him ramble. He could hear Anna's raised voice downstairs.

'Zanzibar sounds like a wonderful place to be from,' Jamal said, but Abbas took no notice.

After what seemed a long time, his father stopped whispering and Jamal guessed from his breathing that the medication had put him to sleep. The noises from downstairs had also stopped. He heard the bedroom door opening gently behind him, and from the stray stairlight he saw that it was his mother. He followed her outside.

'He's asleep,' Jamal said.

'Maybe,' Maryam said. 'Sometimes he just pretends.'

'He was whispering for a long time,' he replied.

'Yes I know,' she said. 'He will do that for days now. He loses his way when he becomes upset. Then he does that whispering in his language as if he has forgotten to speak in English. I think he knew I was telling you about his running away and he has gone into hiding.'

'Has Hanna left?' he asked.

'No, she's downstairs,' Maryam said, smiling in the half-light. 'She found a bottle of wine in one of the kitchen cupboards.'

The next day their father did not get out of bed. When Jamal went to see him, Abbas looked quietly at him and then began to whisper. Jamal pulled up a chair and sat beside him while his Ba hissed away for an hour or more. In the end, Jamal smiled, kissed his father's hand and went back downstairs. Maryam told them some more of what Abbas had told her, but as the day wore on she said there was no point them staying any longer. He had gone into one of his deep places. When he comes back from there, I will get him to continue speaking into the tape. He prefers that now. He sits there on his own and just says whatever he wants, and does not need to look anyone in the eye. She did not want to put any more stress on him, her sick bigamist. The word startled Jamal, but Maryam said she was saying it so that she should become used to it, so that it would not pain her as much as it did at first.

'It isn't so strange for men to have had another family in these situations,' Jamal said when they were on the train to London. 'Think about it. It isn't impossible to imagine how it might happen.'

'By these situations you mean immigrants and refugees,' Anna said, still swollen with outrage.

Jamal smiled. 'You are really rolling that word round your mouth these days,' he said. 'Vile immigrant tragedies, no less.'

'I just wish their stories were not so pathetic and sordid,' Anna said. 'My dad is a bigamist and my mum is a foundling. Can you imagine telling anybody that and not sounding like a character out of a comic melodrama? Of course it's not so strange for immigrant men to be bigamists, and foundlings were everywhere in the 1950s. How perfectly ordinary. We should all of us be more understanding and not make a fuss about it. Is that what you're saying? You should've told that to our father, so he didn't feel that he had to make everyone unhappy with this silent burden he was carrying around. It was wrong of him not to tell us years ago. And what does she mean by telling us now that she was raped by some monstrous Indian boy when she was sixteen. Could she not have just kept that to herself?'

'Not quite raped,' Jamal said. 'And she told us because it hurts her to remember the hurt on her own. Maybe.'

Anna fell silent for a moment and then began again, stopping and starting for a good while before she gradually lapsed into stillness, staring out of the window at the hurtling countryside. Jamal resisted many moments to speak, to protest, to say that Ma was telling them about more than the rape. She was telling them about how these people had treated her well and then later wounded her with such casual misuse, and she was telling them about the guilt she felt for kindnesses she had not understood or repaid. She was telling them about a humiliation she had suppressed and no longer wanted to. But he did not protest or defend, and he sat in front of Hanna while she had her say. There was a cruel edge to Hanna, he thought, as he had thought many times before. She was unkind when nothing could come out of unkindness, when it was nothing more than a flourish of her wit, and she spoke in that aggrieved manner as if everything was intended to hurt and aggravate her. It suited her idea of herself that she was not going to stand for any rubbish, that she would speak her mind and not hide behind courtesies and sentiment.

He told her about Lena and saw her eyes slowly light up with interest and pleasure. He told the story as an entertainment, how he had been secretly besotted with her, tongue-tied with adoration when he was with her, and then how he was so surprised by the kissing after the party and did not know how to proceed afterwards. She shook her head with pity at his fumbling. He told her about the boyfriend Ronnie, and about the postcard, and how she came back from her holiday on the Shannon and took charge. He kept it light, the way she liked her stories. She loved the postcard episode.

'You are such an innocent,' she said. 'She more or less

had to put her life in danger with her super-fit hunk before you realised that she wanted you.'

'I'm an idiot,' he agreed. 'But there's no need to exaggerate. How was her life in danger?'

She brushed aside Marco's attempt at suicide. An exhibitionist escapade, she said. He was going to jump out of that car when the moment was right. He just wanted to scare the living daylights out of his parents. Jamal saw how she hesitated when he told her that Lena's father was Italian, frowning a little at another immigrant story, but she let it pass without remark. Then when he finished telling her what he could for the moment, the silence opened up between them again and her face turned morose. They were on the outer edges of London when she began to tell him how things were between Nick and her. I think he's fucking someone, she said, or several someones. Or that he will sooner or later. Jamal listened silently while she went into detail about her unhappiness with Nick and all that she thought lay ahead for her. The detail surprised him. She had never spoken to him in this way about Nick before. Jamal had thought that Hanna and Nick were permanent, and had long ago learned to keep his opinions on the matter to himself. He could not understand how Hanna could tolerate Nick's egotism, and his flaunting of his intelligence and knowledge. Now as he listened to his sister talking about the failure of her love with such glib misery, he felt sorry that he had lost the habit of speaking openly to her. He watched her as she talked, absently stroking her mobile phone, and he could not find the easy words of reassurance that the moment required.

As they pulled into Liverpool Street station she said, I'd better call our leader. Stay in touch, beautiful one. They went in different directions on the Circle Line, she to Victoria and he to King's Cross. On the train north, his mind turned to his father and the secret he had endured and then forced on them, and to his mother and the unhappiness Ba had caused her. He thought of what Ma had told them, of the woman he had married and how he thought himself tricked, how he cried so much as he spoke of those times and those events. It's no good though, she said. Nothing can be done about these things. The crying does no good now. He should have spoken about all this many years ago.

He felt he should have stayed with them for a few more days.

The Return

4

I T WAS GETTING DARK when Anna arrived home. Nick was sitting in front of the TV watching the evening football. She had rung him from Liverpool Street to tell him what train she was catching, and that he was not to worry about picking her up. She would take a taxi from the station. There was a time when he would have said, Nonsense, I'll be there. She told herself not to be petty, not to fret her mind with these trivial grumbles. He rose to his feet and embraced her, holding her for a long moment, looking concerned.

'Was it terrible? Is everything all right?' he asked gently, steering her to the sofa.

She smiled at his fussing anxiety and kissed him quickly on the lips. 'No, everything is not all right,' she said, sitting down where he wanted her to. 'I saw these two women in Liverpool Street, a mother and a daughter, I think. They were so hopelessly fat, and so much at a loss, so confused in that huge station. It was depressing to see them. Black women. They spoke to each other in a language I did not understand, and were looking around in a terrified way. I don't think they could read English.'

'Then?' Nick asked when she said no more for a while.

'Then nothing. I went to catch my train,' she said. 'Asylum seekers, I suppose. Maybe I should have offered to help, but the sight of them depressed me. They were so helpless and so ugly. Is it really so bad where they come from?'

'Probably,' he said quietly.

She smiled. 'You sound like my saintly brother.'

'How was it at home?' he asked.

She shrugged. 'They had news for us. My mother was raped when she was sixteen and my father is a bigamist,' she told him.

'What!' he said, sitting up in his chair.

'Which apparently is not so strange for people like us,' she said cheerfully. 'How was your conference?'

'Oh, tedious. Same old people saying the same old things. I stayed the night with Matt, that was the best part,' he said, smiling, so she did not believe what he was saying.

'Did your paper go well?' she asked.

'I think so,' he said, frowning modestly. 'It didn't seem that anyone has given much thought to the subject, so my contribution made a bit of an impact.'

'I'm sorry, you never told me what your paper was on,' she said. Or I did not ask in time and you were in such a rush to go.

'It was on CMS missionary activity in Eritrea,' he said. 'Oh, that's Church Missionary Society, a nineteenth-century Anglican evangelical movement. Did you know that the Bible was translated into Ge'ez in the fifth century after Christ? I didn't even know there was a language called Ge'ez until just recently. I didn't know that it had its own alphabet, and the learning to translate the Bible.'

'Yes, you told me. Didn't your friend Julia at work give a paper on that?' she asked.

'That's right,' he said. 'We did a joint paper, Julia and I. She talked about the Ge'ez Bible and I talked about CMS activity. God knows what we were up to in England in the fifth century but it wasn't much to do with Christianity or translating the Bible. That didn't stop us from taking our own improved brand of Christianity to the Eritreans in the nineteenth century, which the miserable wretches rejected. They preferred their outdated Ge'ez variety instead of accepting the opportunity to join the modern world.'

Is it Julia you're fucking then?

'What was that you were saying about your father being a bigamist?' he asked, smiling, inviting her to make what she had said into a joke. So she told him how the visit to Norwich had gone and how she had been unable to contain her irritation with the horribleness of what her mother had told them. After a while she saw that he was no longer attentive to her words, but that his eyes moved slowly over her face and her body. She stopped talking and he came over to the sofa for her. She clung to him as he kissed her, murmuring and groaning in his mouth. She could not help herself. She did not want to help herself. It was ecstacy to lose herself in pleasure so complete that it overwhelmed her whole mind and her whole body.

Afterwards, as they lay in the dark, she said: 'On the way home, I was sitting on the train yearning for you. I even said the words to myself, yearning for you. I was sitting there thinking that soon I will be home and you will make love to me just as you have done.'

He grunted contentedly and turned over towards her. He ran his hand over her belly and breasts. After a moment, she heard his breathing change and knew that he was almost asleep. He usually fell asleep before her and she had become used to waiting for his breathing to change before she opened her mind as a prelude to sleep. It was often a good moment, and she felt a kind of relief as she heard him sleeping. She felt that way most nights, as if she had been released from a watchful presence. Then in the dark she allowed a hidden self to come creeping out, one which entertained secret ambitions and desires. Sometimes she simply replayed happy moments or indulged serial fantasies of her future achievements, when she would become a great success and win fame. When his breathing had become deep and forgetful, she composed herself and selected the narrative she wanted to run through for herself, as if she was selecting a book or a piece of music. If he stirred at such moments, or moved about in his sleep, she waited irritably for him to settle down again so she could return to her secret dramas.

She had always been slow to fall asleep, and when she was younger she had lain awake for hours in the dark because her parents had decreed a time when her light had to be switched off. She thought of how protective her father had been, and how every night before he went to bed, he carefully opened her bedroom door and asked in the softest whisper if she was asleep. She did not answer, and he went away satisfied that his little girl was contentedly sleeping. They stopped bothering her when she started to study for examinations, and then she could read for hours until she became too tired to read any more. At some point, her sleepless hours became a delight, when she played out her daydreams, and undid her inadequacies and fulfilled all her ambitions.

She was still able to do that now, but she had a better idea of her limitations, and it now required an act of will to enact some of her fantasies. Perhaps it was only non-achievers like her who spent hours in the dark living a fantasy life. Perhaps successful people did not need to imagine success, and could fall asleep instantly like Nick after sex. She thought of their lovemaking a short while ago, and replayed what they had done move by move, living again every delicious stroke and thrust. Had he made love to Julia yet? She thought he had, that was her guess. Nick was not inclined to deny himself for long. She did not really want to think about that and what it meant, not at this hour. She wished she could fall asleep, and not be bothered by the sinking sense that her life was adrift, which stole on her when she was unwary.

To keep herself from agitation, she silently recited the first verse of Auden's 'Lullaby' to herself: Lay your sleeping head, my love. Then when she finished that she tried to do the same with 'Ode to a Nightingale': My heart aches, and a drowsy numbness pains my senses. It took her some moments to get the first verse right, and then she recited it again until she could see it in her mind as if it were on the page in front of her. She did the same thing with the second verse, and then waited to see the two verses together before starting on the third. She knew that verse quite well and so she was over that one quickly, more quickly than she would have liked. She struggled through the fourth, and fell asleep when she got to: I cannot see what flowers are at my feet.

That night she had the house dream again. She was walking on a gently rising cobbled street. She could see that it made a turning to the right ahead of her, and on the corner were chairs and a couple of tables outside a small café. There was a smell of wood smoke in the air, and the sound of accordion music and low-pitched voices in conversation. Behind her, she knew, was the sea. There was no one in sight but there were people around. It was a street she recognised, and she marvelled to be there again after having been away for so long. She had never thought she would see this street of her youth again, or feel so comfortable and at leave to stay for as long as she wished. At the corner, the road narrowed and grew dark, and on her right she saw a huge door that was slightly ajar. Against every cautious instinct in her dreaming body, she pushed at the door and entered. Instantaneously she found herself on a terrace looking out to sea and to the town round the curve of the bay. A man spoke softly nearby, and when she turned to look she saw a dark-skinned young man sitting on a stool with his hands in a tub of washing. The sleeves of his baggy shirt were rolled up and he wore an old satiny white cap on his head. He spoke again in the same gentle voice but she could not make out his words. She felt a slight sense of panic and suddenly was eager to leave. She struggled to get a good grip on her suitcase, which she had not been aware she was pulling behind her, and tried to find her way back to the street. Instead she found herself in the derelict house of her dreams, dragging her suitcase up worn wooden stairs and along rotting floorboards, stifled by cobwebs and a steady throb of anxiety. The suitcase was growing heavier and becoming difficult to manoeuvre on the littered floors, but she could not leave it behind even though it was old and battered. Later, in the early hours before morning, she dreamed that she was riding a horse across a beautiful land-scape of gentle hills and sheltered pasture, with the shadow of mountains in the far distance.

Lena and Jamal were invited to tea with their neighbour, whose name, it turned out, was Harun. It said so on the postcard he had pushed through the letterbox. They turned up at four o'clock on Saturday afternoon as instructed. When he opened the door, Jamal saw that he was wearing a suit and an open-necked shirt. The suit was of a similar vintage to the one Ba used to wear, except that Harun's looked less dilapidated. The bruising and swelling on Harun's face had gone down, although there were still some dry scabs on his cheek and on his temple. He seemed very pleased to see them.

'On the dot,' Harun said, extending his hand to Lena and then shaking Jamal's hand. 'Come in, please. When I went back to Sainsbury's to thank them for the way their staff had looked after me after my tumble, the manager reminded me of the shopping I had lost. So instead of my oranges and salad, he sent one of his young men round with an enormous hamper of tins and vegetables and fruit and biscuits and cakes, as if to reward me for my injury. This is a gift from Sainbury's to all of us,' he said, gesturing with a flourish towards the coffee table, on which he had placed a plate of biscuits and another of small cakes decorated with colourful icing.

He left the room to fetch the tea, and Lena gave the biscuits and cakes an expert examination while Jamal looked around. The chairs and sofa were large and old, covered in a faded floral upholstery with wooden insets in the arms. The most faded of the chairs was the one under the window, evidently Harun's chair, with a small table beside it on which he had left a spectacles case and a book. The wallpaper was also floral and faded, and the paintwork was going brown. A small television stood against the inside wall of the house, and next to it was the radio and hi-fi. Everything looked old and worn out. The carpet was matted and bare in places, and of an indeterminate grey colour, which might originally have been a pale shade of green or blue. The room spoke of poverty, or at least lack. Just behind the door stood a bureau. On the bureau, and on two of the walls were framed photographs, sepia with age; there were three framed photographs in all. The two on the walls were of groups, one taken in a studio, and the other in a garden. The one on the bureau was a head and shoulders photograph of a woman.

Jamal stood up to have a closer look at the photograph of the woman, taking her to be a wife passed away. Her face was composed, as if she had made her whole body come to rest moments before the photograph was taken. The small tolerant smile on her lips, patient and forbearing, had spread to her eyes, and her whole face looked as if it would burst into a broad grin if the photographer did not hurry up and take the picture. Jamal guessed that she would have been in her mid-thirties when the photo was taken. She was sitting slightly sideways, leaning forward, her head turned towards her left shoulder facing the camera, a classic studio pose.

He heard the kettle click and headed back to the sofa, in case he should seem too curious too soon. As he went back to sit down he glanced at the two photographs that hung on the walls. One was a group of three, two women sitting down and a man standing behind the small ornamental table that stood between them. He guessed they were siblings. The other was of two men and a teenaged boy. The men were both on the portly side, buttoned up in waistcoated suits and wearing hats. The boy stood between them, in shirtsleeves, and the hand of one of the men was on his shoulder. They were standing in a garden, the men smiling, the boy grinning. In the background, light glinted off a pond, beside which stood a stone bench. From the style of dress, he guessed that both photographs were taken in the period between the wars. He wondered if they were part of the woman's family.

Jamal sat down beside Lena, who asked him in a whisper if that was Harun's wife. As Harun poured the tea, he made conversation. He took two brief sips of tea and then put his cup down on the table beside him. 'As you will have seen on my card, my name is Harun,' he continued in his unhurried way. He paused for a moment and then added, as if unsure whether to provide this additional information: 'Harun Sharif.'

'How are you feeling now, Mr Sharif?' Lena asked. 'I hope the nurse has been coming to look after you.'

Harun made a disapproving noise. 'Tssk, not Mr anything, I would much prefer Harun. The nurse only came to check that I had survived the night, and since I had, I was able to persuade her to go away and never come back. There was no need for her to waste time on me when there are many others who require her skills. I am perfectly well, Lena, apart from the usual aches and pains, and that quite unexpected tumble the other day.'

'The infirmities of age,' Lena said.

'Precisely,' Harun said, laughing and nodding, acknowledging his own phrase. 'I hope you don't mind my asking, but I assume you are students. What are you studying?'

Long before half an hour had passed, it was clear that Harun was making ready for them to go. He offered them more tea, which they declined, and after a short pause as if to make certain that they would not have any more, he gathered the cups and saucers and put them on the tray. Then he sat back in his chair, smiled at them and glanced out of the window. 'Well, that was very nice,' he said after a moment, making as if to get to his feet. 'We must arrange another session of tea very soon. I know you are very busy with your work, but when you can spare a little time, then it would be very nice to have a chat again.'

'Well, we didn't waste too much of his afternoon, did we?' Lena said to Jamal when they got back. Lisa and Jim were back from their Berlin trip, and they told them the story of their tea with the neighbour. 'We can't have been in there for twenty minutes,' said Lena.

Jamal laughed. 'He reminds me of my Ba,' he said. 'Here's your tea, drink it and goodbye, thank you. He more or less kicked us out in the end.'

'I thought he was a very gracious man, though,' Lena replied, joining in the joke. 'Apart from his style of saying goodbye. He had a very clear way of speaking, don't you think? A kind of eloquence.'

'What do you think he does?' Lisa asked. 'Or did, rather. I should think he's retired now, wouldn't you?'

Lena shrugged. 'Jamal was poking around like a detective. I don't know if he picked up any clues. Jamal, what was that book he had on the table? That should tell us something.'

'The Essays of Montaigne,' Jamal said, and laughed out loud at their stunned silence. 'I don't know what book he had on the table! I just wondered what you would make of the possibility that he might be reading Montaigne.'

'I think he's a writer,' Lena said later, when they were on their own. Jamal looked sceptical. 'Just the way he spoke, and all the things he knew about Irish literature.'

That night they heard the banging and the shouting again next door as they lay in bed. Jamal got up and started to dress, but the noises stopped before he had his shoes on, and after a moment of tense silence, Lena called his name and he went back to bed. The next afternoon, Jamal knocked on Harun's door.

'I heard shouting and banging last night,' he said, standing on the pavement outside Harun's house. 'You should call the police.'

'I have called the police, but they tell me there is nothing they can do,' Harun said wearily. 'It has been like this since Pat died. They never used to do this when she was here. I have seen these young people. At least I think it's them, some youths that I see down this street. I don't know if they all live around here or just come to make mischief, but I have seen a group of them and seen their grins as I walk past them. I think they are the ones who come and do all the shouting. But listen, I'll survive. They are probably more frightened about what they are doing than I am. I have seen enough in my life not to be frightened by children shouting abuse.'

Jamal could imagine his Ba saying the same thing. Me, I'm not afraid of these children. I'm more afraid of the police. But Jamal had no faith in children and did not think they could be disarmed by being ignored. They were as evil as everyone else. Just think for a moment of the tortures child soldiers were committing in African wars. He did not want to insist with Harun when he had come to offer sympathy, so after a moment he asked: 'Have you read Montaigne?'

'Yes, some years ago,' Harun said, surprised. 'With some pleasure, I must say. Why do you ask?'

'Oh I just wondered. I heard someone talking about Montaigne on the radio the other day, someone working on a new edition of the essays,' Jamal lied. 'I just wondered if you had read him. I haven't, but I think I will.'

'You'll enjoy him, I'm sure. He is very entertaining, and wise. When I read him for the first time, I was taken completely by surprise. The style was quite unexpected, so accessible and intelligent and frank, not always something you expect when you read a writer from another century and one who you think will have a different view of the world. Come in, let's have a talk about Montaigne,' Harun said, opening the front door wide and standing back.

'Well, I'll read him first and then we can talk,' Jamal said, grinning.

'Come in anyway, let's not stand here at the door like strangers.'

Inside, Jamal's eyes were drawn to the photograph of the woman on the bureau, and without hesitation he asked if that was his wife. Pat. Harun shook his head and motioned for Jamal to sit while he took the chair by the window.

'I don't know who the woman is,' he said, smiling, apparently not minding Jamal's directness. 'We found the pictures in one of the kitchen drawers when we moved into this house more than twenty years ago. The house was empty when we bought it. All the furniture was cleared out, the floors were bare or covered with bits of broken lino here and there. It felt like a house where someone had lived his or her last days in. Then perhaps a relative or the solicitors cleared the house for sale. Well, whoever cleared the house missed the photographs in the drawer. Pat was for throwing them away but I managed to keep them. Then a year or two ago I put them up on the walls.'

Harun stopped as if that explained everything.

'Why did you put photographs of people you don't know on your walls? They are nothing to do with you,' Jamal said politely.

'They are something to do with me,' Harun replied, equally politely. 'I found it comforting to think these were people who may have been part of the life of this house. They look far too grand to have lived in such a humble house, but perhaps they visited here. Possibly the gentry in the pictures were the employers of the people who lived here, or even possibly their relatives who may have fallen on hard times and may have been forced to come down in the world. I enjoyed entertaining all these possibilities, and up there on the walls, they looked benignly on this space that I now occupy. I have grown fond of them, and without their kindly gaze, this would feel a far emptier place than it does.'

Jamal had heard the *a year or two ago*, and assumed these photographs replaced others that were there before, perhaps of Pat. He guessed that the pictures were a decoy, a way of obscuring a reality, offering one story instead of another. But obscure it from whom? Who would come to his house to read his life?

'The pictures seem to have put you in deep thought, Jamal,' Harun said. 'It is just a frivolity, don't let it trouble you. Sometimes I pretend that a stranger comes to the house and asks me to reveal the story behind the photographs because he or she assumes they belong to me. I imagine that I say that yes, they are my pictures, but I have forgotten the people and the places in them. Think just how absurd that story would strike anybody who heard it. I wonder if it could ever be true, that you would reach a time when the mementos of your life would say nothing to you, when you could look around you and have no story to tell. It would feel as if you were not there with these nameless and memoryless objects, as if you were no longer present among the bits and pieces of your life, as if you did not exist.'

Jamal asked. 'Are you play-acting your non-existence?'

'No, I imagine how it would feel to arrive at that condition, not wish for it,' Harun said, giving every sign of enjoying the exchange. 'Not yet, anyway. I don't think this play with the pictures is a kind of death wish. I lament the passing of each day, as if it is something I have lost. I don't wish for my days to end yet.'

'I still don't understand,' Jamal said, encouraged by his smiles to press for something clearer. 'What is this drama with the images an enactment of? What does it mean?'

'I am not sure what it means, just a frivolity on my part,' Harun said again. 'When the idea occurred to me I was amused by what someone would read from this, like wearing a disguise and walking the streets and seeing how the world looked at you differently. Medieval princes found this very entertaining, for example. But since I did not expect anyone to come and see the drama, it was, as you say, a game I played by myself. And since you are forcing me to think so hard about this little frivolity, which I entered into intuitively, I should confess that the pictures may also have been an evasion.'

'Pat,' Jamal said, almost involuntarily.

'Yes, Pat,' Harun replied, and then turned to look out of the window for what seemed to Jamal a long time. He guessed he was running images of her through his mind, remembering her. Then he looked back at Jamal and nodded, smiling wryly in a way he was beginning to recognise. He thought the smile was a courteous rebuke which meant *I don't want to talk about this matter right now*, or perhaps *this is not something that I can talk about with you when I hardly know you*. Another old man hoarding his memories. It made him think of Ba. So much about Harun made him think about Ba, how he might have been.

'I'd better leave you in peace,' Jamal said. 'I'm sorry if I intruded, but thank you for talking to me about the pictures.'

'No no, you have not intruded. It gives me pleasure to talk to you. Like someone I have known for a long time,' Harun said.

'What was your work?' Jamal asked.

'Many years ago I was a journalist. Then when we moved here I became a teacher of journalism at the Polytechnic,'

Harun said, waving these matters aside. 'Now I write stories for children.'

'You are a writer,' Jamal said, delighted.

Harun grinned to have made him happy. 'Well, that is to flatter me. I write children's versions of great stories, and I make up one or two of my own in the same register, although these are not for publication. I have done episodes from Firdausi's *Shahnameh* and some from Homer, and most recently a version of the original *Hamlet*. They are published in small cheap editions for children and sold in South Asia and Africa. It is work that gives me pleasure.'

'I would love to read them,' Jamal said.

'Then you shall,' Harun said. 'Is that what you want to do? Be a writer?'

'Me?' Jamal said, quite astounded by this suggestion.

Then Harun got up and went to the bureau. He opened the desk doors and Jamal saw him reach into a heavy, battered old bag. He brought out a framed photograph and handed it to him. Pat, he said. There were two of them, standing on a wide beach with their backs to the sea. He recognised a much younger Harun, perhaps in his late thirties with long black hair, and Pat beside him. She wore a short, sleeveless cotton dress, splashes of mauve and white, and on her face was a small intimate smile. Jamal thought she looked beautiful and pleased with herself, as if everything was going according to plan. She was as tall as Harun, and perhaps slightly heavier. It must have been a calm day, because her long black hair lay unruffled round her face.

'That was taken at Sennen Cove in Cornwall,' Harun said. 'We went there for a holiday in that wonderful summer of 1976.'

Jamal looked at the photograph for a moment longer and then handed it back. 'She looks lovely,' he said.

'She died, as perhaps you have guessed. She was here with me for so many years and then she was gone, for ever. There used to be a picture of her on the bureau, taken when she was about your age, over there, where the picture of that woman is now. And behind you was that one with the two of us together on holiday in Cornwall. Over there above the television was a picture of me taken when I was a student, just arrived in England. I took them down after Pat died because they made me sad, and forced my mind to think about things that caused me pain. They interfered with the living form of her that I had in my mind. I preferred to have her appear to me in various sudden visions than to have her looking at me in that fixed way. It was so sudden, how after so many years she was gone and there was no one to talk to. Sometimes I'm struck with amazement when I consider exactly how I have found myself here. But then I suppose many people can say that about their lives. It may be that events constantly take us by surprise, or perhaps traces of what is to become of us are present in our past, and we only need to look behind us to see what we have become, and there is really no need for amazement.'

Harun smiled wryly at Jamal, apologetically, his eyes glistening. 'You are a very good listener, Jamal. I was watching you in case you fidgeted or looked wearied, so I would know to stop, but you did not. It is a handy skill for an aspiring writer. Now you see, you have indulged the ego of an old man and he has pounced on your sympathy to burden you with these miserable thoughts.'

'You have not burdened me,' Jamal said, moved by the sight of the grieving old man. They sat silently for a while, and then Jamal said again: 'You have not burdened me.'

It was after six when he left, and by then he knew that Harun came from Uganda in 1960 to study journalism.

His family were of Yemeni Shia origin, very orthodox in their piety. Yazids, Jamal said. Exactly, Harun said, pleased with him. They did not like it when he met Pat.

'I would love to hear about your time here when you first came,' Jamal said.

'Do you want to include me in your research?' Harun asked, teasing him.

'No, no, I love hearing those stories, of how people coped, what it was like,' Jamal said.

'It was very exciting, coming to London,' Harun said. 'After all the things I had read and the pictures I had seen. All those great buildings and the quiet squares. Funnily enough, one of the things that struck me and the thought that comes unbidden when I think of first arrival, is how plump were the chickens in the butchers' shops and how large were the eggs. The mind preserves the oddest things sometimes. Well, I made friends with one of the lecturers who taught me at the university. His class was quite late in the day, and afterwards we went out for a drink a couple of times. He was only a little older than me and had briefly lived in Cape Town as a child, so he made it seem like we had something in common. We were both Africans, he said. His name was Allan, and I liked his calm unsmiling manner. I think some of the younger students found his manner earnest and unsettling.

'It was through Allan that I met Pat. She was his wife. He invited me to dinner at their flat and a few weeks later I stole her from him. Actually, it was she who stole me. I was very naïve about such things. I was brought up in a family that was very watchful of such matters, and to be truthful, I was a complete novice in love. I had no idea how terrible having an affair with the wife of a friend would feel. It went against everything that friendship implied to me, the treachery, the betrayal of trust, the lying, furtive arrangements. I wished the affair would end, but I also did not want the affair to end. Pat was a beautiful and passionate woman, and I felt undeservedly fortunate to have won her love. She was also very determined and obstinate, and admired herself immensely. She made me see how timorous my scruples were and how self-deluding I was to entertain them as if they were a high ethical conviction. I had a duty to fulfil my desires, she told me, which was a completely new idea to me at the time, but one that became more commonplace in the decades to come.

'Anyway, that was how we met. And after Pat and I moved in together, I fully understood that I had lost control of my life because now I had no choice but to stay. It was a decision that caused me hardship. My father did not reply when I wrote to tell him the reason for my decision. My uncle wrote instead and said that I had best come back and explain myself in person, but I knew that if I did that I would never be able to defy them and leave. They would overwhelm me with my obligations. You do understand what I am describing, don't you? You don't find it too intimate and vulgar to hear these things about an old man's life, do you? I stayed in London, and promised to return some time soon to see them and talk things over, but I never did. Over the years, whenever someone asked me how long I'd been living here, it was as if I had to confess to a crime.'

On Sunday evening Anna rang her mother as she had every night during that week. Their conversation was brief. No there was no change. He was taking his medication and eating properly, but he was still not talking. It will be a few days yet.

Oh Ma. She felt sorry about the way she had spoken the previous weekend, not about what she said, but that she was out of control. And she had not listened properly to her mother, and had not offered sympathy when she deserved it. She did not know how to tell her mother these things. Instead she gave her advice, telling her to be firm and not to miss her stint at the Refugee Centre. Oh well, she wasn't perfect.

Don't worry too much about us, miss, her mother said. And don't worry about him. He'll come out of it all right. But now I must go before he gets too stressed.

When she came off the phone, Nick said: 'Any news of the absconder? You know, I've been thinking. I wonder why it doesn't surprise me that he did that, run away, I mean.'

It took her by surprise. He had hardly said anything about her father since she came back from Norwich, and now he only spoke to make fun of him. She had done that too, calling him a bigamist, but she could do that if she wanted. He couldn't. Her Ba was her father, not his. What did he mean it didn't surprise him? She insisted that he explain what he meant and he winced at her voice. She saw that he was beginning to get angry, that she had irritated him again, but she was determined that he should explain the insinuation in his remark.

'Please don't make such a fuss about this. It's hardly anything serious, just a flippant remark, an exaggeration, forget it,' he said, conciliatory words spoken through tight lips. She hated the way he did that, as if he could barely control his frustration with her.

'I want you to explain what you meant by it, however unserious it is. What do you mean that it does not surprise you?'

'All right then,' he said. 'It doesn't surprise me because

219

running away is the kind of thing I would have expected him to do.'

'Why would you expect that of him? Because you think he is a weak man. You despise him, don't you?' she said.

He gave her one of his knowing grins. 'It's a tough world and no intelligent person has the right to expect sympathy because they hurt. Your father always acts as if he has more right to hurt than anyone else. I didn't say despise, you did. You are the one putting words in my mouth. Forget it. I'm sorry if I seemed to be making light of what happened to him.'

He spread his arms out helplessly, in a gesture that was meant to say let's leave it now. Let's not argue.

'Anyway, I've just had an email from Mum,' he said, smiling, looking to please. 'Anthony and Laura have separated. They had a fight and he physically threw her out of the house. It's not the first time he's done that. She got in through the back door and he threw her out again. They had scaffolding round the house for roof repairs, and she climbed on that and tried to get in, but he made sure that every window was locked. She spent most of the night on the scaffold, and in the morning he put a couple of suitcases of her things in the drive, gave her her car keys and handbag and told her to disappear. For ever.'

'What a monster! What does that mean? For ever.'

'I don't know,' Nick said. 'The house belongs to him. He's a partner in the firm she works for. So I suppose he could be telling her not to return to the house or to work. He is such a beast that she might be just too intimidated to make a fuss.'

'Is he that scary?' Anna asked.

'Don't you think so? I think Laura's scared of him. Sometimes when I see them together I feel sure that she is literally frightened of him, I mean physically frightened of him. Mum didn't say, but I think he hits her.'

'Where is she now?'

'I don't know,' Nick said. 'You can ask Mum when she comes. They said they'd like to come down next weekend.'

Nick was at the window, looking out for them when they arrived on Saturday afternoon. They saw the Volvo drive slowly past looking for a parking space. They went out on the pavement to meet them and Anna saw Beverley next door at her window. She waved to her. Beverley waved back but did not move, evidently curious to know what was going on out there.

Nick put his arm around her shoulder and drew her near, possessing her. Then when his parents were on the pavement and walking towards them, he left her to hurry towards them. Jill had brought them a beautiful blue vase. *To go with your door, my dear*, she said to Anna as she hugged her.

'Did you notice the colour of the front door, Ralph? Did it remind you of anything?' Jill asked, glancing at Anna with a knowing smile. Anna had told Jill some time ago that the blue reminded her of the colours of the doors in Tunis that Ralph had described the first time she met them. Ralph looked slightly alarmed at the questions, not sure what he was being tested on. 'Didn't the colour remind you of Tunis?' Jill asked, nodding at him, helping him out.

'Oh yes, oh yes indeed,' Ralph said without conviction, distracted. Anna thought he looked weary, sagging a little inside his blazer, and without his usual decorous sparkle. Jill's smile faltered slightly, and Ralph took the prod and visibly straightened himself. Jill asked Anna to show her round the house, and Anna laughed and said that would only take a minute. When they were in the upstairs back room, Jill paused suddenly as if she was about to say something, and then shook her head and smiled.

That evening Jill and Ralph took them out to dinner at an expensive restaurant, which they had already researched and where they had booked a table. Ralph could not resist telling them about the restaurant's renown and how fortunate they were to get a table at such short notice. The prices were, of course, ridiculous, but the fare was apparently exceptional. He gave the wine list a cursory glance and signalled for the wine waiter. He ordered something in an undertone, and from the waiter's slight bow Anna guessed it was something very expensive. She heard the date 1954. In recent times Ralph's baronial manner had begun to irritate her, and she thought they were in for another long evening. After everyone was well settled and he was reasonably watered, Ralph began to talk about Laura and Anthony. Anna had wondered if that was what was bothering him earlier.

'Laura was such an energetic and fearless child,' he said. 'It made you wonder where she got it from. Of course, she will have got some of her steel from her mother. They are, on her side, descended from a line of forge masters, so it is reasonable to expect that some of that iron will have found its way into the ancestral veins. She would not have much of that kind of thing from our side of the family. We were slothful prelates, good for nothing much but observing the norm and making God's word sound pompous. You have seen our beloved Digby at work with your own eyes, Anna.

'Her fearlessness was like one of those questing children in Blake, who go wandering into the dark night and lie with lions and serpents without any knowledge of terror. She learned everything so easily and so swiftly, unaware at first of these skills that came to her so naturally. This was as true of physical skills as it was of school work. She learned to swim in minutes and a few days afterwards she was darting about in the water like a little seal. From a young age she could climb a tree with perfect poise, and come safely down again. To her teachers or to the parents of her little friends it must have seemed like recklessness, and I can imagine they had to keep a sharp eye on her in case she got the other children into a scrape. But she was not reckless. Sometimes she misjudged her strength, or the strength of what she had pitted herself against. I don't know where the line is between recklessness and boldness, but at worst she was somewhere on that line. You saw this in the way she chose her ambitions. At first she was going to be a trapeze artiste, then a pilot, then a bridge builder and finally an architect. They were all achievable ambitions, finally bringing her down to earth, designing houses rather than flying through the air.

'Then she went to university and changed. We did not see it immediately, or only saw small things of no importance but we slowly realised she was losing that sureness of touch. It was like watching a batsman misjudging the length of a ball and playing and missing repeatedly, or a footballer failing to control a string of passes from his team mates. I don't mean that she became clumsy. Her judgement no longer seemed natural and assured. She was quarrelsome and aggressive with people in shops and restaurants. She was vehement in her opinions, and she was reckless now when she had not been before, driving too fast, crossing the road dangerously, walking too near the edge of the cliff.'

Ralph glanced at Jill for a moment, perhaps to check that he was not exaggerating. She nodded, and Anna discerned something slightly impatient in the gesture, as if she thought that Ralph was exaggerating and Laura was not like that at all, and above all that she wished Ralph would hurry on with the story so they could talk about something else. Anna wished he would too, pick up speed and get it over with, and so she did not mind making Jill party to this line of thought. Something in his voice was grating on her more than usual, and she was not sure if it was its magisterial tone or its warm egotism. He looked at Nick and finally at Anna, his face still sombre but his eyes beginning to sparkle with the wine. He took a sip, anticipating no interruption, and Anna marvelled at his assurance that his audience would remain obedient. He continued:

'It was meeting men that changed her, I think. Jill and I have talked about these things so much over the years. It's what parents do among themselves, talk endlessly about their children, and after all that talking, it may be that their conclusions become a summary of their conversations. So when I say it was meeting men that changed her, that may well be one of those glib summaries. In any case, she chose men who were a challenge to her, men who made her do risky things. I expect she was a challenge to them too. I expect she provoked them. She told us some of this herself, drinking binges, risky scrapes in the countryside, and perhaps she told you other things that she did not tell us, Nick. That would only be natural.'

'She didn't tell me much about anything,' Nick said shortly. Perhaps he too was getting edgy.

'We only really knew one of the men before Anthony,' Ralph said, looking away from Nick's unhelpful interruption. 'His name was Justin, and she was with him for a long time, a big gangly young man with a huge appetite. I hope I am not being too cruel in describing him that way. An awkward, shy chap, very good mannered. They went everywhere together, travelling, riding, climbing, skiing. Even when they came visiting us, within hours they were off on a long hike to somewhere. Maybe they tired each other out, because after they finished their studies – and architects study for a long time – they went their separate ways as if they had planned it that way all along.

'It was then she found Anthony, when she went to work in his practice, and from the beginning I suspected that he was more than she could handle. If anything was to come out of it, she was going to have to say aye to him whenever he demanded it, and he seemed the kind of man who would demand it frequently. Well, to my surprise she seemed willing enough to do that and the fearless child became the junior partner in a dubious enterprise. I don't call it dubious because I think it is all over between them and that therefore it is permissible to say what I think about their relationship. I don't know if it is all over, despite these recent horrors. For all I know, once these bruises have healed, they will get back together so they can inflict new ones on each other. I say dubious because their partnership seemed to me to be contentious and unequal from the beginning.'

Jill shifted in her chair, and Anna hoped she would say something, change the subject, rap the table impatiently, but she knew that no one was likely to interrupt Ralph when he was this settled. He took another sip of wine while they waited for him to continue.

'Why is Anthony such an angry and bitter man? I have often wondered this. Maybe it is his nature. Some people are just made unreasonable and awkward. Maybe it was his upbringing. He grew up in a violent house in Rhodesia. I believe his father was a restless and disappointed man, quite out of control with anger and drink. Perhaps unavoidably Anthony imbibed some of that bitter brew and now lives his life in a rage. Anyway, there they are, the two of them, Anthony and our Laura, and they have spent nearly ten years pummelling each other, with poor Laura coming off very much the worse. Anthony is so full of rage that he is fearless, and he will never know how to stop his violence on her. This is the drama we have been watching with increasing helplessness over the years, and in recent times I have started to fear the worst.'

Ralph fell silent for a moment, and something about his tone made Anna think that he was composing himself for another chapter. The food arrived just then and created enough confusion for Ralph's spell to be broken. After the waiters left, Jill said: 'Right, now you've got that off your chest, Ralph, let us wish them both well and leave them to it. Come, let us have a toast for Nick and Anna.'

'Nick and Anna,' Ralph said, always game for a toast at any time. It must have taken years of persistent practice for Ralph to have schooled his family into such submission, Anna thought. Rage and caprice were not the only ways to acquire an ascendancy, and Ralph had done it with his gently astute ramblings. As she listened to him, she felt a silent rage building up in her. Stop bullying us with your soft-spoken smugness. She imagined that in her absence she too would be the subject of one of his exhaustive analyses.

Many more toasts were drunk before the end of the evening, and they were all a little drunk as they walked along the waterfront towards Jill's and Ralph's hotel. The night was clear and cold, bright with stars. Ralph claimed Anna's arm as soon as they left the restaurant, his other hand stroking her captive arm. She chafed against his caress but resisted pulling her arm away. As they walked on the promenade, he started to recite 'The Solitary Reaper', pitching his voice towards the sea as if multitudes were gathered there to listen to him. A couple walking by grinned at him and he waved cheerfully back at them:

> Alone she cuts and binds the grain,
> And sings a melancholy strain;
> O listen! for the vale profound
> Is overflowing with the sound.
>
> No nightingale did ever chaunt
> More welcome notes to weary bands
> Of travellers in some shady haunt
> Among Arabian sands:

When he finished the poem, he patted Anna's belly and said, 'When you give us a little jungle bunny we'll give him a Wordsworth lullaby every night.' Anna winced slightly and Ralph tightened his hold, chuckling to himself. They walked on in silence for a while, then Ralph said: 'I'm sorry to hear about your father. It must be terrible to find out something like that.'

Anna recoiled from his words and from his touch, pulling away from him instantly. She took a step away and stared at Ralph with angry disgust. He looked back at her with astonishment, and when he made to speak, she raised her left hand to silence him. She turned to walk on, striding to catch up with the others, and he walked beside her without speaking. At first when he said he was sorry about her father, she thought he meant about his illness. It was the first time he had ever volunteered anything about her father. Her family never came up in conversation with Ralph and Jill, maybe as an exaggerated show of sensitivity after that first Easter weekend at their house. But Nick must have told them about the woman her father abandoned. What Ralph was referring to was that her father was a bigamist.

Jill looked back and must have noticed that they were walking apart and were not speaking, because she looked back again twice. When they were still a few paces from them, Ralph said softly: 'Anna, what did I do wrong? I meant to offer sympathy. I did not mean any harm. I am most terribly sorry to have intruded.'

He briefly touched Anna's arm, looking perplexed and hurt. She nodded to let the moment pass and restrained herself from saying anything. She returned his touch, not wanting to hurt him with her annoyance, not after they had come all this way to see them and had tried so hard to be warm. She did not think they liked her, and she could not make herself like them, not even Jill who had shown her kindness. She thought it was a kindness offered in shame to disguise their distaste.

She had thought of her father as they walked along the waterfront and Ralph recited Wordsworth. It was not because her father recited Wordsworth to her, nor could she remember ever walking along the sea with him on a dark cold night bright with stars, nor was it that Ralph's fumbling caresses reminded her of paternal affection. It was his voice reciting that made her think of him. She wished for his voice. She wished he was there walking beside her and talking to her about something he had read or describing once again the limitless corruption of the powerful, or telling her one of the stories he used to tell her as a child, something with archly wise and cunning animals.

When the moment came to part, she kissed Jill first, and then Ralph embraced her firmly as they kissed goodnight. She saw in his eyes that he was still perplexed about what had happened earlier and she felt sorry to have hurt him.

Nick and Anna started to argue as soon as they got in that night, and the argument went on for hours, accusations going back and forth in some relentless logic, fuelled by another bottle of wine. Much of what they said was familiar, but some of it was not, as they broke new ground in their animosities. In the days that followed, they hardly spoke to each other, and Anna knew that they were approaching the end. She found their sullen antagonisms exhausting. He was going away to another conference in Oxford at the end of the week, and she thought she would use that time to think clearly about what she wanted to do with herself. School was about to start in a couple of weeks and she needed to get herself organised for her new post. She had truly had enough.

Then when the end came, it was less complicated than she anticipated. She went to school on Thursday afternoon to attend a pre-term staff meeting, and afterwards she planned to put some new pictures on the classroom walls. She had not done so before because the room was not hers, but now that she was no longer the supply teacher, she would make the room more congenial to her. The poster of Byron in Albanian costume was going to have to come down and possibly the one of Sydney Harbour, not because she had any great animosity towards either, but because she wanted images that were less grand. Perhaps a glinting stream running through a wood, or a tree-lined city street, or even a map of the world.

Nick was to take the train to Oxford on the same day, to be there for the first session on Friday morning. He was not due back until Sunday evening, so she had the whole weekend to herself. On her way home she considered what she could cook herself for dinner and decided that nothing they had at home appealed. She dropped her bags off in the house and drove to Sainsbury's. She had keys for the car but she rarely got to drive it, so the car and the late shopping on a Thursday evening had a feeling of doing something improper or adventurous, and she did not mind if that sounded pitiable. The traffic was heavy and it took a while to get to the supermarket, but she felt content and unrushed. She bought some bream and asparagus, and a piece of beef for the next day. She also bought two expensive bottles of wine. When she got back home she put the shopping in the fridge and went to sit in the garden in the fading light. She got lost there in her own thoughts for a while, the events of the day, her last conversation with her mother, Nick at his conference. Julia would be there, of course. She felt a stab of pain at the thought, somewhere in the region of her heart, and she wondered at the absurdities of the body's biology. What did the heart have to do with it? That was not where feelings resided, and yet she felt a thud in her heart as she thought of Nick and Julia making love. She went back inside and opened one of the bottles of wine, and then went upstairs to change.

It took her a moment to register the noise, and then she recalled she had heard it before while she was downstairs but it had been too faint to distinguish. Now she realised it was her mobile phone alerting her to a message. She hurried downstairs and found her handbag in the living room where she had left it. When she found her mobile it was switched off, and there was no message. She heard the noise again, fainter this time. It must be Nick's. He must have left his mobile somewhere upstairs. When she got back upstairs she saw it on the desk in the study and she did not hesitate. She opened the phone and read the text: *thinking of you since I opened my eyes cant wait to hold you tonight luv you ju xxxx*. She closed the phone and went to change out of her work clothes. Then sitting on the bed half-naked, she sipped her wine while a slow rush of heat spread through her body. After a moment she went to the bathroom and sat on the toilet while her body emptied itself.

She had thought herself ready for this news but she had not expected to feel this paralysis and terror. She forced herself downstairs, but she found the idea of the bream nauseating. Perhaps she would make herself something simple with toast. She poured herself another glass of wine and sat down, astonished by how her body was betraying her so unexpectedly. After a while she forced herself to think about what needed to be done. She had convinced herself she wanted an end to things as they were between them, and now there was an end approaching. She went back to the kitchen, put the oven on, put away the clean dishes on the draining board, washed the asparagus, and wrapped the bream in foil. The oven light clicked off, so she put the fish in and went upstairs to draw the curtains. There were practical things for her to think about, and although she had given some vague thought to where she would live and so on, now suddenly she was confronted with threatening hints of chaos and disorder. She felt herself retreating, perhaps she should wait to see how serious this was. Must keep moving. Perhaps strip the bed and put clean sheets on, get rid of his smell, but the labour of it was too arduous just then and the smell of him was everywhere.

She could not manage much of the fish but she ate all the asparagus, and drank some more wine. She tried the TV but could not get interested. She went upstairs and rummaged in her bedside drawer, rifling through her passport, looking through her bits of jewellery, and then decided to change the bed anyway. The clean sheets felt good, as they always did, and she wished she had had a bath before going to bed, but she did not feel like getting out of bed again. She tried to read but could not concentrate. The wine was making her sleepy, so she switched the light off and made herself comfortable.

The hours passed but sleep did not come, instead episodes of her life ran through her mind and would not be denied despite her efforts. She thought of her life at home, of her childhood, of Nick, of what would become of her, and all these thoughts were accompanied by memories of embarrassments and by images of her incompetence and failure to act with resolution and kindness. Why had she waited so long? She should have known it would end like this. She struggled against this onset of what she thought of as her feebleness, her stupid uncertainty. By the early hours of the morning she was sobbing uncontrollably, deep in self-pitying anguish and hopelessness.

When he came back she would tell him that she no longer wanted this stifling life they lived together. The affair was part of it, part of his arrogance, a conviction that he could lie to her and cheat on her without fear of discovery. She did not think she could even talk to anyone about what had happened. She hoped he would not ring, most of all she could not bear to talk to him. What should she say to him?

Is this true? Well, of course it's true. All right then, I'm leaving. *Where am I going?*

Is this true? What do you think? All right then, get out. Fuck off, this is my house, you get out. *How are these things done?*

Is this true? How could you think such a thing of me? Of course it's not true. Let me explain.

She woke up early on Sunday morning, and lay in bed with the door and the back-room curtains open so that the light from the window spread across the landing and into the room. Her panic had almost subsided, and in its place there was something that felt like the nervous tremors she had before setting out on a journey to a destination that was new to her and the thought of which intimidated her. None of her journeys had turned out to be as intimidating as she had imagined them, so perhaps this one would be the same.

The seagulls were making an unbearable racket on the roof and forced her out of her mood. So she got up, made some tea, and began the long struggle to get through the day, waiting for him to return. She did not wait in impatience, she just could not concentrate and could not think of anything else to do. So she sat where she was, a book in her lap, waiting. Nick arrived just before five. She heard the taxi stop on the road and a moment later heard his key in the door. He came into the room and kissed her lightly on the lips, smiling. He was wearing a new jacket and was still carrying his overnight bag, and he looked smart and sophisticated, someone who had been out in the world. He put his bag down and took his jacket off, then he sat down in the chair opposite her.

'Was it good?' she asked him.

He smiled more broadly. 'It was very good,' he said. 'I'm sorry I didn't call you. I forgot my mobile and I just couldn't get to a phone at a convenient time to call you.'

She nodded. 'I saw your mobile upstairs,' she said. 'I read Julia's text.'

Nick went upstairs and came back down with the phone open in his hand. They sat in silence for a while, each waiting for the other to speak. He sighed and then said: 'I'm sorry. I hoped that I had switched it off, but obviously I didn't. It wasn't deliberate that you should find out like that.'

Anna shrugged. 'Well, never mind. I thought that was what was going on,' she said.

She thought he was going to speak, explain, justify himself, but he leaned forward in the chair and put his head in his hands, and sat like that for a while. He looked up, she saw there were tears in his eyes. 'I'm sorry. I love her,' he said calmly. 'It just happened. Neither of us could help ourselves. From the beginning.'

She was waiting to hear those words, or something like them, and she thought when they came they would make her wince, but they didn't. It must be because she had already felt the words in her flesh even before he spoke them. She felt exhausted, but there was also relief that they had got here at last, that now there was no turning back, no fudging explanations and pleas for understanding and reconciliation.

They sat in the living room until it began to get dark, talking with increasing heat as they raked over their lives together. He said it wasn't just Julia, that things had been going wrong for them, and he did not always feel that she cared for the things he cared for. She said he had become domineering, and only cared for himself. He said that she had become petty and small-thinking, pleasureless and worrying about utter banalities. He said she was envious that he was beginning to make a success, and she laughed at how correctly she had guessed his egotism. He went to the fridge to see if there was any wine, and he came back with a glass for her too. It was ridiculous, he said, the way she jumped and winced at every little thing he said, as if he was a great bully. That she made his parents so uncomfortable when they had come all the way to see them, just because Ralph said something about her father or some shit like that. Then in the end, quite obviously irritated with her, he said: 'I feel sorry for people like you.'

'What do you mean people like *you*?' she asked, assuming he meant something about *race*.

'I mean I feel sorry for people like you because you don't know how to look after yourselves. Your father was a whingeing tyrant, bullying everyone with one misery or another, in the grip of a psychic crisis, so it seemed. But he only had diabetes, a thoroughly treatable disease, that's all. Your mother was an abandoned baby and doesn't know who she is. Well, it doesn't take a genius to find out that kind of information. Why couldn't she just pay an agency to check it out for her? Or why couldn't you, or your brother, do it for her? She, and all of you, would have known within days. But no, it had to be another festering drama. And then it turns out your father is an absconder and a bigamist but he couldn't just talk about this, the whole crowd of you in the grip of a hopeless melodrama, acting like immigrants.'

Anna was almost drawn into offering a defence but she managed to suppress her words. She had thought all this herself. What he added to what she had thought herself about her family was scorn. It jolted her the way he said that word, immigrants, exactly as she would have said it, with the same degree of disdain.

'And as for you,' he said, and she winced and closed her eyes for a second, knowing how much she had dreaded this moment of contempt. 'You are cringing all the time, expecting to fight people when it isn't even necessary. Mum and Dad did their best to welcome you, but you managed to find them condescending and smug. Instead of making them comfortable and winning them over, you make them feel ashamed. They did not understand the tragedy of being you. Instead of taking charge of your life, you keep waiting for something to happen and then you get depressed when nothing does. You think you have unfulfilled ambitions but you don't, all you have are desires, little fun-filled daydream desires.' After a moment he said, 'I'd better stop.'

They sat like this for some time, not speaking, looking away from each other while Anna slowly calmed herself down. She did not know what time it was but it was dark outside. She would sleep in the study tonight and go to the letting agency tomorrow. Nick rose to his feet and came to where she was sitting on the sofa. He sat beside her for a moment while she sat tense with disbelief. His hand fell on her thigh, and he said: 'One last time? For old times' sake?' He was smiling at her, inviting her to another naughty escapade, but his smile quickly faded when she began to laugh. 'Oh come on, we've had good times,' he said.

She laughed even more, strengthening her defences. 'You're a greedy egotistical bastard,' she said. 'I wouldn't dream of it.'

He tried one more time, reaching for her, smiling once again through her laughter, refusing to take her refusal seriously. She slapped his arm away and rose to her feet, no longer laughing. He rose too and picked up his shoulder bag. 'I'll come back for my things later. You can reach me on the mobile whenever you want.'

That was that, he was gone. She was shaking with anger at the farewell pass he had made, as if he could just play with her, even after what he had done and what he had said. As if he could linger with her for one last fling as a farewell offering before leaving her with her regrets.

She had not thought it would be that quick. Perhaps his love for Julia was already unequivocal and it was only a matter of when, not if, for him. Perhaps Julia was already expecting him that night. Nick being Nick, though, he could not resist going for one last fuck before departure, just to show her that he could have her whenever he wanted. She heard him start the car, and even under the circumstances that made her smile. He knew how to do that, just to take what he wanted. It was the colonial instinct, she thought, not restricted to proper English people either. There were people who just knew how to do that, just take what they wanted, or at least take what they could. Nick did it with a pretence of absent-mindedness, as he had just done with the car, as if he had forgotten to ask, but she was sure he knew what he was doing. Well, she told herself, she had better stop acting like an immigrant and go and take charge of herself. Her life was about to start again and she was twenty-eight years old, a good age, and she should feel full of vigour and hope. She locked the front door and put the chain on.

In the hours before the dawn on 23 September of that year, Abbas suffered a stroke, and after this blessed third stroke he slipped away quietly as he had once done forty-four years before.

Rites

5

I HAVE LIVED LONGER than I ever thought I would. I don't know if everyone thinks like that. I am surprised I am still here and I don't know whose fault that is. I had not thought to be here this long, and I don't know if that is luck or stubbornness. Maybe I really want to stay but will not admit it. What a dirty business dying is. You think you know what's coming, but the pain still catches you out, and this helplessness and feebleness is embarrassing. Although I don't think there is that long to go now.

When I was much younger, I thought it would not be too long, that I would not be here for that much longer, that I would soon be on my way, make my exit in my twenties. Leaving was already a kind of death, and dying again did not seem unbearable. It was not because life was such a tragedy that I desired it to be short but there did not seem any good reason for it to go on as it was. But that was a very long time ago and I am still here, like a tiresome guest in my own life. It upsets her when I say that I would not have come had I been asked, not to this world, not to this life with its tiresome comings and goings. It upsets her because she thinks I mean that I wish for death, or that she has not meant anything to my life. I do not wish for death, and she has illuminated my life, but I am surprised that death has not yet come.

There is a story someone told me in Mogadishu, a Lebanese man whom I met in the docks. This was in the days when Mogadishu was still a port and not a slaughter house. The man looked at me as if he knew me and came to greet me, holding out his hand and smiling, but it turned out he had mistaken me for someone else. It happened so often, in far-flung and unexpected places, people mistaking other people for someone they once knew. It must mean that we look more alike than we think, or more alike than we like to think. We laughed over the mistake, shook hands again, and then the Lebanese man pulled me into the shade of a warehouse to get us out of the bright afternoon sun. He told me this story.

A man who lived in Jerusalem went to Haifa to visit friends and relatives. While he was there and was walking from one friend's house to another, he passed another man who looked at him with surprise, as if he recognised him. He did not stop, though, and the man from Jerusalem walked on, searching his memory to see if he could remember who the tall powerful-looking man might have been. A short while later, when he was sitting in a nearby café having a coffee with his friends, the man from Jerusalem saw the tall man again. The tall man slowed down when he caught sight of him, as if he had been looking for him, and this time he had a good, long fierce look as he walked past the café. Even his friends were surprised at the man's fierce look, but none of them knew who he was. The man from Jerusalem began to worry that this was someone he had once insulted or wronged, perhaps without even knowing he had done so. Such things can happen without intention. Some while afterwards, on his way to his relatives for lunch,

240

he passed the man again, and this time there was no mistaking the annoyance in the man's eyes. The man from Jerusalem panicked, fearing that the man who was following him was an assassin, and said a hasty goodbye to his relatives before heading back to Jerusalem. In the late afternoon he was sitting on the terrace in front of his house in Jerusalem, pleased to have got away from the unpleasantness in Haifa, when he saw the man again. The tall man walked purposefully towards him now, smiling, and then he said: *Salam aleikum, my name is Azraeel. I have come for your soul. What were you doing in Haifa? I was supposed to come for your soul in Jerusalem half an hour before the evening prayer, and there you were fooling around in Haifa. I am so glad you made it back in time.*

I hope I told that right. The Lebanese man enjoyed his story so much I would hate to think I spoiled it.

She wants me to speak, she tells me it will do me good. She says I should speak so the children will know the things I have not told them. She says they are afraid of my secrets. I tell her that parents always have secrets from their children, don't they? How did they know I had secrets for them to be afraid of? My father grew up poor as a child but when I knew him he was hard and frightening, a small tireless man who always gave orders. I don't think I cared what he was not telling me about his life. Even if I did care, I would not have known how to ask him to tell me anything. Even if I did care, and even if I did ask, he would not have told me anything just because I cared. I never heard my mother speak about her childhood or her past. I don't remember wanting to know although that was not because I did not care for her, or she did not have her own stories. Everyone has stories. I had not thought of that before, but I cannot remember her talking about herself in that way, of things she did or wanted to do in her life. She was our mother, working and complaining all the time, as if that is how she was from her first day on earth.

But she says our children are here, in a strange place, and all we have given them are bewildering stories about who we are. She thinks it makes them unsure and afraid about themselves. It makes them lose confidence, she says. As if we should be full of confidence all the time. As if we can know everything we want to know. As if we don't all discover our own fears whatever it is we know. Perhaps even, I tell her, the less we know the more plump and content we become. I don't know, I think we have given them more than just bewildering stories.

After all these years, when she has known nowhere else, she still speaks of here as a strange place. I tell her not to be such a timid hen. This is the only place in the world where she should not feel a stranger. She tells me that is how she has felt all along, and now she feels like an old servant in a large household, allowed to go about her business so long as she is not a nuisance. I no longer have the strength to argue with her about this way of thinking. It has been too much for me, this illness, and I have made her so tired when she has been the happiness of my life. I am the one who has made her a servant, making her clean after my sick waste and repaying her with my sulks. I am too tired for this talking. Why does she force me to do this? Why does she not leave me in peace?

She wants me to talk about my home, that little Unguja of ancient memory. She says this cunningly, so that I should not feel that she is forcing me to speak. Just tell them about the buildings and the streets and the sea, she says, as if I was a tourist guide giving information to strangers. There are two rainy seasons, the long rains and the short rains, and the fish market is best avoided in all seasons.

I can't remember anything, I tell her, but it is a lie. I remember many things and I remember them every day, however hard I try to forget. I thought I would keep quiet about all that for as long as I could. I thought if I started to talk I would not be able to stop. Or I would not know how to say don't ask me about that yet. Or I can't tell you about that now. I thought I would wait until the time came to talk about these things so they did not seem cowardly and shaming, but that time cannot come. I did not know it would take this long to realise that.

It is now such a long time ago and I am caught out in my silences and lies. They keep catching us out in our lies, our betters, hardly listening to the stories about our tolerant, smiling, harmonious ancient civilisations. That is what I would like to have told my children if I had spoken about that little place. That we all lived together in peace, in a forbearing society built as only Muslims know how, even though among us were people of many religions and race. I would have known no other way of talking about it. I would not have told them about the rage that lay just under the surface waiting to break, or the rough justice the children of the enslaved planned to inflict on their sultan and on everyone else who mocked and despised them. I would not have told them about our hatreds, or about the way women were treated like merchandise, how they were traded and inherited by their uncles and brothers and brothers-in-law. I would not have told them how enthusiastically the women themselves performed their worthlessness. And I would not have told them about our tyrannical ways with children. Why are we such a lying, deceitful rabble?

*   *   *

How? She wants me to talk about how I ran away. I turned into a seabird and took to the air. I changed into a sea creature and picked my way over the crags and the boulders of the ocean floor. I floated out on a raft made from the broken timbers of my cowardice. How else could I run away from an island? I stowed away on a ship, that was how. Or I tried to stow away because the sailors found me as soon as I opened the door to come out of the hold. I must have set off an alarm. I was in there for three days. Everything blessed happens in threes, and on my third day I found my way into the open. They took me back down with a torch and made me clean up the mess I had made. These days they throw stowaways overboard, so we hear, but I was lucky because the ship was short of hands and I was signed on. That was how I became a sailor. The ship's name was the SS *Java Star*. My first home on the sea.

It was easy after that, because I liked the work and lived a hooligan life on ships and in all parts of the world. I was never short of work for long. Sometimes I lived in places for a few weeks and then found another ship, and there was so much of everything to see and do. When I met her I had been living like that for fifteen years. Just imagine how much life happens in fifteen years, and then to put that aside and begin another new life. When I met her I was thirty-four, twice her age, even though I told her at first that I was twenty-eight. I did not want her to think I was too old for her.

How exactly did you stow away? She does not want to be spared the smallest detail. She does not want me to deny her the briefest moment of my cowardly flight. But I can't live it all again, not like this. I have lived it for decades, until now my mind is numb with the story of that moment. Every time I open my mouth to speak, I hate what is going to come out of it. She won't let me say no. She insists, you must say exactly how you stowed away, otherwise how can we know.

Somehow I found the hardness of heart and the unexpected will to board a lighter that was headed to one of the ships anchored in the roads. The idea to go in this way came to me a few days before. In those days, everyone was talking politics and independence, and the air was filled with that kind of language, full of outrage and complaint. It was an exciting time, rallies and marches and long speeches about the hatefulness of the British. At about this time, an enormous aircraft carrier paid the island a visit. It was the HMS *Ark Royal*. This was how the British liked to soothe our nerves. The Royal Navy sent along a big warship and flew a couple of jets over the island, breaking the sound barrier and stampeding children and animals. Instructions were sent to headmasters of certain reliable schools, and groups of school children and students, the well-behaved and obedient ones, were selected and invited to a tour of the ship and an on-board tea. I was one of those chosen from the college, even though by then I had finished my examinations and left, because I had always been a respectful and reliable student.

It must have seemed a good idea to our rulers, to awe the natives with British power and then soothe their children with jellies and cakes and pastries. What those who organised these events did not know was that every one of their young guests believed the food to contain pig products. That was what some of their parents had said, and the word was passed round to the rest. Haram, they put pig fat in everything. So the young guests either did not touch the food, or the more daring among them superciliously threw it overboard. I can see the sailors standing silently along the side, staring ahead with arms crossed behind their backs, while the juvenile monkeys spurned their party fare. We were all doing what we could for the war of independence. But before the feast, they had shown us round the ship. They showed us the fighter planes and the helicopters, some on the flight deck and some in the hangar below decks. They even allowed some of us to get into the cockpits. If the idea was to frighten us with their knowledge and their power, it worked with me. I was thoroughly frightened and intimidated by their knowledge and their power. But not every corner of my mind was cowed in this way. As we walked round the ship's nooks and crannies, the idea came to me that it would be easy to find a place to hide in a ship.

I had been thinking for weeks about how I might get away, but this thinking was theoretical. If I wanted to escape, how would I do it? How can it be done? That visit to the warship made the idea concrete. A few days later a large cargo ship anchored in the roads, and somehow I managed to get myself on board. Those lightermen on the early morning trip must have known exactly what I was doing, and must have chuckled to themselves when I said I had some business on board. They must have known what I was up to as soon as I appeared on that pier. It was not as if I was one of those ragged young men who hang around the docks, their bodies as sleek as seals, and who go back and forth to the ships for work. I was a student, about to become a teacher, thin as a worm, dressed as you would imagine such a person to be. I expect I looked as frightened as I felt as the lighter made out to sea.

It was fear of ridicule that made me do what I did, made me do what now seems impossible to imagine that I did, but it was also anger at the way I had been trapped and the way my happiness had been ruined. I'll tell you about that another time, before you hear this. Or she will tell you. She knows all about it. It drives her mad, the thought of that woman I married and then ran away from. And the child I abandoned. I tell her that *she* is my wife, and you are my children. But she says not according to the law. What law? She is my wife. According to the law it is the woman I ran away from who is my wife. I see it in her eyes, her anger. I was trapped into doing those things I did in my youth. They fooled me. They were getting ready to have a good long laugh at me. They trapped me. That rage kept me going for months whenever I trembled or felt foolish about what I had done. Why could they not have left me alone, the scheming miserable bastards? Why did they take away the simple pleasures I had found for myself? It was that rage that helped me keep my secret to myself, and for a long time it helped me to suppress feelings of regret and shame.

Because the moment the engines of that ship started to turn, I was overwhelmed with regret and shame. What will people say about me? What will my father say? He will gloat at my brother Kassim and say this is what you wanted for him. This is what those khinzirs at the college have done to that boy. They have taught him to run away. What will happen to them all? But I raged at them too and learned to suppress my shame.

Everything was new and the world was so big that I lost myself in it. I tried very hard to lose myself in it but the hardest was not to be afraid. I got used to it after some time, just letting events take me from place to place, just letting things happen to me. It did not always feel so bad. I lived like that for a long time, and that place I had left moved further and further behind me. I pushed it even further and further behind me whenever I could. The violence and cruelty that took place there after independence and went on for years made it easier to put to one side any idea of going back. It was impossible to forget anything, and the most difficult was to forget her or to feel that I had done right to abandon her. Sometimes, often, I wondered if I might have been wrong about her, and if the baby was really ours but maybe it was a monster that was growing fast inside her. If I was wrong about her, I imagined how my wife would have worried about my disappearance and how wounded she would have been when she realised I had deserted her. Sometimes I calculated the child's age and wondered what it had grown up like. Then I would have to start all over again so I could feel once more the anger that had driven me away. Sometimes I dreamed that I returned and she did not recognise me, and was perplexed by my persistent stare. That was how I lived for years, never anywhere for long, roaming the seas in any direction where work presented itself, and without any idea how to make my life different. Then I met her in Exeter and all at once I saw something possible ahead of me.

She says they know about Exeter. We have told them about that so often. Tell them about all those years before, when you were a hooligan roaming the world. She is a stupid persistent bitch. When I switch this machine off, she comes and listens, and then tells me say more about this, say more about that. There is nothing more, they know the best of it, and what they don't know is sordid and pathetic. Now they also know the big secret I had thought to save them the trouble of knowing. I ran away from my home and abandoned a wife and unborn child, a terrible enough crime in any scheme of things. I might say that what I did to myself was also bad enough. I was nothing but a little shit, a frightened little shit and I cut the heart out of my own life with what I did. What was there to tell about all that?

When I left there I did not know how much I was leaving behind. Wherever I wandered or came to live after that nothing was expected of me. I was a man without responsibility, without a purpose. Nothing was required of me. I would have wanted to explain that to you, how I had lost that place, and at the same time lost my place in the world. That's what it means, this wandering. That's what it means to be a stranger in another people's land. I would have wanted to talk about that with you, but now too much time has passed and I have not found a way of talking about these things. You would have wanted to know more, and I didn't know how I could tell you more. I had not thought I would wait this long to tell you all this, but it worked out like that. I could not bring myself to do it and thought you would be better off not knowing. I thought we could all make something new and better for ourselves. Now that's enough of this.

She has switched the machine back on and put it beside me. Say more about Zanzibar, she says. I'll go and make you some tea. She is a parasite, her teeth are sunk into my flesh. Every day and every night she is here beside me, tormenting the life out of me. She gives me medicine to keep me alive so she can go on sucking my blood. I wonder what has happened to them all, whether they survived the killings and the expulsions. If only one person survived, it would be my scheming sister. I do not have the strength for this. Have

I not said enough? I don't know anything about Zanzibar any more. It is no longer a real place to me. Whenever I hear the word I hurry away from there. Whenever I see the word I look away or turn the page. What more do you want me to say about that old latrine?

I picked up the school bus on the corner of Hollis Road, which at that time was still a bridge over the creek. One side of the creek was being filled in. The other side eventually opened out to sea. When the sea was in, which it never was in the morning, the creek shone and glittered in sunlight. When the water was out, the creek bed was dark with sewage and human waste. People who lived by the waterside in Funguni built platforms over the water so they could sit in their houses and shit right into the creek. The bus followed the shore of the creek for about a mile before making another stop at Gulioni to pick up more students. Soon after that the bus was out in the country and it felt as if we had been let out of a crowded room. After Mtoni we could see the sea from the road all the time until we reached the college. That was my journey to school every day, and I missed it for years.

In those weeks after I ran away, I was either angry or frightened, not of anything in particular, it must have been just panic. Even the people I was with frightened me. I had not so much as spoken to an English person before, and the only ones I had seen close to were the sailors on the warship and the principal of the college, and he had never had any reason to speak directly to me even once. Now I was to find myself surrounded by these people, with their red faces and untruthful smiles and their fearful aura. We stepped out of their way when we saw them coming, not only on that ship but everywhere. I don't know how the world learned to fear them so, but I know I have still not learned to rid myself of it even now. I have to be firm with myself not to step aside, not to defer, to say I'm afraid of nothing.

But nothing terrible happened to me on that ship, and that became the important thing as time passed, that I had survived my reckless treachery. I began to feel safe, safer than I had ever felt before, and there were so many surprising joys. It was all new to me, to see land alongside us as the sun was rising, to approach a great harbour like Calcutta or Hong Kong in daylight, and to think that all this had been going on, all that coming and going and commotion, while I had been sitting under that mfenesi tree, shelling groundnuts. Then there was the sea itself, so big and so rough, glittering with utter wickedness, I don't have the words to tell you, I don't know how to describe that to you. It is terrifying when it is in a rage, and it is terrifying when it is beautiful. The sea, it isn't something I can ever forget, the grip of its terror.

So the newness of everything, and that nothing terrible happened to me, those were the things that replaced the panic. Even the work they gave me to do at first was new, cleaning toilets, sweeping and scrubbing floors, fetching and carrying, dirty work it would have shamed me for anyone I knew to see me do. That thought made me smile sometimes, how before I would have imagined what I was doing as something demeaning, but I did not feel demeaned at all. The British officers were aloof and did not seem surprised to see me doing that dirty work. It was what they expected of me, and that helped me not to feel embarrassed myself. Not everyone on that first ship was British. There were some Malays and Filipinos, and two of them became my friends. Raja worked in the kitchen, and Alvin worked in the engine room. I have never forgotten those two. Alvin took me to the engine room with its giant clockwork cranks and shafts like the throbbing heart of a huge beast. He loved that engine, and he showed it to me like he was letting me into a secret. These two were my companions whenever we had a few hours to wander around a port city, but at first they left me to myself as I coped with the crew and their mockery. For if the officers were aloof and superior, their juniors were chatty and aggressive, full of abusive and scorning words. They were proud of their roughness and mocked each other and everyone else all the time. I did not understand that at first and took silent offence, but later I learned to respond just as roughly when I could, forcing myself to do so as if this way of speaking was familiar to me. That first ship took me to Bombay, Madras, Calcutta, Singapore, Manilla, Hong Kong and then Jakarta and back to Singapore. My Malay friend, Raja, left the ship in Singapore, and I managed to manoeuvre myself into his job in the kitchen.

I took a walk in Singapore, which I still remember today. I was on my own, walking down a tree-lined street downtown, and I remember thinking to myself: I am free. It was not that I had thought of myself as confined before, or at least not until those last few weeks before I ran away, and that was a special feeling of being trapped. What I felt in Singapore was something quite different, something I had not known before. I felt as if I could choose freely what I wanted, or what work I did, or where I lived. In any practical way, this was just an illusion. I had no money, no papers, no skills, but that did not stop me thinking I was free. I had lost my fear of the world. I thought that no one would be able to make me do anything I did not want to do again. Everything around me provided so much pleasure, the sights, the smells, even the anxieties. I even mistook an attempt to con me out of a few coins for an offer of friendship and welcome. That same night the ship left Singapore for Madras, Bombay, Durban, Cape Town, Freetown and Liverpool, and at the end of that journey I knew that my life was changed beyond recovery, beyond any chance of returning to what it had been before.

I could have said something and hidden something. I could have told you about some of it even if not everything. Maybe I did not have the wisdom to do things by halves. By the time I might have told you about my treachery, I was used to living with my own silence, to managing the gap in my life. I committed an unkind and thoughtless act, and silence was a way of coping with the memory of it, offering a deadpan face to the burden of it. Our lives were full and complicated as it was, your mother, your childhood and this difficult place, and what I did in my teens was something for me to handle. Maybe it was because I was afraid you would be ashamed of me if you knew, and that you would lose respect for me. Maybe it was that, but I think it was also easier to say nothing and hope for the best. Well, that will do, I had not meant for my silence to make you afraid. I had meant to save you from this sordid knowledge so that you would look ahead and be brave and not be paralysed by these shameful memories.

This morning I made a list of the places I lived in during those years. It is surprising how speaking about those times in my life has made me want to go back in my memory and how so much has survived my desire to suppress it. Sometimes when a job ended I was not ready to join another ship, and lived for a while wherever I found myself. That was how I lived in Durban for some months. I fell in love there, but that was not the first reason for staying. I did not like the ship I was on, and after an argument with an officer, I impetuously asked to be relieved of my duties, and found myself wandering the streets of Durban. I ended up in the Indian part of the city and immediately felt comfortable there. The cafés and the food were familiar. The buildings reminded me of my home, as had buildings in Bombay and in Madras and even Colombo. I heard the muadhin calling people to prayer, and was tempted, but decided to stay on at the café and have another mug of sweet tea.

As I sat there, a tall man of about my age came into the café. He looked in my direction and then looked again as if he had recognised me. I began to smile because I knew what was going to happen next. He smiled back and came to my table. He asked me if we knew each other and I said no, but he thought we did. It happened to me all the time, in different places in the world, except in England. I kept meeting people who thought they knew me. That was how I met Ibrahim, and in no time at all, it was as if we did really know each other from before. He helped me find cheap lodgings and a few days later found work for me in his uncle's scrapyard. In the evenings we went wandering the cafés and sometimes had a few surreptitious beers. He came from a religious family and did not want to embarrass his relatives by drinking openly.

He lived in a large household, two brothers with all their families living in one house. They were Iranian. One of the brothers was the scrap-metal merchant whose yard I worked in. The other brother was Ibrahim's father, who was an imam. The part of Durban they lived in was so densely packed with Indians that no one they did not want could find an inch of living space in there. That was how the Indians liked it. It kept the savages out of their midst, although they did not mind so much the Arabs, as the rest of the Muslims were called. That was the official name the government had for them. Even Muslim Indians were Arabs. It was important not to be called native, because then you would be subject to bad laws, and anyway, none of them wanted to be called African then.

Ibrahim's grandfather had been an Ithnaasheri imam, travelling huge distances in South Africa to see to the needs of his scattered congregation, conducting weddings and memorials and other holy rites. He was already gone by the time Ibrahim could remember anything, but the grandfather always felt nearby during his childhood. I never had anything like that as a child. I knew nothing about my father or my mother, and never knew any of their relatives or anything like that. But in Ibrahim's family, the grandfather's name was invoked every day, and some of his stories were repeated like ritual. One that I still remember was of the grandfather being called hurriedly to read for a man who had suddenly died. When he got there he discovered that the man had been buried too quickly. His relatives noticed on the morning following the funeral that the mound over the grave had shifted, and fearing desecration had opened the grave. They found his body twisted out of the trench where he had been laid on his side as custom required, and his mouth was full of soil, and so they knew that there would still have been a spark of life in him when he was buried and these were his last struggles to breathe. That story made a great impact on me, and sometimes when I remembered it I struggled to breathe.

When Ibrahim's uncle found out I could read and write, he moved me to work in the office, which was on the ground floor of the house they lived in. At lunchtime I was sent food from upstairs, and that was how I came to know Ibrahim's sister and fell in love with her. Nothing could come of it, of course. They were a big family and I was a hooligan sailor passing through, and I already knew what came of exchanging longing looks with a rich merchant's daughter. We hardly spoke a word to each other, but somehow Ibrahim knew about our hesitant smiles and the brief sparkle in her eyes when she brought my bowl of food to me. Perhaps these things are obvious to everyone except to the two people who believe they share a secret. Ibrahim took the trouble to tell me about his mother. I suppose it was some kind of warning, and I heeded the warning and left the job in their family business immediately, and moved from my lodgings on the same day. I left Durban a short while afterwards, as soon as I found a berth. This is the story Ibrahim told me about his mother, and I always associate Durban with it, in ways that I find impossible to explain.

His mother, he said, sometimes became strange. Her mind drifted from its moorings, and her eyes turned blank and depthless. She broke things and hurt herself. She talked unstoppably, saying real words as well as gibberish, which made what she was saying very difficult to understand. It happened perhaps once a season, out of the blue without very much warning. There was a pattern to what she did when she became strange, but it was not predictable. Sometimes she broke things silently and stared with her unblinking gaze, at other times she talked without breaking a thing.

As soon as the first sign of turning strange showed itself, her daughter (the one I had grown to like) or her husband or one of the servants tied her hands behind her back and her feet together, and gagged her. She never resisted this restraint unless she was too far gone to know what she was doing. In fact, she was often the one who called out when she felt the approach of a strange spell, calling for whoever was with her to tie her up. Then her eyes turned blank and her mind drifted away. She hardly ever went out and was never left alone for long.

She was an intelligent woman, he said, but in her state she was likely to shame herself and her family with one of her mad outbursts. That was how they spoke of her, poor mad Zahra. No one needed to explain to her why it was necessary to tie her up and gag her, and restrict her as much as possible to the house. Madness is a cataclysm, an act of nature whose meaning is explicable only to itself, because it serves neither human nor divine purpose. Ibrahim's father said this from time to time, invoking his own father, the imam, as the author of this wisdom.

I understood that Ibrahim was warning me not to disturb these arrangements in his family, and not to bring shame to them with my attentions to his sister. I said goodbye to him that evening and took to wandering the docks like an old-fashioned water rat. Apartheid was well entrenched by then, but they did not bother too much with us sailors and I had my British-protected papers, which made me safe from harassment even from jinns and afreets, let alone boers. I wandered the streets of Durban for days, avoiding the places Ibrahim and I used to visit, and I felt once again as if I had been freed from the misery of human sanctimony. Perhaps, I told myself, I have a weakness for sidelong glances and lingering tremulous looks, and only merchants' daughters who spend their youth locked away from shame can provide these. I regretted my eviction from the pleasure I had found in Durban, but I regretted even more the loss of Ibrahim's friendship. I had even begun to think that I might seek his help to find a way to stay in Durban and put an end to my wanderings. There is always a way, but after he told me about his mother, I knew that was no longer to be.

She told me I should not stop because talking is doing me good, but that I should say more about Zanzibar. My time in Durban is very interesting but they all wanted to hear more about Zanzibar, not about that little slut of a merchant's daughter. I got angry with her, which is not hard to do when the bitch is being such a nag. Leave me alone, I told her. I don't want to say more about Zanzibar, I don't want to say more about anything. I threw the machine across the room hoping it would break and she would leave me alone, but I have no strength and it did not and here it is beside me again. Oh Maryam, I don't want to think about that place any more. I have thought about it every day for all these years, even when I was not thinking about it. I don't want to think about that woman I abandoned and what she had to cope with, or of the child and what it grew up to do and what it must think about me. I don't want to think of my mother and how I did not have an opportunity to say to her how sorry I was that her life had been so wretched because of us. I don't want to think about what happened to them, and what they must have thought of me as their world became ugly. Did you want me to talk about the breeze that blows through the trees at twilight or the murmurs of the silent lanes early in the morning? I don't want to think about these things that cause me pain. I am going to switch this thing off and I never want to see it again.

She insists I should try. She says I should try. She says I don't realise how much good it is doing me, my therapist. I have agreed to speak into this thing one more time and then that's it, whatever she thinks. I intended to talk about her, my tiresome harpy, how she found me just in time and what a lucky day that was for me. But I find I don't know where to begin. How beautiful she looked when I met her, and how her laughter was electric? Shall I tell her that? I did not know how ridiculous and lonely my hooligan life was until I met her. Shall I tell her about the joy the children brought and how empty everything would have been without them and without her? Shall I tell her that I cannot imagine my life without her companionship? She knows all these things.

Just now as I imagined how she looked when I first met her, I remembered another place I went through, and another woman I loved briefly. Maybe that is what happens to someone who leads a vagabond life. He catches glimpses of reprieve when he sees a woman he can love, a woman for whom he can end his wandering, and perhaps that is what happened to me in Port Louis. I haven't thought of her for years, but I did think of her when I first met Maryam in Exeter. It was all the more strange when she told me that her foster mother came from Mauritius, because the memory that had come to my mind was also about someone I met in Mauritius. It happened to me several years before, when we stopped in Port Louis to pick up a cargo of sugar bound for Bristol. It was my first and only visit to Mauritius.

There was a delay with the delivery of the cargo, so I went to explore the town and I got carried away with the sights. They reminded me of home. Many places reminded me of home, the look of the houses, the fruit in the market, a crowd outside a mosque. I could not stop seeing the similarities. On a beach in Port Louis I saw an old man sitting amid the reek of sun-burn fishscales, and I stood watching him for a few minutes, surprised by the familiar grace with which he pulled the needle through the sailcloth he was sewing. After walking for a long time, I found myself heading out of town, which was not my intention. As I passed a country lane, I caught sight of someone crossing in the other direction. I stopped and took a step back, and the other man did the same thing, so for a moment it was a funny sight, both of us taking a step back simultaneously across a country lane. The man laughed and waved, and I waved back. We both started towards each other and met somewhere in the middle of that country lane. I wanted to ask him for directions back to the port, although I was not particularly worried where I was. When you live that kind of life you stop caring about getting lost. The man was pleased when he found out I was a foreigner, and said that if I wanted the port I was heading in the wrong direction completely, which I had already guessed by then. He told me he was heading back to town and I could walk with him if I wished. So we walked back together, talking in the way you do when you have found a new friend. He told me I looked Mauritian and I said so did he, and we laughed so much we shook hands over it.

He came all the way to the port with me. When we got there it was already dark and the gates were shut and the security guard said there was no launch scheduled until the morning. My new friend, whose name was Pascal, said I should go and stay with him and get back to my ship the following morning. As I said, when you live that roaming life, you stop worrying about many things. My friend's house was a small bungalow, and we went in through the back door, which was in the garden. I smelled the perfume of the flowers before I saw that beautiful garden the next day. My friend explained what had happened to his sister and she smiled and fetched some food for us. She said they only ate a light supper in the evening and apologised for the modesty of the table. I remember that, because I had never heard that expression before or since, the modesty of the table.

Her name was Claire and she was beautiful, although not as beautiful as this nag was when I first met her. The three of us ate our meal and then talked for hours. They told me about their father, whom they called Sir as if it was his name, and their mother who had died only just recently. Sir was a senior clerk in one of the big firms in Port Louis but he was also a renowned amateur botanist. It was he who grew the garden, which I would see and marvel at the next morning. I wished I could see it immediately. They made it sound so magical, describing for me the different flowers and fragrances that grew in it, but they said, no, wait until the morning. That is when it is at its best.

That night I stayed awake for a long time thinking about many things but mostly about Claire, and the next morning, after I was shown the garden, I reluctantly left to go to the port with my friend Pascal without seeing her again. But the delivery was still delayed, so I rang the number Pascal had given me and went back to my new friend's house for lunch. When I left late in the afternoon, I shook hands with Claire and I felt sad. I thought she looked sad too. I promised to write to them and to come to Port Louis again. At the time I thought I could not bear not to see her again. But I never did write, and never went back to Port Louis.

When I saw Maryam for the third time in that factory, it made me think of Claire and how for many years I thought of her with regret. God knows what the old nag will make of this when she listens to it. I have not thought of Claire for a long time. Nor did they look alike or anything like that. It was the feeling that I recalled, a chance of happiness that I should not be stupid and lazy enough to miss this time.

Anna played the tape on the hi-fi, and her father's voice came out of the speakers like a public performance, like something on radio. None the less, she played it softly, as if she did not want to be overheard. She listened to it with strange pride and an unexpected elation. She had not thought he would be lucid. She had expected him to rant or whisper, muttering and grumbling to himself, the way he had so often in his last months. She had expected a broken-down tearful shambles of a voice and had dreaded listening to it for that reason. What good would it do relive that misery again? So she was surprised that his voice and what he had to say disarmed her so fully. His voice was clear and composed, most of the time, and even the difficult parts were calm and eloquent. There were moments when he talked as she had never heard him speak before, humble and reflective in a way she understood. Her own stream of thought sometimes took that tone, but she had never heard that from him before. She recognised it as a kind of unfor-giving honesty, which she did not usually expect to hear in someone's voice, let alone in her father's. He was their father: he instructed, cajoled, encouraged and commanded when that was necessary. He did not sit and muse aloud on his blunders and his regrets, and on the slow moments of reprieve.

She would have liked to hear more about that solitary walk in Singapore, or that reckless stroll in Port Louis. She would have liked to hear more of him, and it made her sad when the tape stopped. Nick's departure had made her melancholy, and then Ba's death on top of that was such an unexpected shock. She thought she was ready for the news about Ba, but when Maryam called to tell her, she howled on the phone like one of those demented women you see on the TV news. Listening to him talking on the tape made her wish for him, and she shed tears and mourned him for a moment, and felt sad that he had lived so long with such a feeling of wrong and such an expectation of disgrace. She took the tape upstairs and played it again on her radio cassette, listening to it through her earphones. This time she was not as much on edge, and she heard the long pauses between words and the catch in his voice in some places. She shut her eyes and she saw him sitting in his chair talking, and imagined him hurling the tape machine across the room, if he really did do that and was not just saying it to seem the capricious old man. She imagined her mother keeping him at it while he grumbled.

She reached for the phone to call her mother and tell her that she had listened to the tape. She had not spoken to her for several days, and had planned to do just this, listen to the tape and then call her afterwards. But when she called there was no reply. She leaned back in her chair and replayed the story her father had narrated in her mind, and it came to her in a series of pictures that ran swiftly past her, many of them imprecise and out of focus because she did not know enough to make them concrete and still. Her mother Maryam had told them about his life at the college and the woman he used to watch from his storeroom. Again and again she went back to the image of a lonely youth looking out of a slit in the wall, over the top of trees at a glimmering sea. She said that was a happy time for him, and perhaps it was, but what she could feel in her image of him was his loneliness. She could not see the woman or the terrace, it was too much for her. Probably a skinny teenager just out of her childhood. She would have to read and look at pictures to get a better idea of that, to see what she might have worn or what kind of terrace it might have been. She had meant to do that, ever since her mother told them he came from Zanzibar, and told them about the woman he had abandoned, the poor, pregnant sad bitch. That was only a few weeks before he died, and she had other business to deal with in that time, and not much time for reading about Zanzibar women on their terraces. Then his death and her mother's grief put her crisis about Nick in perspective. It forced her out of her wistfulness about him and returned her to all that she disliked about him and about herself with him. One fire puts out another's burning, slowly.

She had browsed the internet and read all the improbable descriptions of holidays and hotels, and excursions and festivals, and thought there was another place she wanted to find out about, not this one. She expected Jamal, in his methodical style, was already halfway through the appropriate literature, but he had a university library at his disposal and time on his hands. That was her excuse, anyway.

She returned to the images of his story, and realised how much she was enjoying this way of thinking about what he had said. She imagined him on that bus ride to college that he had remembered so often later, and she wondered why that journey was so memorable. Perhaps it was the clarity of it as an image, an early morning bus ride, or the difference between the black stinking creek and the distant view of the sea as they rode out of town with the breeze blowing through the open sides of the bus. Maybe it was the feeling of it that was memorable, and not the sight. She herself had pictures like that, which came back to her for no reason, a street corner near the cathedral in Norwich or a train platform in London in early evening, but she did not think of these moments with the craving he described, and so perhaps she had never known such longing. Then she saw him walking down that tree-lined street in Singapore again exulting over his freedom, and then leaning against the ship's railings as they entered Cape Town harbour. All illusion, of course, but she could imagine how the swelling moment could carry you away. She saw him at the college, a thin youth in shirtsleeves, strolling with other youths across the grounds. She had never imagined him a college student, only ever a sailor, and when she knew him he worked as an engineer in an electronics factory. She had thought of his reading and his knowledge as something he acquired on the side, out of interest, something he'd had no time for when he was young. She had thought of their going to university, Jamal and her, as a new high point in their family's fortunes.

Dear Jamal. How's your beard doing? Growing fast? Apparently it has to be at least four inches below the chin before you can describe yourself as properly pious. Did you know that? Not much hope for you, I don't think. I listened to Ba's tape today, twice. I expected croaking and muttering, all that scary weirdness he did so well. Instead he was clear and made complete sense, and really moved me with the story of his youth and all that wandering around the world. Feeling free in Singapore. Do you suppose he was doing all that weirdness to scare us? Keep us at arm's length? Keep away from me, whelps. It helped to know even before I started listening what *the secret* was, rather than listening in dread for the moment when he would jump out of the bushes with an unbearably dreadful story. I know it's unbearable enough, abandoning that poor woman, girl really, and then in explanation coming out with that frantic and panic-stricken story of *that* plot against him, the foisting of someone else's child on him. But it could have been worse. Why do you think he really ran away? Just to escape, maybe. Perhaps nothing tragic or profound at all. I don't know how Ma managed to keep him at it, and how she kept him from mumbling and cursing. Because I'm sure it took some work. What do you make of that dreamy couple in Port Louis? Do you think that really happened? Pascal and Claire, a chance friendship and budding love spurned. Then many years of ancient mariner stuff before he ran into Ma in Exeter. But he told it well, though, don't you think? I liked the idea of walking all over the island as he did, not caring about getting lost. I think this is the longest email I've written. It shouldn't be allowed. I tried to ring Ma after I listened to the tape but she wasn't there, gallivanting in Matalan probably xxx.

Jamal wrote: On what you said about getting Ma sorted out with her paperwork, next time you speak to her ask for the surname of Vijay the accountant. It might be worth checking to see if he did set up that firm and then it should be easy enough to find his business address. I can do it, I need a break from this gruelling intellectual sweat-work now and then. I am lying low with Ma at the moment. She is threatening to come visiting in Leeds, and I fear that when she sees the filth and chaos I live in she will feel forced to reform me. Someone appears to have told her about Lena, I can't imagine who, and I think she is curious.

Obviously they don't give her enough work to keep her busy at that infidel charity where she gives her labour for nought xx.

Anna wrote: She is threatening a visit just to panic you. I don't think she plans to go anywhere much at the moment. She is appearing in a play that the women's group is putting on at the Centre and she is too busy rehearsing. They wrote the play themselves, and she is playing a lady doctor, probably a stubborn Spanish one called Dr Mendez. The story is something to do with asylum, and she says it has everything – birth, death and marriage, as well as some songs. She told me all the parts and who is playing what, but you need to have followed the whole serial to know who Halima is and who Lydie is, and so I'll spare you that. I asked her about Vijay's surname, and she said it is Gopal. She was a bit tense about the question at first, but I said we were just talking about it after the funeral, and wondered how to find her foster family, if she was interested. She said she thinks she has already found his business address. V. K. Gopal Accountants. Someone at the Centre showed her how to use the Companies House website and she searched for him there and thinks she has found him. He must be ancient, but she said he would be in his mid-seventies and she did not think that would deter Vijay from working. She hasn't followed it up yet because she is so busy (you see) so I think a little weekend conference might be a good idea. Perhaps we can go down to Norwich to see the play and then make plans about following up? She might be just nervous about doing it on her own xxx.

Anna wrote later: The drama is unfolding. In the first place, although not in order of importance, the play is on this Friday and Ma would be honoured by your presence, as you are well aware. It's the last Friday of the school term, and I had to negotiate hard to be released from all the fun events on the last day of school before Christmas. In the second place, I have just spoken to Ma and she has received a reply from the dreadful cousin Dinesh who used to menace her all those years ago. It said that he has passed on her request and Mrs Ferooz Gopal has agreed to hear from her but does not want to meet her. Mr Vijay Krishna Gopal is now retired and rather unwell, and she will agree to nothing that will upset him. Mrs Gopal has nominated Saturday afternoon at 2.00 p.m. as a time when Ma can call. Ma – this is the new Ma, for God's sake – immediately rang the number and spoke to Ferooz. Can you believe it? The woman who used to treat the telephone as if it were some kind of a trap? In short, through some kind of ancient magic, probably abject apologies and tears, they managed to make up enough for Ferooz to agree to see her after all. I think the children, that is you and I, were part of the magic. So Immigrant Family Abbas is off to Exeter at the crack of dawn on Saturday morning. I just checked the trains. I don't think Ma needs us for support or anything like that. Our role will be to act as decoys to draw enemy fire. Oh well, we'll find out if there is anything to find out, and that will be something. It has been a wonderful term at the school. I think I've got my favourite class hooked on Keats. And, I am pleased to say, the melodrama of my life down here diminishes by the day. Some time very soon I'll even stop thinking about that fuck-head. Love to Lena xx.

Jamal replied almost immediately: Bravo! Down with melodrama. This is your first email in two days. Don't you realise that people who spend all day in front of the computer rely on emails for their sanity? Yallah, we're going to Exeter.

*   *   *

The Refugee Centre looked as if it might once have been the premises of a small business. There were two large rooms downstairs and several offices upstairs. The play was to be performed in the inner of the two large rooms, and drinks and snacks could be bought in the room nearer the front door, which was normally the reception area for the Centre. The makeshift theatre otherwise served as a crèche, an activities area for various voluntary groups, a meeting room, and even as a concert venue when required.

The play began at three in the afternoon and finished at around four. The chairs were arranged in a rough semicircle, leaving a space clear at the end of the room nearest the large doors. There was a drum set just inside the door. The room was crowded with women and children, many of them already seated, and a few men who lounged against the walls, looking as if they were there only temporarily. Judging from appearance, the audience was made up of people from Africa and Asia, and a family or two of Central Europeans. Many of them seemed to know each other. Jamal, from professional curiosity, had already found out that they were mostly Somali, Eritrean, Afghanis and Romanian Roma. There was constant coming and going, children wandering about, and a great hum of talk and laughter.

Finally, the lights went down, and a spotlight high on a rafter at the back came on. In the spotlight they saw that a young man had slipped in and was sitting at the drum set. There was instant applause while the young man grinned with delight, waving his sticks in the air at this welcome. More lights came on and turned the cleared area into a stage. All the cast were women and children. The play was a series of narrations, women telling stories of disrupted lives. Some of it was dramatised, some of it was comic, and there were passages of song, accompanied by someone behind the audience playing a flute. The drummer built up tension when required and signalled changes of scenes. The audience still moved in and out, although less so now, and the children were constantly on the point of wandering on to the stage area.

As the play progressed, the movement among the audience slowly died down and the number of men in the room increased. Ma was the doctor who gave the women stern advice about themselves and the children, and told them something about the nature of the modern world they had fled to. Some of the figures and statistics sounded familiar to Anna from what she had heard Jamal say at times. She glanced at him and he smiled at her, acknowledging his contribution. Feeding her propaganda, she whispered. When an actress delivered what she thought was a powerful line, she turned to the audience for a reaction, and the audience generously applauded while the drummer showed his appreciation with a swelling roll on his drums. The climax of the play was a wedding. The groom was played by a youth who could not have been more than thirteen, but he was just an excuse. All the women in the room, African and Asian and European, burst into a raucous joyous song in Somali, which they had been rehearsing for weeks. Their voices rang with such clarity that they needed no accompaniment. Their faces, and the faces of everyone else, glittered with smiles, and the room was full of song and laughter.

They were up early the next morning for the 7.10 to Liverpool Street, then across London to Paddington for the Exeter train. They arrived in Exeter just after 12.00, having travelled across England from east to west. Maryam said little during the train journey, looking out of the window most of the time, or listening to her children's conversation with a placid smile. They left her to her thoughts, and Anna expected they would be turbulent and anxious ones, despite her appearance of calm. She tried to imagine Ferooz, a thin woman who smiled a lot, her mother had said, and Anna wondered whether she would receive them with bitterness or courtesy. Whichever way, it had to be done, to find out what could be found out.

In the taxi from the station, Maryam looked around with eyes sparking with memory. It was her first time back in Exeter since she left so suddenly thirty years before, and everything was so changed. She seemed much less tense than she had been on the train, especially before they took the tube across London. The address Ferooz had given her was different from the place where she had lived with them before, and was in a prosperous area unfamiliar to Maryam, who fell silent as they approached their destination. It was a large new house with a drive spacious enough to allow a big car to turn around. There was a grey Mercedes Benz parked in front of the garage. A Christmas garland hung on the door. The door was opened by a young Indian woman who smiled at them cheerfully and knowingly, and introduced herself as Asha. She ushered them in. The hallway was ample, with a four-foot-wide staircase leading to the upper floor. Christmas decorations crowded the hallway. It was obvious that this was a rich man's house.

The young woman led them to the sitting room and stepped inside, and then stood to one side to let them come in, Maryam first, then Anna and Jamal hanging back. The room ran the full width of the house, with windows at the back and the front. Standing in front of the rear windows was a thin tall woman in a flowered dress, her arms stiffly by her side, her body tense and somehow disapproving, her lined face taut. Jamal had not expected Ferooz to look so frail, so anxious. In his mind, he realised, he had pictured her as an antagonist, and had figured her as more robust than this. Then almost in spite of herself Ferooz broke into a smile, which she quickly suppressed, clamping her lips over her large teeth as if in rebuke, but in the meantime her body had changed, and she walked forward and took Maryam's hand. Very gently, she raised her hand to her lips and kissed it. In turn, Maryam leaned forward and kissed Ferooz on her right hand, and then on her left cheek and then on her right. It gave Jamal an anguishing pleasure to watch this exchange of courtesies and affection, as if he was witnessing the completion of an unfinished rite.

'Maryam,' Ferooz said, smiling now without restraint. 'Maryam, Maryam. It is so good of you to come and see us. But to stay away for so long!'

'It was bad of me,' Maryam said, her eyes glistening. 'You look just the same.'

'Oh don't, you're such a liar. I'm old and skinny,' Ferooz said, waving Maryam's flattery away. 'And these are the children. So grown up, so lovely. Who would have imagined. Hanna and Jamal, please, you are welcome. Come and sit down, Asha will bring us some snacks.'

It was only after these exchanges that they noticed a man sitting silently on the other side of the rear windows, shaded from the light by a partly drawn heavy curtain. He was old and dark with a large wart on his cheek. Vijay. Ma had never mentioned a wart on his cheek. When they sat down he too was part of the circle, although he was withdrawn in his shaded corner.

'Vijay too is pleased that you came,' Ferooz said, indicating the silent man. 'If you knew him well you would be able to see his smile. Poor Vijay had to have a hip replacement operation, and he suffered a stroke after surgery. He recovered but not fully and now all the time he's under heavy medication for the pain. He lost mobility and he can't speak, but he can hear. He knows you're here and he welcomes you too. There Vijay, you see, he's smiling. Can you see he's smiling?'

Jamal could not see that he was smiling, but he smiled back anyway. Asha brought a tray of snacks and soft drinks, and they nibbled at these while Ferooz told them about Vijay's misfortune and its impact on his life. 'Vijay loves to work,' Ferooz said. 'Do you remember, Maryam? He is now seventy-seven years old, and he has worked hard all his life. So now imagine the torment for the poor man when he has to sit there all day and worry about what his partners are getting up to. Dinesh runs the business now, and he does it very well. It's a big firm, very successful, but poor Vijay cannot stop worrying. I know what he's like. Never mind, he's using this opportunity to catch up on all the reading he never did. Just now he is listening to an audio book of a history of Gujarat. We went back to India to visit, before he fell ill, and it was wonderful for him to see his family again. It was like a festival and he was handing out presents like a prince. He was very proud of what has become of his country, and now he wants to know all about Gujarat.

'But you must tell me about what you have been doing all these years while you have been hiding from us,' Ferooz said smiling, her eyes moving between them amiably to take any blame out of her words.

Maryam told her about Norwich and about Ba's illness

and death, and then after a while, she raised the matter they had come to see them about. Ferooz nodded and said she would tell her all that she knew. When they fostered her they were given her birth certificate and were told her history. As she spoke, she handed Maryam a piece of paper that she had ready on the little table beside her. Maryam accepted the birth certificate and looked at it briefly before putting it down on her lap. With that brief look she had seen that her name appeared only as Maryam, no second name.

'Much of this I told you when you first came to live with us, when you were nine years old,' Ferooz said with a smile. 'There may be certain things I did not tell you then because I did not think a child would understand, but I tried to remember to tell you later. Is there something in particular you would like to know?'

'I would like to find out who my mother was, if it is possible to know something about her,' Maryam said, picking up the birth certificate and holding it up for a few seconds.

'The official story was that you were left at the hospital entrance, and the search for the mother was unsuccessful,' Ferooz said, looking at Anna and Jamal at this point, perhaps to mitigate the starkness of the information she had just given them, or because she could not help smiling at the sight of Maryam's children. 'The caseworker we dealt with told us more. She told us that the police investigation could not come to any conclusion because the most likely woman to have been the mother disappeared. They heard about her from a neighbour who came forward after an appeal. She told the police that the people who used to live down her street had a daughter who fell pregnant, and she was unmarried. They were refugees after the war, Polish.

They couldn't go back because of the communists, so they stayed on in England for a few years. She knew they were planning to emigrate, but she wasn't sure if it was to Australia or South Africa. It was one of those two, that's for sure. When she first heard about their plans they still had not decided between the two, but she thought they decided on Australia in the end. She saw the family leaving but it was all very rushed, and she did not have time to talk to them. She said she did not want to be nosy, but she did notice that the girl was no longer pregnant and there was no sign of a baby. People were very alert to such things then. It was only a couple of weeks later, when she heard about the appeal for information that she wondered if there might be a connection.

'The police investigated and found out where the young woman worked, and questioned some of her co-workers. They said she had left months ago and they knew nothing about where she had gone to. She used to see a soldier, not British, a darkie with a light complexion. People said things like that without embarrassment then. That was what the caseworker told us, and she said those were the words quoted in the file. A darkie with a light complexion could mean anything, and since we were not really worried to trace any of these people, we did not ask for names. I should have thought that one day you would want to know, but we did not think like that then. Anyway, this is only like a rumour, because the woman had disappeared and the police were never able to confirm an identification.'

After she finished telling this meagre history, Ferooz turned towards Vijay, as if to see if he had anything to add, but really, Jamal thought, to escape Ma's wide-eyed intensity.

'Why did you take me?' Maryam asked. 'Were you not

worried about taking a bastard child of unknown people? A dark child. And all the trouble I had with those other parents. Did that not worry you? What made you take me?'

Ferooz did not reply at once. She looked again at Vijay, and Jamal thought she was composing herself, selecting which answer to give, the simple one or the complicated one. In the end, he thought, she decided on the simple one.

'We wanted to help someone,' Ferooz said, a note of pleading in her voice. 'It was his idea at first. He said we had been fortunate in our lives. We had health, we had happiness, we had prosperity, and we should help a child whose life was unfortunate since we could not have one of our own. So we asked for a child to look after and they gave you to us. We thought we would give you care and shelter as if you were our child, until you were able to find your own way. To me you were like my own.'

Maryam rose to her feet and went to Ferooz. She hugged her and kissed her, and then went to Vijay and did the same. They headed back to Norwich on the late-afternoon train. Ferooz was tearful in farewell, hugging Maryam and both Anna and Jamal. They all shook Vijay's limp hand while Ferooz pointed to his invisible smile. On the train, they left Maryam to her thoughts until she was ready to speak.

'It is very likely that I'm Polish,' she said, amused by this additional complication in her life.

'Half Polish,' Jamal said. 'Don't forget the darkie.'

'But what Pole would call her daughter Maryam?' their mother asked.

'A Jewish Pole,' Jamal said. Maryam shook her head but Jamal pressed on. 'If that turns out to be the case, and since

276

Jewishness travels in the maternal line, that makes all of us Jewish and entitled to be citizens of Israel if we wish.'

'Maryam is not a Jewish name,' Maryam said.

'On the other hand,' Jamal continued, 'the darkie with the light complexion could be an Arab on some special training in a Military College nearby. Maryam was the name of his beloved mother, and when your mother gave birth to you, she named you after his mother.'

'Maryam is not a Jewish name,' Maryam said again, firmly. 'I checked. I already thought if the name is Jewish and I checked. The Hebrew form of the name is Miryam.'

'In that case there can be no further doubt in the matter. Our Polish grandmother was seeing an Arab and not a Jew,' Jamal said.

Anna wrote: Think about that critical vowel! She is already following up, talking of Freedom of Information and calling in police files for her alleged mother's name. She is even using the language – 'calling in files' and 'alleged mother' – all that sort of legal-sounding speak. She must have picked up something working at the Refugee Centre. When she has the name, she plans to check passenger lists to Australia and South Africa in the weeks after her birth, and continue following the woman's tracks until she finds her. I doubt that she'll get very far with police files. Her mother committed a crime in abandoning her, and her case is still open. The police will not release the file of a continuing investigation.

Jamal wrote: My writer friend next door loves the critical vowel. He and Lena have really hit it off, and Lena is beginning to claim him as her discovery. If I were Ma, I don't think I would want to chase all this up. Like I don't think I really want to find the woman Ba abandoned or her child. Our brother or sister, I should say. Not desperately. Do you? Is it bad of me? But I want to go to Zanzibar, definitely.

Anna wrote: Will we really go to Zanzibar? Or will it remain a nice story, a pleasing possibility, a happy myth? When I think about it sometimes I feel anxious, as if I'm approaching new disappointments and possibilities of rejection. It's not because I feel I belong there or that I'm owed a welcome, but since knowing these things, I feel myself suspended between a real place, in which I live, and another imagined place, which is also real but in a disturbing way. Maybe suspended is too dramatic, tugged then, tugged in a direction that I sometimes find myself trying to resist. I am looking at a picture of an Eritrean woman holding her daughter in her arms, maybe two or three years old, and behind them a shelter made of tin and old rubbish. They are both wearing rags, but the woman's hair is carefully coiled as if she had prepared herself for this photograph. She very nearly manages a smile for the photographer. It was in one of Nick's magazines, which had fallen behind the desk. The woman is frowning, and looks weary and worn out, a beautiful woman whose body has been cut and slashed by hunger and custom. Almost certainly her genitals and her daughter's genitals have been mutilated, and both she and her daughter are hungry. My mind is crowded with my little thoughts when our world is full of so many unspeakable anguishes. Sometimes knowing about such things makes me feel ashamed to be well. xxx.

Jamal wrote: She makes me think of Ma's women at the refuge. It's not all hopeless. Talking of Ma, here's the latest: she is thinking of buying an exercise machine. These are critical times. Do you think she's met someone? Of course we'll go to Zanzibar. I want to see that tree where our father was shelling groundnuts while the great world was churning just out of eyeshot. I'm writing a short story. Another father story. Such a predictable immigrant subject. I am going to call it *The Monkey from Africa!*

A NOTE ON THE AUTHOR

ABDULRAZAK GURNAH was born in 1948 in Zanzibar and teaches at the University of Kent. He is the author of seven novels which include *Paradise* (shortlisted for both the Booker and the Whitbread Prizes), *By the Sea* (longlisted for the Booker Prize and awarded the RFI Témoin du Monde Prize) and *Desertion* (shortlisted for the Commonwealth Writers' Prize).